FORBIDDEN
EMPIRE OF SECRETS

FORBIDDEN
EMPIRE OF SECRETS

Jax

Forbidden Empire of Secrets

Copyright © 2019 by Jax. All rights reserved.

No part of this publication may be reproduced, stored in a retrieval system or transmitted in any way by any means, electronic, mechanical, photocopy, recording or otherwise without the prior permission of the author except as provided by USA copyright law.

This novel is a work of fiction. Names, descriptions, entities, and incidents included in the story are products of the author's imagination. Any resemblance to actual persons, events, and entities is entirely coincidental.

The opinions expressed by the author are not necessarily those of URLink Print and Media.

1603 Capitol Ave., Suite 310 Cheyenne, Wyoming USA 82001
1-888-980-6523 | admin@urlinkpublishing.com

URLink Print and Media is committed to excellence in the publishing industry.

Book design copyright © 2018 by URLink Print and Media. All rights reserved.

Published in the United States of America
ISBN 978-1-64367-184-0 (Paperback)
ISBN 978-1-64367-185-7 (Digital)

Fiction
15.01.19

Always...

    I wanted to make this dedication fancy but sometimes I think simple is the best....

    Joey, I dedicate this book to you, you have listened through hours upon hours of editing until I am sure, you know my book better than I do. You have also listened to all my ideas, until I am sure you were ready to pull out all your hair. Most of all, you have been there to encourage me to reach for my dreams.

    Thank you does not seem like enough, but there it is. I thank you with all of my heart, without you in my life there would be no me.

TABLE OF CONTENTS

Chapter One: Wedding Rituals 11

Chapter Two: Kali 18

Chapter Three: She is Gone 28

Chapter Four: The Great Escape 33

Chapter Five: The King 39

Chapter Six: Justine is Pregnant 49

Chapter Seven: Mother Nature 55

Chapter Eight: The Shark 61

Chapter Nine: Bart's Childhood 81

Chapter Ten: Here Piggy Piggy Piggy 89

Chapter Eleven: Promised 108

Chapter Twelve: Manu Island 115

Chapter Thirteen: A New King 130

Chapter Fourteen: Promising Ceremony 144

Chapter Fifteen: It's Not Easy Being the King 155

Chapter Sixteen: Growing Up Royal 167

Chapter Seventeen: The Gig Is Up 181

Epilogue 201

About the Author 205

ACKNOWLEDGMENTS...

    I believe my calling in life is to write. With the love and support of my family, I have found the courage to pursue my dream.

    Joseph March, Erin Haun, Bree'Anna Haun, Katryna Freels, Megan Freels, Gary March, Jazzy March, Chris Fraticello, Alicia Fraticello, Carolyn Oxford, Ashley Bailey & Becca Flessas.

    A special thanks to someone who believed in me and changed my life, Bill Haack, thank you from the bottom of my heart.

    I also want to recognize a special lady that has been my biggest fan and strongest supporter, Linda Galvao – this is just the beginning, thank you for being there.

    I love you all to the moon and back

In my dreams...

My love is a secret now; days hold nothing but pain,
A future that is not of my making.

We met as children; grew and changed, doomed from the start,

Being with you meant certain death.
However, .not mine.

I am Royalty, you are not, now, I must look away,
You must be a stranger to me, to keep you safe I must obey.

To have anything and everything your heart desires,

Yet to be denied that which makes you feel alive and burn with fire,

This is a fate worse than death, however, .not mine.

In my dreams now is where I find you,
Your smile is just for me,

Forbidden love
Dreams do always set us free.

CHAPTER ONE

WEDDING RITUALS

He worked in my father's house and every time I saw him, I would catch myself holding my breath. He was a servant and the king forbade me from being with anyone beneath my station. I knew this, but my heart.... My heart seemed to have a mind of its own and did not play by the rules. Internally, I waged a constant battle. Very soon, I was to go to one of the other neighboring islands to learn everything a queen must know to rule a kingdom. I had never looked so forward to leaving. Normally, I would follow my mother's lead and she would teach me. I have no mother so that is not possible. One of the other royal queens has offered to apprentice me. I will be gone for two years; surely, by the time I return I will have forgotten my silly girlish crush on this mere servant boy.

It matters not…he never looks my way. I cannot blame him in this matter. For me, it would be nothing more than a stern reprimand, for him....for my servant boy, it would mean certain death. That is something I would never allow, so I just secretly watch him and worship from afar. Another time perhaps, another life.... not now.

As for being in royalty, we are given unlimited freedom when we are children. We are actually encouraged to play with the children of the palace servants. We make what we think will be lifetime friends and even first love. The harsh reality is that when you grow up, your freedom is sacrificed for the good of your kingdom. Recognize that your playmates and confidantes of yesteryear must now be looked upon for what they are, mere servants. I cannot go against my father in this. This was the King's (My father's) rule. His law in this matter, was very clear. In most things, my father is a fair and righteous ruler however since I am his only daughter

In addition, whomever I wed will rule in my father's place when the time comes, he has to be very careful in his choice. I can promise you that it will definitely not be a servant boy with an impure bloodline. I am already promised to marry another, a Prince that will bring strength and riches to our small island kingdom. We have never met or even seen any photographs of each other. All I know of him is that his name is Prince Micho Branoi. I guess Yana Branoi sounds all right. Our fathers have been friends for a very long time and arranged our marriage when we were children. Neither the Prince nor I have a choice in the matter. It seems so surreal that in the twentieth century things like this still go on. Here on the island the outside world does not exist. The laws were never broken or questioned just simply obeyed.

When I turn eighteen, the prince I am to be wedded to will, journey here. He will leave his life and everything he knows to come here and compete in deadly challenges vying for the chance to rule Zanzi someday and wed the princess (who happens to be me.) My father will provide a grand feast to welcome him. I will not be allowed to attend this event. This feast is pretty much where my father will question the Prince and "size him up." Once my father gives him his blessing, that is when I will be permitted to meet him. We are only given a few moments together. There is barely time to mutter our awkward hellos but at least we get to see whom we will rule next to and bear children with. Even then, though, we are strictly chaperoned. There must never be a question of my virtue.

This is not a love match, this is a match that is made to better both kingdoms, love (hopefully) will come later.

After what I like to call the "meet and greet", we will both go our separate ways and will not see each other again until our wedding ceremony (if Prince Micho bests my father's challenges that is.). The wedding rituals for the intended bride and groom each take six days. For the prince, the rituals are quite rigorous and physical. He will have to prove his prowess in hunting as well as his strength and cunning in hand to hand combat among other tasks that will be set before him. The Challenges are kept secret so I am not sure what all they entail. For the most part, my father has to follow the ancient customs, but I am sure he has thrown in a few "new customs" of his own. Since I have had no mother, I have turned to my father for everything and we are extremely close. I cannot see him letting the Prince off very easy. He has to pass every challenge before my father as well as the kingdom will accept him as the future ruler and give him marital rights to me. When my father can no Longer lead and has to step down that is when Prince Micho will be given the "keys to my kingdom. "If he is victorious, then he is worthy to be the king and to take my hand in marriage. If he fails, he will ultimately be sentenced to death.

What use is a Prince that cannot rule a kingdom? No decent woman would or should bear him children. If she does, then she will be chastised and ridiculed by everyone. She will be considered no better than a whore and will be treated as such. Their offspring will suffer a worse fate. They are guilty by association and will be considered outcasts and shunned. The children will not be allowed to attend school or partake in any activity that would help them to better their positions. If anyone (friend or family) is caught helping in any way, they too will be considered no better and lose their station in life. The sons would be beggars on the street and the daughters will be considered whores like their mother. The progeny of such a union will never be of any importance or own any land. They would be born paupers and through no fault of their own die as paupers or worse. It is a cruel but necessary practice. No one will fight for or lay down their life for a king they do not respect, fear and worship. A king needs to be the right hand of God or be a mortal god to his subjects. My father was that and more to everyone he ruled. It all seems very boring and extremely exhausting to me.

I have watched my father and I know firsthand that the king never sullies himself in combat. If asked to fight, the king will appoint someone to fight and defend his honor. Do not get me wrong, the king is very fit and able to fight for himself but if something were to happen to him the kingdom would be lost because there would be no one to rule in his place. When the king needs someone to battle in his stead every abled-bodied male on the island steps up to volunteer because this is quite an honor. To bleed for your king is one of the greatest sacrifices you can make. If the man is successful and does not perish in the skirmish, he and his entire family will never want for anything for the rest of their lives. They will become very wealthy and highly respected pillars of the community. If I had been born a son I would have fought in my father's place until I married or had to rule a kingdom myself. I do not pretend to understand any of this but that is how it is and has been for as long as I

Can remember. My wedding rituals are nothing like that of the prince. The only thing uncomfortable that I have to endure is the examination to confirm that I am still a maiden and intact. There must never be a question of my innocence and virtue. On the first night, I am to be bathed in floral scented water and my personal handmaidens will remove every bit of hair from my body (except the hair on my head.) I must come to the marriage bed as pure as a newborn babe. The next day is spent scrubbing my fingernails, bleaching my teeth, pinking my lips. Lastly, as the sun sets on the second day the rituals my ears are pierced and the Apothecary come and covet the drops of blood. This is the very last ingredient in my Cleansing Ceremony shampoo. I guess it is a signature on the shampoo that makes it only mine.

Day 3 is my most favorite, a soak in a warm luxurious bath full of creams and sacred oils. This has quite a few purposes. A Royal princess never works a day in her life and her skin must be free of blemishes and as smooth as silk. Her fingernails need to be impeccable, her hair luxurious and she must never sport any type of callousing or scars etc. The fragrant oils that are used are very intense and the healing properties are phenomenal. Whatever the reasoning for using these creams and oils during the wedding ritual is, I really do not care. The most amazing thing to me is what happens afterwards. After they have been infused into my body and I am dried and dressed, whenever I walk into a room, everyone will turn their eyes in my direction. I am not sure of the nature of the oils but everyone smells something different. When I was younger, it was fun to go around and find out what each person sensed when the prospective princess bride would enter the room. Some named similar scents yet to others the aroma was something I would have never guessed. The real magic to these potions though is that the princess can leave, wait a bit to let the scent dissipate and then re-enter the room and everyone will waft something very different from what they previously thought. It is as if it were magical.

Another part of the wedding preparation is the Cleansing Ritual. This is an extremely important part of the wedding preparations. This ritual is only for the princess brides. It is also only for their hair. The shampoo that is used has been likened to that of the "Nectar of the Gods." You have probably already guessed that on the Island of Zanzi long hair is one of the g r e a t e s t endowments a woman especially a Royal Princess can possess. The base recipe for the sacred shampoo used in the Cleansing Ritual is always the same; the special ingredients are only added when a new princess prepares for her wedding. The Royal Guardsman that has protected the base recipe from its inception is the same guardsman that will protect the finished product until it is no more. He will forfeit his life to protect the recipe if he must. If you think about it, this guard will watch over and kill for something that they know nothing about. The shampoo is so pure and sacred that only virgins are allowed to have a hand in its creation lest the unclean contaminate it. After the shampoo is finished, the young maidens that took part in its creation must forfeit their tongues.

When a new princess is born, the young girls that will assist in their wedding ritual are chosen for her. These girls and their families will be segregated from the rest of the village. They are immediately moved into special houses that are located on the palace grounds. They achieve instant fame and are revered and very well respected. It is quite an honor for your child to be chosen for this sacred task… For years as the princess grows up, the maidens are schooled on exactly what is to be expected of them. They are also made aware of the sacrifice. All of the girls understand how being chosen has improved not only their lives but the lives of their families as well. The gods show favor and smile down on these "selected ones" and the rewards in this life are nothing compared to the rewards that await them when they go on to their next life. As far as the forfeiture of their tongues, the Apothecary have tested and continue to practice many less painful and less barbaric ways for the extraction. The girls are assured that when the time comes there will be no discomfort or else it will be minimal. The everyday tongue extractions are for torture and punishment. They are meant to be as painful as they can make it.

To quell their fears, it is explained to the girls repeatedly that the tongue extraction is for their protection as well as the lives and well-being of their families. After an exciting day of lessons, many of the young maidens like to go home and confide in their siblings and parents. Sometimes, something that was not to be repeated is said. To avoid this, when the time comes to actually work with the ingredients and put the Shampoo together the young girls are removed from their homes and will reside in the palace under lock, and key until their tongues are no more. Only then, are they allowed to return to their parent's homes. The monarchy takes no chances when it comes to protecting the sacred recipe. The rival palaces want all of the recipes. They especially want the shampoo recipe for the unbelievable healing properties that it possesses. They have roughish young men from their own villages infiltrate and pose as servants of the Zanzi palace. These imposters court and woo the young impressionable maidens and make many promises to them to acquire the recipes. If the rival charlatans are found out, they are immediately apprehended and beheaded for all to see. It is for this reason that the temptation to talk is removed from the maidens and their tongues are humanely extricated. This is another cruel but necessary practice and a very important part of the sacred wedding rituals.

Just as every maiden and servant boy are specifically chosen for each part of the Wedding Ceremony, each individual bottle of shampoo that is used for the Cleansing Ceremony is also made for a specific princess bride to-be, from the moment of her birth.

Throughout the years as the princess grows up the Apothecary collects samples of her bodily fluids, her hair, skin and nails to create it. It takes years to come up with exactly the correct recipe

CHAPTER TWO

KALI

    I do remember one wedding that as hard as I try I cannot erase from my memory. It was supposed to be my cousin Soneji's wedding day; it turned out to be quite scandalous and absolutely horrible.

    You see, one of the maidens named Kali decided to take some of the shampoo from the Cleansing Ritual for herself. Had she never said a word about it (well at least until her tongue was removed) no one would have been the wiser. She saw no harm in what she did. The shampoo that the princess did not use in the cleansing Ritual is disposed of and she only took a small amount. In her mind, she was not stealing it; to justify her actions, she convinced herself that she was just being frugal and not wasteful and besides she thought, I should get some type of compensation for having to lose my tongue (it is only fair after all.) Unfortunately, she unwisely told one of the other maidens whose name is Ricci. Ricci of course promised secrecy but some secrets are too tempting not to tell. I believe that had she known what the telling of this particular secret would lead to she would have taken it to her grave. I can imagine that to this day she still blames herself and bears the scars for the horrific story that I am about to tell. As it went, Ricci told another maiden who told someone else and soon all the servants knew.

Normally, the servants (although they do gossip) are able to keep secrets especially this serious in nature. That was not to be the case this time. Ricci had been one of the maidens that was specifically chosen as a child to have a part in the Royal Wedding for the Princess. She was given a very important task; she was to assist in the creation of the sacred shampoo for the Cleansing Ceremony. Groomed from a very young age, she knew exactly what was expected of her when the time came. Honored, as she was to have this position, she had never gotten over the fear of having to forfeit her tongue. Throughout her years of preparation she secretly hoped that they would do away with this part of the custom by the time it was her turn to fulfill her role. Sadly, they had not; she had felt all but doomed until Kali told her what she had done. Even while swearing an oath of secrecy to Kali, she was plotting in her head exactly how this information would benefit her. She devised that if she did her due diligence, went to the Royal House, and divulged the terrible secret she might have some advantage in keeping her tongue. It all sounded good but the problem with that theory is that the one thing my father hated more than a thief was a traitor.

Ricci went straight away to the Royal House to request an audience with the King. The King was quite intrigued as to why a mere servant girl wanted to see him. He walked to his throne and sat down. Ricci began by telling the king that she had been sworn to an oath of secrecy but felt it was her duty to break the confidence that had been bestowed on her. The King stood up and put his hand out motioning for her to stop talking. He looked down at Ricci and said, "My child, think wisely before you break someone's confidence. All you really have is your word. When you die and move on people are not going to remember whether you were important or wealthy, they are going to remember the things you said. They will remember if you were trustworthy or a liar. So I beseech you to stop and think before you utter another word." With that, he sat back down and looked at Ricci. Poor simple-minded Ricci did not grasp the meaning or forewarning in the King's words and spilled her guts anyways. After she divulged her secret she looked up at the King expecting praise, instead she saw him bend his head down, rub his temples, and look up signaling to his guard. Ricci could not figure out what they were doing. The guard had walked over to the king and bent down so that King Rayno could whisper something in his ear.... Very peculiar Ricci thought as she watched this exchange. The guard nodded and before Ricci knew, what was happening the guard had her restrained and they were following the King to the Great Hall. Ricci struggled against the guard; she was frightened and very confused. She tried to question the guard that was brusquely dragging her along but he ignored her pleas. There is a large table in the room and the king instructed the other guard that was present to clear everything off the table. Once that was done, Ricci was pinned to the table by both guardsmen and the king himself performed the gruesome surgery of removing Ricci's tongue with his personal blade. While all this was going on a very crude sign was constructed. As the blood started to drip onto the table, a guard reached into the puddle and with his fingers, he wrote Traitor on the sign in her own blood. The King looked and her and said, "You were warned, you did not heed my warning. This sign is to be displayed around your neck every day until bedtime. When it starts to fall apart and fray, you will fashion another one. Only when I deem that that the punishment has fit the crime and I feel that you learned your lesson then and only then is when you may remove it. If I ever see you without it, you will forfeit another body part.

    Ricci was then carried out of the Royal House and left on the steps of the servants quarters not only with blood oozing from the fresh gaping hole that used to house her tongue, now she also bore the sign that was crudely tied around her neck. The servants that passed by spat in her direction. Not one of them dared to come to her aide. Word had passed quickly through the kingdom and they all knew what she had done.

For the most part, my father was a generous king; He always listened to both sides of an argument and thought long and hard before he passed out a sentence. Here on the island though, the caste system was very prevalent among the islanders. Rarely did you find them trying to better their situations in life. The belief was that you were born in a certain caste, you accepted your lot in life and if you were a good person then in your next life you would be greatly rewarded with a higher caste. It was considered a disgrace against the gods to not accept your lot in life and make the best of it. Ricci apparently was not satisfied with the life the gods had granted her and the very important job she had been groomed to do. Being a part of a Royal Wedding was a great honor." Yes, she would have had to forfeit her tongue but she was to have been rewarded not only in this life but also in the next. In the large scheme of things, that is a small sacrifice to pay.

Back at the Royal House, the King quickly gave the order to dispatch a guard to seize the maiden named Kali. The door to her family home was destroyed as the guard kicked it in. Kali was ripped out of the arms of her weeping mother. She kept screaming, "Why are you doing this? What have I done? Mother… Mother please do not let them take me!" As the guard clasped the metal irons around her neck, wrists and Ankles, she pleaded to her father, "Papa, Papa please help me. Papa…I do…Not…." The guard put a gag in her mouth and that was the end of the pleading. Her parents just hugged each other and sobbed in fear and disbelief. Her father (Cato) worked at the Island Mill and he had already heard the gossip about one of the maidens. Apparently, a maiden from the wedding party had stolen some of the sacred shampoo. He remembered the night before when Kali had come home from the Palace bragging about the shampoo. He warned her to discretely return the shampoo from whence it came and never say a word about it to anyone….ever! "Kali," her Papa said, "You have no idea what a grave sin you have committed wretched girl. Please child for once use your head…go put the sacred shampoo back where you found it….I pray it has not already been discovered to be missing. Please listen to me, Kali I beg you." She responded with, "Oh Papa, you worry too much. I have done nothing wrong.

They always make too much and the unused shampoo is thrown out anyway, so why can I not have it? After-all, it may as well be mine for I made it." Her father simply shook his head and walked away. He thought to himself, "No good can come of this."

Kali was taken to what can only be described as the "bowels of hell." She endured being tortured and raped as well as severely beaten. On the second day of her captivity (which was to be my cousin's wedding day,) she was to be made an example of in front of the entire kingdom. Very early that morning, they drug her from the dungeon into the open market place. There, for everyone to see, the guards stripped her naked. The crowd gasped at the sight of her battered and bruised body. She was to be branded with a hot iron as a thief. If I close my eyes, I can still smell her burning, smoldering flesh as the branding iron did its damaged to her skin. It haunts me to this day. We wanted to look away but everyone was warned that the king had forbade it. He wanted this day etched in the minds of every peasant, servant and anyone else that resided in his Kingdom. He made a speech for everyone to hear, "My subjects heed my words, (he pointed at Kali) as I speak look upon this wretched young girl who on this day will wish for the sweet release of death many times before she succumbs to it and her wish is finally granted. My word is law. Do not question or break my laws or you will suffer greatly just as this miscreant is about to. Anyone and I mean anyone (with that my father the king looked directly at me) that is caught looking away will be flogged or worse. I was fourteen years of age at that time and what I saw still makes me shudder with fear when I think on it.

The first thing they were going to do to Kali was use the branding iron that had been sitting in the hot coals for over an hour. Forcing her to watch, one of the guards removed the red and very angry looking branding iron from the coals and dripped a few drops of water on it; it immediately sizzled and hissed as steam billowed off it. Kali was shaking with fear and begging the king for mercy. She made herself as small as she could trying to meld her body into the wooden pole on which she was bound. She no longer felt the blisters and raw burns from the ropes that held her wrists above her head. She no longer cared that she was completely naked for all to see. The only thing she was concentrating on at that moment was that hot branding iron that was coming ever nearer to her and the pain she knew it was about to inflict on her body. She was shaking so much that one of the guards had to push her body into the pole so that the branding iron could leave its indelible mark on her porcelain skin. As the guard that held the branding iron got closer to Kali, she made one more plea for mercy to the king, this fell on deaf ears. Not even acknowledging her presence my father signaled for the guard to begin. Taking his signal from the king, the guard brusquely swung Kali around so her bare back was facing out to her spectators. Her hair seemed to be in the guard's way so he took his sword out and callously chopped it off. "No one will ever dare to marry you if you survive this day," He said as he laughed and threw her hair into the roaring fire. We were all paying attention to the guard with Kali's hair that is until I heard the most god- awful noise I have ever heard in my life. (Kali's deep guttural scream,) that scream came from A place way down deep inside. You could actually hear the raw pain she was feeling; if you closed your eyes (which we dared not do), I am sure you could have felt her pain as well. When the steam finally cleared, and you could see her it was enough to turn the strongest stomach. Her face was white as a ghost and you could see the beads of sweat dripping off her body. She looked as if she were having spasms because she was shaking so hard. It was the flesh on her back though that still makes my skin crawl. It looked as if it had melted off her body where the hot iron had touched her and her spine was exposed. (Nightmares were made of this stuff.) The skin that had not melted or seared to her spine was just hanging and some of it was still aflame. One of the guards noticed this; he took the heel of his boot and ground it into her back to put out the flame. Kali screamed again and then passed out from the pain and the shock. Her blood-curdling scream still wakes me from my sleep to this day. I can still relive every gruesome detail of what she suffered that day. I wondered how much more she could handle. She was as of yet still tied to the pole and as her body hung like a limp ragdoll, they beat and kicked her until she regained consciousness. Her jaw now hung down at an unnatural angle as if her skin was the only thing that held it together.

Most of the bones in her face were broken. One of the guards said he was tired of hearing her screech and beg; he roughly reached into her mouth and pulled out her tongue. "Take what you have coming to you wretched whore" he said. Kali futilely struggled against him, she knew what was about to happen. She was no match for his brute strength and there was nothing she could do to stop him. She desperately looked at the crowd pleading with her eyes that someone help but no aide came. She gave up, took a deep breath, looked the guard in the eyes, and said, "Take it, for after today when I sit with my maker I will have no need for it. My soul will speak for me. No words are necessary." He laughed nervously at her, took out his blade and crudely sliced through her tongue. Blood spurted from the open wound; her body once again slumped and strained against the ropes and chains that held her. The guard turned away from her limp body and held his prize up in the air spinning around so everyone could see it. When he was done showing off, he unceremoniously dropped it to the ground and as her blood ran down his arm, he used his boot to grind her tongue into the dirt as if it were a piece of trash or a cigarette that needed extinguishing. He turned towards the king seeking approval and laughed as he did this. At that point, the king signaled one of the other Guards to hand everyone rotten food and rocks. They threw these things at her. I am not sure they really wanted to do that to this poor girl but they were afraid not to. One of the guards sensing the apprehension in the crowd said, "Throw these at her or you can join her and share in death." With that warning in the air, everyone obeyed and pelted her with the rotten food and rocks. Most of the rocks hit their intended target, leaving angry welts, as they ripped through her already compromised skin. Now she had more seeping angry gashes adorning her body, these treacherous guards under direction from the king once more used the hot branding iron to cauterize Kali's open wounds. One of them laughingly said, "We cannot let infection set in now can we?" All the guards laughed at this.

    Kali's eyes opened and were as big as saucers as her flesh burned once more, there were tears streaming down her blood stained face. I had never in my life wished for death but at that moment, I desperately wished for hers. I quickly glanced around and the shock and horror I saw on everyone's faces matched my own. I could only imagine what other sadistic forms of torture she was to endure. I knew this would not and could not end until her body had taken its last breath. My heart ached for this poor girl. Yes, it is true, she had broken the law, but to be so severely tortured over shampoo....this was something that my young mind could not grasp. Even now, I do not pretend to understand the brutality she had to go through. I reasoned, if they were going to punish her and sentence her to death, it could have been swift and humane. Sadly, that was not to be on this day. She lasted many hours and we (the kingdom as a whole) had to watch it play out in entirety. The guards on the other hand seemed to take pleasure in torturing this poor waif. There were four of them and they took turns removing parts of her body. They cut off her ears and threw them into the fire. Kali was made to watch in horror and excruciating pain as they removed her fingers and toes one by one. These guards treated her no better than a stray dog that had gotten into the garbage. Every time she lost consciousness, her body would slump forward. The ropes that bound her wrists and across the middle of her torso were the only things holding her up. One of the guards came up with a game to play with her almost lifeless body. He grabbed the end of the rope that was not attached to Kali and pulled it taut until her feet no longer touched the ground. The other three guards would then strategically stand one on each side of her and make a sport out of knocking her from side to side like a piñata. As we watched Kali, swing from side to side there was a sick popping noise and sadly, we all knew that now her arms were dislocated and freed from the sockets that had held them. The last time she slumped forward, they were not able to rouse her by beating her. I hoped and prayed she was gone. They took something very pungent that is similar to smelling salts and placed it next to a jagged gaping hole in her face where her nose had once been. She once more revived again. You would think that they would have run out of ways to torment this poor girl by now. Not the case, the guards then unsheathed their swords and after heating them up in the hot coals, they took turns poking different areas of her torso. The more she squirmed and writhed in pain the more they poked and sliced at her leaving angry wounds and gashes all over her body. They wrote things on her exposed flesh. On her forehead, they wrote whore. Across her bare chest, they wrote traitor. They also made a sport of seeing who could remove her eyes with the point of a hot sword. (I learned that day that if you poke an eyeball with something hot it explodes.) Against my will, I watched all of this in horror. Tears were streaming down her face now but she could no longer scream or beg for death. She only had one eye, which was swollen and bleeding because of the failed attempts to remove it. I am not sure; I think she was blind by then. I just wanted her to die. "Why won't you die?" my mind screamed. "Enough is enough. She has been made an example of; can we please just end it now?" I knew that if I could at that moment I definitely would do it myself. It is then that I looked over at my father; hoping he would see the desperation in my eyes and end her life. What I saw stopped me cold and chilled me to the bone. My father, the man that comforted me when I had a nightmare. The man that read to me on stormy nights until I fell asleep. This caring, loving and ever doting father was not the man I saw that day. The man I was looking at had a smug pompous look on his face. His arms crossed his chest as if he were bored with the events. It was his eyes though; his eyes froze the blood in my veins and drained my face of all its color…his eyes were for lack of a better word….dead. I saw no remorse and no pity for this young girl. I saw only hate and disdain in the look on his face as well as in his posturing stance. I could not bear it and had to look away in shock and disbelief. I did not know this man…this man was not my father…. If I broke the law would he do to me what was being done to her…I wondered.

Although she was very petite and small in stature, Kali fought hard to endure every inconceivable thing those guards put her through on that day. I think in a way my father's idea of using her as an example of what happens when you break his laws backfired on him. When it all started early in the morning you could feel only hate and disgust for this girl from her audience. By the end of this outrageous horrible ordeal, people actually respected her for her strength. Later the mantra for Kali was, "They had broken her body but they were never able to break her spirit." I think the King's "example" became everyone's "Martyr." She was not thought of as a thief, a wretch, or a whore anymore. After that day, Kali was referred to as a fighter and a very brave young maiden that was needlessly tortured and killed. To this day, if ever anyone complains, all you have to do is simply whisper the name "Kali." Everyone from the very young to the elderly know the reference behind her name.

CHAPTER THREE

SHE IS GONE

After her body could take no more and finally expired you would think that it was over, it was not to be so. The guards looked to the King for guidance and asked…" Your Majesty, the girl is dead; shall we cut her down and let her family have her remains to prepare her for burial?" The King needed to think for a moment. All of us (his subjects) thought for sure that this horrible spectacle was over. Everything in me wanted to go over and cut Kali down from the pole to provide her a little dignity in death by covering up her battered naked body. As I started to cross the courtyard heading to her lifeless body, I looked around to see if I could see any of her family members. I had never met her or them before this day but by the looks of Kali,

I figured she probably had favored her mother. I spied a small group of people that were huddled together comforting each other. I started to walk over to them to get some help in cutting her down. Out of the corner of my eye, I saw that my father was making his way back over to us.

The King cleared his throat and started to speak, "I have decided what is to be done with this Ingrate's body. I do not feel that her death has yet paid her debt in full. I do not feel she needs to be rewarded by resting peacefully in hallowed ground." The crowd suddenly let out a gasp. (You see, the island folk believed that without blessed ground to rest in a soul would walk the plain of existence between Earth, Heaven and Hell.) She would never know rest, peace, or forgiveness for all of eternity. This would be worse than Hell. (Hell consisted of fire, brimstone and great lazy rivers of scalding molten hot lava. The damned souls that resided there earned their right to be there, but not Kali, she did not deserve to be there and we all knew it.) The King continued...."She has desecrated a sacred ritualistic custom which plays a very important part in the wedding ceremony. She may as well have spat in your cousin Soneji's face for the blatant disrespect she has shown her. The wedding may be ruined or at the very least have to be postponed." (Then he stopped mid-sentence at the shock and disbelief he saw on my face.) He came over to me, kneeled and then softly cupped my face in his hands. With a tone that was not so harsh, he began to explain all of it to me. "Yana, my beautiful Yana, you are still very young and I know you do not understand what transpired here today. You probably, no I take that back. By the look on your face, you think that the punishment was too harsh. Well, I am here to tell you that it was not harsh enough. You see my daughter; this wedding was going to save your cousin's palace from a marauding band of renegade cutthroats and thieves. These scourges had at one time been highly respected and honored guardsmen in King Malaki's Royal Guard. Now their mission is to take over, enslave her family, and brutally kill anyone that opposes them. Had she married Marek today then King Tula (Marek's father) would have defeated the mongrels and Soneji would still have a home. Because there was no wedding performed, by law he was not able to dispatch his troops.

During the execution this morning, I sent out a scout to see if King Malaki (Soneji's father) was safe. The scout was not able to physically see the king himself but he reported that the palace was set ablaze and many of the kingdom's guardsmen's severed heads adorned the wall that surrounded the kingdom. The fires lit up the early morning sky for miles as the smell of their burning flesh permeated throughout the land. I am not a betting man, but if I had to venture a guess, I would say that King Malaki's head is probably adorning the leader of the Ravager's spike or spear as we speak. According to their customs, in order to assume control the leader would have to perform a disembowelment on the ruler of the palace. Their usual practice is to slice open his gut while he still has breath in his body and as his intestines spill forth they hold his head and force him to watch as they are fed to the ravenous hogs. It is a slow painful death. What that wretched girl endured on this day is nothing compared to that or to the horror the women and children of that doomed kingdom would experience. They most likely forced the mothers to watch as their children (both boys and girls) were raped and burned alive. I am sure that the last sounds those poor mothers would have heard was the agonizing screams of their children as the flames claimed their young innocent victims.' Then most likely, the same men that raped and killed their children would have (for sport) raped and slit the throats of the grieving mothers. Yana put her head down so that her father would not see the tears that threatened to spill from her eyes and cascade down her face. When she could control her emotions once more, she then looked up at her father as if she were willing him to continue his story. Her father watched and patiently waited until his daughter composed herself enough to hear the rest. As her head came up he knew that was his signal to continue. The king began again, "You see Yana, the thoughtless act that imp embarked on has a dire consequence. Not just one life was forfeited on this day, an entire kingdom was lost." He looked deep into her eyes and said, "I always want you to remember that for every action there is a reaction. Before you make a decision that, you know is wrong, think long and hard because careless thinking can have deadly consequences that will affect more than the person or persons committing the act. Sometimes innocent lives will pay the price." Yana shook her head, not in acceptance but in understanding. Now the dead eyes from this morning made sense to her. The king gave her arm a squeeze and stood up to address his people, "It is for this reason alone that girl will also be disemboweled, tied to a horse and drug through the kingdom. Whatever part of her body is still intact after that will burn in the hot coals until there is nothing left but ash. That rogue will find no peace here. There will be no resting place for her. She is to be erased from existence as if she were never born. Her name is to be stricken from any written documentation. She is never to be mentioned in my presence. Her family will also pay the price for her actions. They must forfeit all their worldly belongings and leave the castle and the island never to return. Since I allow the trees to grow and I alone grant permission as to when they are cut down for canoes. This miserable excuse for a family will have to find their own means of leaving my island. They are denied anything from this island. No food, no water, no shelter and definitely no boat. If any of them or their future generations return, they will suffer a fate similar to that of hers. If anyone comes to his or her aide, you and your family and generations after that will suffer the same fate. From this day forward, they are to be shunned. No one looks in their direction….they do not exist." The king took a deep breath and continued, "I King Rayno decree from this day forward that the acts that transpired this morning will be but the first of many such events. Do not break or question my laws. The only reason you breathe is that I allow it. You have homes because I grant you that privilege. You eat because I provide you the means to grow your food. Your lives are mine to do with, as I will. Break my laws and you will pay with your life and those lives of your families and the lives of your unborn future generations. Never mention that depraved girl's name in my presence. Her family and generations to come will be ostracized until the last of her bloodline take their final breath. They will all meet up again in hell for their disgrace." With that, the King signaled his guardsmen to carry out the final humiliation and doom

Kali's soul for eternity. When Yana was sure, her father had left the area she once again scoured the crowd looking for Kali's family.

However, it has been said that they disappeared never to have been seen again. The rumor is that they walked out into the ocean and never came out. Mind you, that was just a rumor.

CHAPTER FOUR

THE GREAT ESCAPE

After Kali's ruthless death and the orders that the king had given. Kali's father (Cato) quickly took his wife and remaining children and attempted to leave the marketplace. His wife Menia struggled against him. She had not listened to a word of what the king was bellowing. All she had eyes for was her daughter. Her Kali was still hanging from that pole. She tried to stop Cato from leaving, "What are you doing? Husband, we have to take her with us," she cried to him. "We cannot just leave her here. We have to put her soul to rest. Please husband, please, give me my daughter that I may wash her and wrap her wounds. I must perform this last act of love for her; please I need to prepare her body for burial. I beg of you Cato, let me hold my sweet girl one last time." Cato heard the pain and anguish in Menia's voice so he stopped and looked deep into her eyes. He sweetly said to her, "Menia, my sweet Menia, Kali is gone love." Menia started to protest and Cato put his fingers to her lips, "Menia, the king means to have us killed on this day. Do you want to mourn one or all?" Kali's mother understood and hung her head down. She no longer fought against her husband; she just meekly let him lead her and their children from the marketplace as silent tears streamed down her face. She said no more until they reached their home. Whence they got there and everyone was safely inside Cato barricaded the door. He looked at the frightened faces of his remaining children and said to them with a weak smile, "Once you lock the door, the outside stays outside." They seemed to accept that and it put them at ease if for only a little while. Cato sent his family to the cellar, "Do not come out until I fetch for you." He had to think about what to do. He knew he was alone in this. He daren't ask anyone to help them. Everyone he knew had his or her own families to worry about and this would be too great a risk. If they left in the black of the night, there might be a chance for their survival. However, how? He had no canoe. He could go to the Mill and take enough wood to fashion a raft. How though without taking the chance of being seen? He had no tools and besides there was just not enough time. They could try to swim it. Maybe, he and Menia were strong enough, the children though….No, damn, none of these ideas had a chance in hell of working. Sadly, when Cato awoke this morning he had steeled his emotions and prepared himself for the task of burying his eldest daughter. When she had been drug off in Irons, she might as well have already been dead. She had sealed her fate when she took the sacred shampoo. He just never thought that they would all pay the price of his stupid impetuous daughter. She had never been one to think things through. Now, unless he could come up with a plan his entire family would parish. He understood why the king did what he did to Kali. Although he never expected to watch, his child go through such horrendous torture. A tear slid down his face when he thought about all that she had experienced. When he closed his eyes, he could see her writhe and strain against the bonds that held her.

This young maiden, his daughter; he was there when she struggled to take her first breath and today he watched her struggle as she fought to take her last. If that were not enough, it pained him even more to know that her soul will never find peace. As a father, all you want to do is protect your family and he had failed them. He vowed they were not going to die, not here and not now. Cato was so deep in thought that he did not hear the quiet knock on the door. Then, there was a louder knock and that one he heard. Fear quickly crept into his heart for he thought the king had sent guards to take them away and torture or kill them all. Tentatively he said, "Who-who is there?" A young feminine voice responded, "Mr. Sula, please let me in lest I be seen by someone. I have come to help you and your family." Quickly Cato opened the door and was utterly shocked at who he saw on the other side of his door. "Your Highness, please-please come in." He muttered. There before him stood Princess Yana. She quickly entered the crude home and glanced around nervously fearing the worse, "Where is your family Mr. Sula? "I have them hidden Your Highness." Cato responded. Yana began again, "Mr. Sula, we do not have much time. I have heard that the king is going to dispatch the guards to come and burn down your home and kill whomever they find. I have a plan but we must move quickly." Cato was puzzled, "Your Highness, you are not immune to your father's wrath. If he finds out that, you have helped us he will have no choice but to punish even you as he decreed. You are risking your life for people you have never met." Yana stopped what she was doing and looked him square in the eyes, "Mr. Sula, while I understand that Kali broke the law she did not deserve what was done to her and she does not deserve to be damned. If I am to be a fair ruler someday, I have to do what I know to be just and right. I have to stand up to opposition even if it is my father. Sometimes, when you know you are right in your actions you stand alone and fight alone because the majority of the people are too afraid to stand with you or simply do not care. If caught I will accept my fate. I know if it be death then I will meet my maker with a true soul." Cato looked at this young girl of fourteen with such awe and respect. "Your Highness we are indebted to you for our entire lives. I will never be able to repay your kindness or your bravery." Yana looked at him and smiled, "Seeing you and your family safe is all the repayment that I require…now we must hurry! Please gather your family…I have a large canoe waiting on the other side of the island." With that, Cato fetched his family out of the cellar. His wife was shocked and eyed Yana cautiously; she pulled her husband aside and asked him why the princess was here. "Dear wife, she is here to save us….gather a few provisions', have the children put on a few layers of clothes (not too many that anyone will notice that they are missing.)" Yana tried to hurry them along, "There is not much time and we have to hurry!" Within a few minutes, Parents and children were ready to go. Yana carefully peaked out the back door, she saw no one so she motioned them one-by-one to come out and run for the overgrown brush that led to the path and to their freedom. The trek through the brush was treacherous; normally if anyone took this way at night, a torch would light the night for them. This group dared not don a torch lest it draw unwanted attention their way. "Do not look back, keep your eyes forward and try not to make any sounds." Yana instructed. The Sula family obeyed. It took many hours to get to the secluded cove where true to her word a large canoe was tethered to a limb that hung over the edge of the shore. "There it is." Yana pointed her finger towards the canoe. Cato got on one knee and blessed Yana, "Thank you Princess, you have saved my family from certain death. I will find a way to repay you." She looked into his eyes and said, "Keep your family safe, paddle swiftly, use no light and never look back. Go to the island O'Sangha, which is due east. Do not stop until you get there." She then reached into her pocket and pulled out a beautiful bracelet and a few rings that were just as exquisite. She quickly handed them to Cato. "Take these and pawn them. They should be worth enough money to book you passage on the Supply Ship. Do not tell them your names, many of the islanders cannot read or write….you must pretend the same. Sign your name with an "x" and do not speak to anyone. Once you reach the Mainland quickly disappear." She grabbed Cato's hand and gave him something else that was wrapped in a handkerchief with a crude string holding it closed. He looked at her puzzled once more. She wiped a tear from her face and looked up at him, "Mr. Sula, this is all that I could find…it-it's Kali's finger (or part of it.) You do not need her entire body to lay her at rest. Find hallowed ground on the Mainland and bury her. Please give her soul peace and forgiveness." Cato had tears streaming down his face. He was so deeply grateful to this brave young Princess. He had no words. When he looked at his wife, she too was crying. She went over and hugged Yana. "Go; go quickly now….we have wasted too much time. You have to be well out to sea before the sun rises. Remember, stay east. Good luck…. now go!" With that, the Sula's got in the canoe and disappeared into the black night. It was almost dawn when Yana arrived back at the castle. Her father was in such a rage that he had forgotten to check on her. She quickly made it up to her room before the Changing of the Guard and changed her clothes. She noticed that the sticker bushes had cut her legs up pretty badly so she would have to cover them up and make sure no one noticed. Seeing her father so angry only meant one thing. She smiled to herself because she knew that while she could not help Kali in her time of need she was able to help her family escape death and eventually lay her soul to rest. There was one more thing she had to do….

She was going to take a page out of her father's book. She smiled to herself; she was going to make sure that no one went looking for the Sula's….She was going to use the servants to start a rumor. She knew just where to go and who to tell. Off to the kitchen she went. Yana entered the kitchen where she was going to put the last part of her plan into action. Just as she had hoped, the Palace staff were all huddled in front of the oven gossiping. They glanced in her direction barely paying her any mind. Yana slowly walked over with a somber look on her face and said, "Poor family, can you believe what they did?" One of the house cleaners stopped mid- sentence and looked up at her. Yana continued…."Just something I heard." She had their attention now, "So sad." Then a house cleaner interjected with, "I know…Poor things…Can you believe? Oh my no, such a shame." Yana knew she had them now and casually said, "I heard that Kali's family was so distraught and with no way out, they all held hands and walked out into the surf." The Palace staff looked at her and nodded in agreement.

Yana went on...."but this is only a rumor. I did not see this for myself." Her plan went perfectly, later that same afternoon it was spread all over the palace as well as the island that the poor distraught Sula family saw no alternative and took their own lives by walking out into the surf never to return. Mind you, this is just simply a rumor.

CHAPTER FIVE

THE KING

My father had become a very powerful king although this had not always been the case. Let me explain…After Soneji's debacle of a wedding day I accidently stumbled onto my Mother's journal. It was quite a revelation. I found out things I would have never believed to be true of the man that I fondly called "my father." Firstly, the name "Rayno" is fictitious.

My father was not born of royal blood, nor did he marry into the royal family. I have gathered bits and pieces through my 16 years and my mother (although she was not here) confirmed it from the grave through the words I read in her journal. It is quite a tale to tell, if it were not my family I would never believe it to be true. About 16 years ago, my father was on the run from the law. Wanted for murder, he started out as a petty thief to support his habits. His quick temper was fueled by his use of drugs and his abuse of alcohol.

He used to get drunk and high on a daily basis. When he would run out, he would start an argument with my mother thinking that she was hiding money from him or stealing his drugs to sell. Maybe it was just an excuse to beat her. She obviously never touched his drugs or hid his money. His paranoia led him to such thoughts. She loved him though and no one understood why…. It became normal to see her sporting a black eye or a fat lip so no one thought anything about it when she was not at bible study. Bart (my father's real name) made some lame excuse saying she fell down the basement steps while doing laundry and was recovering at home. Everyone figured he beat her as usual and she was too embarrassed to leave her house. Seriously, how many times in a week can you run into the cabinet or trip off the porch and yes, the basement excuse was used often too. Bart was a big man who was quick to temper. Everyone in their small town tried to stay on his good side. It is true what they say about small towns, everyone knows everyone else's business.

Bart's drug and alcohol abuse were common knowledge but no one ever said anything about it (especially not to Bart.) When he asked to borrow money, whether it was for their groceries or it was their bill paying money, they did not hesitate to give him everything they had. Most of the time, to remain on his good side they insisted that it was a gift and did not need to be repaid. No one, I mean no one ever dared to ask what the money was for (they knew already.) "Sometimes it is best to let the sleeping bear lie and not poke him." They justified it in their minds by telling themselves that they saved Justine (my mother) from a beating on that day. People normally tried to avoid him. As far as the murder goes, you are probably thinking it was a drug deal gone badly or maybe he got in a fight and he hit someone too hard. Sadly, it was none of the above. Bart Randolph murdered his wife of 10 years. Yes, my father murdered my mother and if you do the math it happened on the day, I was born. Apparently, my mother went into labor and my father was in a very bad mood. Initially, when he found out she was pregnant he had no feelings of joy about becoming a father. He actually had no feelings at all other than irritation over the fact that with a baby there would be less money for him to spend on his drugs and alcohol. He looked at her with disgust when she told him and he said…."I guess an abortion is out of the question? I can always get a coat hanger and get rid of it for you." My mom did not miss a beat, she crossed the room to stand next to him and wrapped her arms around his neck and assured him that everything would be fine. Dear old dad did not reciprocate her hug or affection he just stood there stoic, with his arms hanging at his sides glaring at her. "Keep it away from me he said in a menacing voice…I have no time for a screaming

brat." Mom knew better than to push the issue so she backed off. She had been so sure, he would warm up to the idea of being a dad but now she was questioning herself. She was lost in her own thoughts and not paying any attention to Bart when all of a sudden she was snapped back to reality by a sharp searing pain to the side of her face and a horrible ringing in her left ear. The sheer force of his punch had hurled her to the floor, left her dazed, and confused. Bart was standing over her, "Are you paying attention to me now?" He bellowed. He had his fist clenched poised and ready to continue the assault with a very icy evil grin on his face…"There is more where that came from dear wife." Justine had recovered a bit and used her left arm to protectively cover her belly. Her right hand shot out in front of her as she pleaded with him to stop.

"Good, now that I have your attention there are a few ground rules about this parasite that you insist on giving birth to. Make sure you listen very closely, "Number one….Keep the damn thing quiet or I will, number two….You are not spending any of my money on it. I do not care if you have to put a paper bag over your head and sell your body just make sure you use your own money. Number three….If it breaks anything or gets into anything of mine it will rue the day it did and so will you. Number four and this is very important….nothing changes, I do not care if you are sick or tired but the house will stay clean, my meals will be hot and homemade and my clothes will be clean and ironed every day. If I find out you are using processed food I will make you wish you never met me. If I see any clothes in the laundry basket then I will give you a real excuse for not being able to do the laundry….I will break your damn arm. If it cries a lot, I will break its jaw so it cannot make any noise and then I will break yours for letting it cry and disturb me".

With that, Bart walked out of the house to go find an open window so he could get the money to take care of his sudden craving. He had money, a lot of money but he enjoyed the thrill that breaking and entering gave him. He also knew no one would dare turn him in. He ruled that town; there was no question about that... Justine still sat on the floor all the way against the wall. Her heart was racing and she was shaking so much she could not pull herself up. Always, she was careful around Bart. Could she protect his child from him? Would he actually hurt his own flesh and blood she wondered as she subconsciously rubbed the side of her face.

When she was finally able to stand on her wobbly legs, she made her way over to the bathroom to look in the corner of the mirror that was not shattered. She cringed at what she saw. It was another black eye and her cheek split open and already starting to swell and turn purple. She put her head down; she was supposed to have her first prenatal appointment the next day…how could she go looking like this. What if they called Bart and questioned him? She hoped that would not happen, but she could not think about that now. She had no idea if he was going to be home for dinner but she knew it better be ready especially after today's episode. With that, she busied herself making his food. Although it hurt, she found herself smiling and humming. She had a little person growing in her belly and she knew that when he or she made their appearance in this world their daddy's cold heart would melt and a wonderful doting father would appear. As she cut up the broccoli, she imagined Bart, the baby and herself going to the park as normal families did, having a picnic, and laughing. She could see the love in his eyes for his wife and child. This is what she prayed and longed for.

Everyone tried to warn her about Bart. He has a short violent temper. He will throw a punch to get your attention rather than ask a question. Justine had met him at a party; he treated her with nothing but kindness. She knew that he was from the wrong side of the tracks. "He's just misunderstood," she would say. "You do not know the real Bart like I do." Bart on the other hand knew that Justine was a good girl from a rich family. She was very gullible and naïve, he saw an easy mark and he took it. After a few sweet lies he had her convinced that he loved her. He could be quite the charmer when he wanted something. She had money, well, she was getting ready to come into a lot of money and he meant to have it. He scowled to himself though; he knew in order to control her money he would have to marry her.

Within three months, my parents were married. Justine's trust fund was to be signed over to her when she turned 34. For one year, Bart would have to lay on the charm thick. For the first year of their marriage, it was everything Justine had hoped for and more. Bart was loving, kind and attentive to her every need. He took her out for dinner and dancing almost every week. He was the perfect husband and she was very happy. A couple of months into their marriage Bart nonchalantly asked my mother what she planned on doing with her inheritance. My mom responded, "Hmmm, honey, I hadn't really thought about it much. What do you think I should do? I hate thinking about money. I really do not have the head for figures." She giggled and ran her fingers up his arm. Dad saw his way in and took it, "Babe, why don't you sign it over to me? I can take care of the finances that way you don't have to worry your pretty little head over it." My mother smiled up at him, "You really do love me don't you Bart?" "Justine how can you ask that Doll? I worship you." She sighed real big, leaned over the side of the couch and put her head on the top of her crossed arms, "Well then, how do we go about doing it? I don't even know who to talk to or any of that. Daddy always handles all the money stuff." Bart smiled and squeezed her arm, "Don't worry baby, I will talk to dear old Pops for you."

Eight months later my mother gave my father control over her trust fund without thinking twice about it. Her reasoning was that when you marry someone you are supposed to trust in them 100%. The day of the signing, they walked arm-in-arm into the lawyer's office; he even pulled the chair out for her to sit down in. My mom's family lawyer had some concerns about this so he tried to explain the legalities of what she was doing to my mother. My father fearing that she might change her mind leaned in and whispered something into her ear that made my mom blush. "Oh stop it Bart, you are a bad, bad boy." Dad looked at her and said, "Babe, you honestly have no idea." He once again knew he had mom right where he wanted her looked at the lawyer and said…"Yeah, yeah, yeah…can we get on with it; I have things I need to do. Justine just sign the damn paper giving me the rights and then I'll sign it and we'll be done." My dad started loudly tapping his foot on the floor and leaned back in his chair with his arms crossed on his chest. He had a very bored look on his face. Impatiently he said, "Why is this taking so long? It's just a piece of paper and it is just money"…he smiled and laughingly said, "A Lot of Money!" Mom signed the paperwork; after my father confirmed that there was no waiting period. He grabbed his coat, looked at his wife, and said, "Move your ass, I'm dropping you off at home and I'm going out with all my money and getting drunk." Mom playfully asked if she could go and my father looked at her and said, "Sweetheart, the honeymoon is over." He laughed and walked out the door not bothering to look back. My mom looked a little bewildered she stood there and watched him leave the office. Quickly she realized that all eyes were on her so she composed herself and said, "Oh, don't mind that, you don't know him….He is such a kidder." Nervous laughter followed her she gathered her coat and left the office. Once Bart got in the car, he laid on the horn impatiently waiting for my mother to get across the busy street. "If you had been any slower I would have made you walk." My mother opened the front door and was about to get in the car when he pushed her out and told her to get in the back seat. She thought he was joking and attempted to get in the front seat again but this time he pushed her unceremoniously out of the door with his foot. I think she got the message that time and climbed in the backseat. He hit the gas and they sped off. Every time she tried to talk to him, he would just turn the radio up louder until she finally gave up and just stared out the window. That was the beginning of the end.

Things started to get bad quickly for Justine. At first, she would make excuses to herself as to why he hit her. After a while, she just started expecting to be slapped around. Her fairytale marriage was over. If Bart had a bad day then my mom got beat. If his boss yelled at him, he came home and beat my mom. Other times, he would come home, she would be in the kitchen cooking, and he would just walk up behind her and punch her in the back of the head unprovoked. Sometimes there was an excuse but mostly I think he enjoyed having that kind of power over another human being. Yet she loved him and so she stayed. She hardly ever went out because she hated the pity she saw in everyone's eyes.

    The only place she was allowed to go was her Bible Study class. She was there every Wednesday night without fail. She loved it, they sang and laughed and found the beauty in life by reading and learning the scripture. No one cared how she looked or what Bart made her wear; she was always accepted no matter what. It was always a warm and happy environment. This was the only thing she had to look forward to each week. A warm hug waited for her. She sang and laughed, for just a moment in time she could forget everything. She was not someone's daughter, she was not someone's wife, and she was simply Justine. No one could tell her what to do or not do. Nothing was expected of her. She was free and the only regret she ever had was when it was time to go home. If she could stay there forever, she most definitely would. Bart never allowed her to attend the retreats or the picnics or any other church activity. Bible Study though, that was her happy place. Sometimes though it did bother her that if her "brother and sisters" from her Bible Study class saw her anywhere else but in class they would go out of their way to avoid her, especially if she was in the company of her husband. She did not blame them, everyone was afraid of Bart. Mostly they just looked away. Justine felt like a pariah in the town that she had grown up in. Bart had turned her into a shell of the happy bubbly teenager from yester-year that used to skip happily down Main Street. She always had a warm smile for everyone she met. Growing up she had big plans for herself, now she felt worthless and lower than the dirt on the bottom of a shoe. After you are told repeatedly that, you are nothing that you are no good and a waste of human breath from the person that is supposed to love you unconditionally it is hard to believe anything else. When the person that is supposed to be your biggest supporter treats you as if you are the biggest failure you start to feel that way. When you constantly hear about what a disappointment you are then when you look in the mirror that is what you see. When you hear every day, that you are not the woman he married, and that you are the one that makes him do the things to you that he does because you deserve no better, then you accept your fate and even start looking forward to the harsh words and the beatings. You might think that is a very misconstrued way of looking at things. When you are starved for any type of attention then positive attention and negative attention are still exactly that….attention. Bart destroyed her self-esteem. If they were out in public together, he always made her walk behind him. "Women are inferior beings and do not deserve to be a man's equal, therefore you my wife must walk no less than ten paces behind me always." He even treated her like a dog around her own family.

"Every year, towards the end of the summer, Mom's family would throw a huge party. They invited the entire town. Once, Fred (Justine's older brother) confronted Bart about the way he treated his wife. Bart who was sitting down having a conversation with a pretty young thing ignored him at first. Justine who was being made to stand behind her husband (as usual) quickly spoke up and said that it was fine. She said as she tried to warn Fred with her eyes, "Oh Fred you are being silly, Bart is very good to me. Please do not think for one minute that he mistreats me." At that, Bart shot out of his chair and glared at Justine, "Were you told you have permission to speak?" Justine put her head down and shook her head no. "Bart continued, "No one cares what you have to say dear wife so shut up before I make you. I do not and I'll repeat, I do not need you to explain my actions or make excuses for me to anyone." Justine started to mumble something and Bart raised his hand and slapped her across the face. "Are you stupid? Do you like when I hit you? Are you trying to make me look bad? I did not give you permission to say a word." Justine started to look up at him, big tears were streaming down her face and her cheek was red and puffy as was her eye. He looked at her with such hate and started to raise his hand again to hit her once more. Something stopped him; Fred had interfered and grabbed his forearm to prevent it. As soon as Bart realized that Fred had his arm, he looked at him and snarled, "Do not interfere in my business. She is my wife and my property and I will treat her anyway I want. If you know what is good for you, you will release my arm now!" Fred thinking the situation had been defused released Bart's arm and started to walk away.

Without a second thought Bart balled up his fist and with all his strength spun around and buried his fist in the side of his wife's head…"See what you started and now I have to finish it. This is why I treat you the way I do. You are an imbecile Remember this wifey because what is about to happen next is all your fault, you did this and you have no one else to blame for it." The assault on Justine was so unexpected and happened so fast that no one had time to react. Fred was unaware of what transpired because he had his back to Bart and Justine and was almost to the back steps that led into the kitchen. He had worked up quite a thirst after confronting Bart. He felt pretty proud of himself for standing up for his sister. "It was about time someone did," he thought to himself as he went to grab a glass off the shelf. Bart crossed the distance between himself and the back door to the house in a few easy strides. He slammed open the back door and before Fred knew what hit him, Bart had one hand around his throat and the other fist was pummeling Fred in the face over and over again. Fred was unsuccessfully trying to defend himself. The hand that had Fred by the throat slammed his head on the stone counter top and slid the side of his face over the entire surface. As he got to the end of it, he brought his knee up and drove Fred's head directly into his knee. Fred's head had been hit so many times now he was very dizzy and could not keep his focus on what was happening to him. His eyes were almost completely swollen shut, which made his vision blurry and out of focus. He was moaning and begging Bart to stop. Bart drug Fred outside and continued to beat him until his face was swollen, bloody and unrecognizable. Bart was in a rage and completely focused on the task at hand when he heard a voice yell, "Bart, for god's sake Bart stop or you are going to kill him. He has learned his lesson, please let me help him." Bart recognized the voice….it was Justine's father.

Bart ceased his assault, grabbed a drink, and sat down to enjoy the rest of the party as if this was an everyday occurrence. Justine used to look so forward to this. Before Bart, she would get together with her girlfriends months in advance and plan what they were going to wear and who they were going to talk and flirt with etc. Now, Bart picked out what she was to wear and instructed her under threat of violence that she was not to speak to anyone. She obeyed and stood behind him with her shoulders slumped and eyes cast down to the ground. People that were her childhood friends would quickly glance in her direction and look away when Bart would glare at them. Justine had no friends and even her family were all afraid of Bart. She had no one to turn to for help. Yet she loved him. Maybe she loved him because he was all she had anymore. He alienated her from everyone. She asked him once why he treated her the way he did. "Because I can, and now I own you. There is nothing you or anyone else can do about it." "Do you hate me that much? What have I ever done to you except love you? "She asked. He sneered and growled back…"You and your kind have always looked down on me. You all thought you were better than I was. Well honey, the laugh is on you now, I took the most popular sought after girl and made her mine. I took all your money and made you broke and completely dependent on me. I took something and made it into nothing. I did all of this because I hate you and what you stand for. Now everyone looks at you and laughs when they see what you have become. I have the respect now baby and you…. you my dear have nothing. You are nothing and I am the richest most desirable man in the town. I should thank you for being so naïve and stupid. Instead, I think I will spit in your face. That is exactly what my father did, he spit in her face.

CHAPTER SIX

JUSTINE IS PREGNANT

My dad loved to hear my mother scream. He was never gentle in anything he did. That night he took my mother against her will. That is the night my mother got pregnant with me.

That is how my mother's life went for the most part, no better and no worse. She almost became immune to the beatings. She tried to be obedient but it did not matter he beat her anyway. Mom realized she was pregnant about 3 months later. You would have thought she would resent me but she did not. The more of her journal that I read the more I found out how much she protected me from my father's wrath. As a matter of a fact, she protected my unborn life with her own on the day I was born.

Since my father wanted nothing to do with me, he refused to take her to the doctor. When he found out, she was going to prenatal appointments on her own he beat her until she promised she would never go again. He told her...."you wanted the thing growing in you so you have it all by yourself. Go squat in the yard with a stick in your mouth for all I care." My mother tried to take care of herself the best she could but Dad never bought much food. The food he bought was for himself. When he went to the grocery store, he stocked up mostly on liquor. My mother knew better than to complain though because as big as her belly was it would be an easy target if he decided to hit her there. She scrounged what she could and rationed everything. Sometimes she wrote..."I cried and asked god what I did to deserve this?" She begged god, "Please watch over my baby, I have a bad feeling that I will not be around to see her or him grow up." When I read that, it sent shivers up and down my spine.

I put the journal down for a minute. The man I am reading about, this Bart Randolph....This cannot be my father. The father I know is loving and kind to me. My father took time to explain the things I did not understand. He walked with me and held my hand. He read me bedtime stories and sang songs that we made up when there were storms so I would not be afraid. He stayed up with me all night if I was running a fever or was sick. As I read the words from my mother so many years ago, I could see some similarities in the way he treated the subjects. I was confused though because for someone that did not want me, I knew his love was genuine. Yet, I sometimes saw the smug satisfaction in his eyes and his demeanor when he gave the command to the Head of the Royal Guardsman to flog or torture someone. I could see glimpses of the man my mother described in detail...I just wondered when it came to me....What had made him change? My father reveled in controlling someone and here he had an entire Island of people willing to obey his every command and lay down their lives for him if they had to with no questions asked. For a control freak, this was heaven. There was no better life for my father than being a king. He was a natural at it. Seeing him in action, you would never believe he was not born into the role. After reading my mother's journal, so many unasked questions I have had about dear old dad were answered. I had read enough to know though not to ask him any questions about my mother, just to go along with the stories he always told me about her death. He insisted that it was a private matter just between us. "Yana" he would say, "The people must never see me as weak. I am a god to them. "I agreed" and waited patiently for him to (in a trembling voice) start off by saying, "Daughter, your mother loved you so much she died for you." I had felt guilty for many years because of that statement. Now though, I know the truth, my mother wrote about part of that day. Of course, she did not write about her actual moment of death. It is hard to say…."Excuse me, Bart, before you kill me, will you please let me jot down what you are doing play-by-play so that anyone that finds and reads this will know how I died, why I died and who killed me." All I really know is what I saw on a newspaper clipping that my father had stashed away. My mother's journal ends that day. Her last entry talked about how bad a mood he was in that morning. Apparently, whatever type of drug he had picked up the night before had fallen out of his pocket. All the anticipation he had at the thought of getting high was squashed when he reached into his pocket and all he pulled out was lint. He flew into a rage and tore his car apart. Again, he came up empty handed. He even retraced his steps but that was also a dead end. He just ended up going home. Justine had been having contractions all night and when Bart got home, she told him as much. He shrugged his shoulders and said to her, "Not my problem, you wanted it now you deal with it. Remember what I said…no doctors and no hospitals….you figure it out and leave me out of it. Now get out of my face I am busy." As Justine started to walk away, he stopped her by grabbing her arm and in a very cold and deadly tone he said, "You better not make a mess or I'll mop it up with your face, that's a promise or a threat you take your pick. Do not test me." Justine backed away very quickly and got out of the room. She took her journal and locked herself in the bathroom. "It's just you and me baby…we can do this. "She said. With that, she sat down on the cold floor, pulled her knees up to her chest, and waited for the pain to come. She was in labor all night; she tried to stay as quiet as possible. Sometimes she let out a gasp or a whimper but mostly she just bit her lip and clenched her fists, and waited until the contraction stopped. That was the last entry in her journal....

The rest of the story of my mother's death at the hands of my father I found in this newspaper clipping…I replaced the article where I found it. What had originally been a normal rebellious act of a bored teenager curious to see what was in boxes marked "Personal / Private." Became a trip into a past that Yana never wanted to know about. Her mother had suffered horrific abuse at the hands of the man that had sworn to love, honor and protect her all the days of his life. How can I hate the man from my mother's journal? I have never known this man. The man my mother talks about is not my father….it just cannot be. Thinking back, I had never seen my father do any drugs, a beer or two on occasion. I had never even seen him so much as smoke a cigarette.

Before I stumbled onto my mother's journal I had known nothing about her other than I had supposedly killed her while I was being born. When in private, if I asked my father to tell me about my mother he weaves an elaborate tale of a sickly woman that had defied the doctors and become pregnant anyway. According to my father, she had a very weak heart. In order not to harm you, she would have to stop taking her heart medication during the pregnancy. The doctors had told both her and my father that if Justine got pregnant she probably would not survive. They defied the doctor's orders because they had wanted a baby so badly they thought if they monitored everything and were extremely careful that they could beat the odds and survive the pregnancy and the birth. They loved each other so much they wanted a piece of each one of them rolled up into one perfect little person. "Yana, you are a testament to the love that your mother and I had for each other. Why do you think I have never remarried? There is no one else that can ever take the place of your mother in my heart. When I look at you, I can see her in the way you smile and shrug your shoulders, and yes, especially the way you roll your eyes as you are doing right now." Bart went on, "The pregnancy was pretty easy for your mom, I waited on her hand and foot. We attended every prenatal appointment and I read every book on raising babies that I could get my hands on. To avoid any unnecessary stress on your mom's heart we had a pre-scheduled C-Section already setup. Everything was going great until your mom went into premature labor. On the way to the hospital, she started having chest pains and then trouble breathing. Yana I tried to get her to the hospital as quickly as possible. I even contemplated pulling over to try to help her. There was nothing I could do so I decided the best thing was to pray that she could hold on until we got to the ER. I kept trying to talk to her but soon; she was just slurring her words and then not responding at all. When I got to the hospital, she was no longer breathing and she was the color of gray ash. I screeched the tires and laid on the horn shouting that my wife needed help. The hospital staff quickly started CPR and gave her oxygen. As she died in front of my eyes, I suddenly remembered that you were in her belly. I started jumping up and down and yelling like a crazy man, "My Wife, she is pregnant, she was having contractions…please save our baby!" The Emergency staff quickly realized that she was indeed pregnant. They put her on life support machine, prepped her body for an emergency C-Section, and whisked her away to surgery. Dad's voice breaks and he tears up every time he tells me this story, "An hour later they placed you my beautiful Yana in my arms. You were perfect and I knew that from that moment it would be you and I against the world." After that, my dad always said it is too painful to talk about so we leave the story there.

Now I know in order for him to remember all the lies he tells he uses the "less is more" thought process. "The less you tell the easier it is to remember what you told. I guess if you lie about something as often as he does about my mother you actually begin to believe your own lies. That is what happened to my father, he now believes his own lies. No one ever dares to check him on anything; he is after- all the King. I was in shock at everything I found out that rainy gloomy day. My adventure had turned into a horror movie and the star actors were my mother, my father and myself.

CHAPTER SEVEN

MOTHER NATURE

I do not know exactly how we made it to this island castle other than my father was very good at gambling and he won somebody's boat passage ticket to this island in a card game. Wanted by the authorities for the murder of his wife, he was relieved to have the means of escaping to somewhere that the US authorities had no jurisdiction. I was only a few days old at that point and stuffed into his duffle bag asleep while all this was going on.

While we were waiting for the boat to leave the harbor, my father decided a beer sounded good and slipped into a small pub. He overheard someone rambling on about being a Prince and going to the island where he was to rule. He was quite drunk as he regaled his story. He, had never met the Royals, which ruled that island, they were distant cousins. The king took ill and being the last living heir, he had a duty as a Royal to leave his life and his future wife to go rule an island in the middle of the Pacific Ocean that he knew nothing about. He got up to relieve himself and my father followed him into the bathroom. My father quickly strangled him took his identification and discarded the body out the back window. He left the bathroom, grabbed his duffle bag and headed for the boat. That is the story of how my father became the king that he is today. I do not remember much from when I was little but I do here the stories of how we ended up on the shores of Zanzi Island. If I had to venture a guess, I am sure my father's intentions were to get rid of the duffle bag with me in it once we were safely out of US Waters. If he had intended for people to know about me, why would he keep me stuffed in his duffle bag? I think he removed me from my dying mothers belly either so that I would have been a bargaining tool if he got caught or maybe because he did not want to be wanted for two murders? I do not know his reasoning and that is something I will probably never know. From another newspaper clipping, that I found apparently Mother Nature had other things in mind.

Honestly, though this is only conjecture on my part, I think this may have thwarted my father's plans and saved my life. It amazes me how my father is able to take every tragedy that occurs in his life and turn it into something that somehow is always a benefit to him. Think about it, what he did to my mother should have had him swinging in the gallows or riding the lightening on the electric chair that is fondly referred to as "Old Smokey," he outsmarts the law and escapes. He does not only escape his fate though, he becomes a king. How many people can say that? For the life of me, I do not understand why my father has kept so much proof against him. Personally, I think I would have gotten rid of it long ago. So far, the newspaper clippings I have found are about a man found strangled with no identification. I am thinking this is the real Prince Rayno. If there were an investigation, they would find that the real King was not married and definitely did not have an infant daughter. That is not the case and lest you forget that this all took place 16 years ago. I think by now, they have quit looking for my father.

Ever diligent about not being caught, one of the first things my father changed when he took the throne was the tourists' visits. The new monarchy (my father) said that we needed to preserve the original native customs. We could not accomplish that with the influences of a Westerner's way of life pulling up to our shores every week. He decreed Zanzi a private island. Anyone that wanted to come to Zanzi had to have permission from the King (my father.) I can tell you that was not happening any time soon if ever. He also convinced the island elders that the Western Technology aka. Computers, Cell Phones, Laptops....All of that had a detrimental effect on preserving the ancient ways. Pretty soon, he got his way and we were totally cut off from technology; there is no cable or internet on the island. We never have visitors unless they are dignitaries from the neighboring islands. I have never seen a Mainlander here other than ourselves. No one ever leaves the island unless they are going to O'Sangha to collect supplies; Dear old dad has that covered as well. Since one of his favorite punishments is the removal of tongues he always makes sure he sends someone that is illiterate and tongue less to collect the supplies This way, even if they heard or saw something about my father they could not read the article nor tell anyone about what they found out. It was ingenious on the part of my father. I do imagine how tired my father must get from having to remember everything about the life; oh, I mean the lie that he lives every day. He can never relax, he always has to be one-step ahead of everyone, and He has to be aware of everything that goes on around him.

He covered his tracks so well that no one ever recognized him as anyone other than the identity he had assumed sixteen years ago in a small pub in an alleyway of a seldom-used seaport.

As I read and reread that clipping, it both infuriated and saddened me that my father could take advantage of all that tragedy and benefit from it. I hoped that as I grew up I would be nothing like him. He was proud of all the ways he hurt and duped people into doing exactly what he wanted them to do or not to do. I think that is why he saved all the incriminating evidence against himself. The rest of my father's rise to power I learned by listening to the servants gossip. They never paid much attention to the things that they said around the children. If you wanted to learn something or catch up on the gossip all you needed to do was stand outside the kitchen door. Those Palace house cleaners and cooks cackled like hens. They knew everything that went on in the entire kingdom. Some of it was pure gossip and conjecture but some of it was truth. I learned very quickly what was factual and what is not.

The stories about my father though, have never been embellished. This story was as true as "King Rayno had led everyone to believe. No one dared lie about the king lest it get back to him. He seemed to like the tales about himself. Every night he would have his informants summoned to his private bedchambers. Once there he would have them regale all the gossip, they had heard that day. He laughed at some of it and made mental notes on other things he heard. You never knew whom he planted where; he was after-all a very cunning man with a very bad past that he intended on keeping well hidden. Sometimes he even had his spies plant some of the gossip. I think he did this so he could see who was embellishing things and who was not. We could not have a king that went around and killed people for no apparent reason....or could we? He was very clever and yes, he was very much in charge.

When we got to Zanzi, I was taken straight to the island doctor (Doctor Tenjin) and his staff. After they examined me, they were very concerned with what they found. I was suffering from severe malnourishment and very jaundiced. Of course, my father explained that away too. He said that the porter forgot one of our bags on the dock. The forgotten bag had happened to be the one that held all of my things. My mother had been working with the chef to make a suitable replacement formula since they did not stock this type of thing on the ship. Apparently, I had a very sensitive stomach and everything they tried I could not keep down. They then put the word out that they were looking for a mother that was still nursing. They had no luck there either. My diet therefore consisted of heavy cream and diluted with water. The doctor accepted that explanation because my father seemed genuinely worried about my wellbeing. They had also heard that the Prince had lost his wife (my mother) during the tornado. The doctor then smiled and patted my father on the back and said, "Do not worry, we'll fatten her up in no time. We have many wet nurses on the island that would love to help you with your daughter Your Highness. What is her name if you don't mind my asking?" Bart had to think quickly, he looked around and spied a crate of Oranges that had the label "Yandel Oranges" so he looked up at the doctor and said, "Her name is Yana. She is named after my dear deceased wife. "With that, the doctor took me from my father's awkward arms and handed me to one of the nurses. "Put the word out Island wide that we need a wet nurse for little Yana." The nurse that was holding me scurried away to get me cleaned up and find me a wet nurse. The doctor then turned to my father and said, "Yana will stay here with us in the infirmary for a while. Since you do not have even a birth certificate for her, we will need to run a series of tests to make sure she is healthy." Dr. Tenjin started to walk away from Bart and then he paused and turned, "It is still very odd to me that they allowed an infant so very young to cross the sea on a ship." He shook his head a little and said, "Oh well, no harm and no foul. Yana is in good hands now.... Besides, with her here with us this will also give you the time you need to settled in and rest before your challenges begin. You have been through quite an ordeal." My father nodded and hastily made his retreat. As he was walking back to the Palace he thought to himself that at least as the king, he would not have to take care of the brat. No diaper changing, no sleepless nights that thought put a smile on his face as he waved to all the subjects he passed on his walk. It will be good to be the king.

At first, the "Challenges" that Dr. Tenjin referred to seemed pretty simple if you asked Bart. The first challenge my father faced was the hand-to- hand combat this was very easy for him. The second challenge was a hunting skills test. It was also a breeze for him. This one consisted of killing a bird with a blowgun. As a boy, he enjoyed hunting, trapping and killing animals in the woods behind his house. Bart killed the bird on the first try. He found that the third challenge was quite a bit harder and fraught with danger.

Because they were on an island, it was only fitting that the third challenge take place in the sea. The prey that Bart was to hunt was a shark. While this was new to him, he relished the challenge. He was only allowed three items for this test. He was given a very crude spear, a small one-person canoe and a stone that had been blessed by the island priest. In order to complete the challenge he had to capture, kill and bring the dead shark back to the Palace. The spear was extremely dull as the young boys of the island used them to capture and kill coconut crabs. The canoe was very lightweight, flimsy and small as most of the subjects of Zanzi Island were not more than 5'3" tall. Bart was almost 6'5" tall. Then there was the blessed stone. This was how he was supposed to humanely kill the animal once he caught it. This custom of catching and killing one of the strongest and most cunning of sea creatures was used to prove that if the island were ever attacked the king would be not only strong enough but smart enough to defeat the enemy. Not many of the challengers were able to do this the first time so per the custom they would be given three tries (one every month for three months.) My father however announced that he would return triumphant before the sun set on the first day. Everyone let out a gasp of dis-belief for no one had ever accomplished that. The challenge was to take place at sunrise the next morning so my father excused himself saying he needed to go check on me, meditate and rest before the big event. Of course, he did not check on me and he did not meditate or rest. He went into his room and behind closed doors; he got high and very drunk on the drugs and whiskey he had brought in the duffle bag that I had been stuffed into. By the time sunrise came, he had been up all night and was quite high. The drunkenness had worn off, as he did not have very much alcohol left. This was a good thing as he knelt in front of the island priest for a blessing before heading out into the sea to complete the first of many challenges.

CHAPTER EIGHT

THE SHARK

Prayer of Protection

Protect this Prince as he ventures into your lair
One of your sons he attempts to snare

A fair fight to the death this day
One will survive and one will be no more
A soul will fly
A soul will soar

Prey will dine with the gods on this night
Victor will live for another fight

Hunter may your aim be true
Hunted
The sacrifice is you...

    Sunrise of day one of the Shark Challenge came at 5:30am. Bart was up, dressed, and ready to go. He had not yet seen the canoe or the spear. First, he was subjected to a Full-Body Strip Search. Once that was over and it was proven that, he did not have anything other than the three items allotted to him for this Challenge. Then the rules were explained to him. Although he pretended to listen intently to every word the elder was saying, all he heard was....blah.... Blah.... Blah.... He was ready to inspect his equipment and get the show on the road. The biggest part of the challenge for him he reasoned to himself was going to be how to lure the shark to the surface. He did not know much if anything about these creatures except if they can breathe then like anything else they can die. In addition, he knew that they have very sharp teeth and he did not intend to get close to that part of the animal. He figured that if push came to shove, he would just simply jump in and grab one; it is just a fish after-all.... Really, how hard could it be? Sharks normally feed at dawn and dusk. As Bart peered outside of the crude building, he took note that dawn was quickly ebbing away. Another obstacle was that he had no type of bait (other than himself) and that was not going to happen.

    All he had to make any noise with was this silly rock. He did not think the pounding of a rock sounded anything like a fish in distress so how would he attract the creature to the surface. If they had supplied him or allowed him to take, at least a fishing pole this task would have been much simpler to complete. That however was not the case. The third problem that Bart saw with this challenge, was if he was able to lure a shark to the surface, he knew that their skin was tough and looking at the spear it was definitely dull. He decided he would have to use his brute strength, wrestle the animal onto the boat, and then stab it with the spear with all of his might. He prayed this would work and he hoped he would not put a hole in this canoe.

The spear was nothing special just the run of the mill island spear that they used to kill coconut crabs. It was dull because the chore of killing the coconut crabs goes to the very young boys and the elders did not want them to accidently stab themselves or their partners. The elders wanted the boys from a very young age to learn to help the Palace and the Island survive. Everyone had to do his or her part. Even now, this tradition is active and when you watch, the boys come back to the Palace triumphant it is quite comical. Their chests are puffed out and they are walking tall. You would think they had wrestled and killed a bear. This is a necessary chore because the coconut crab meat has many uses. None of the crab is wasted; the shell used to make poultices for infected wounds as well as mixed with the coconut milk to soothe an upset tummy. The men in the Palace prize the eyes of the crab for it makes them quite virile for their wives. The claw makes fishing hooks and so on. Right now, though the would-be king (my father) was about to use one of these very lacking spears to catch and kill a ferocious and dangerous oceanic predator. He frowned as he held the spear. There was not much weight to it and the fact that it was extremely dull was disconcerting. Nonetheless he would make it work, he always did.

Were they serious though about this canoe? Bart was a big man and as he looked over the canoe, he was not at all sure he would even fit in it let alone float in it. He thought for sure that the moment he sat in it he would sink. If it did not sink, he knew that it would definitely not hold his weight and that of the shark that he was to bring back to the Palace. For the first time he questioned whether or not he was facing certain failure. Bart decided to ask a few questions concerning the canoe "Excuse me, is there a bigger canoe? I am probably one of the biggest and heaviest men on this island. I really do not think that this canoe will hold me. Once I capture and kill the shark, it is definitely not going to hold both of us. Does anyone have any suggestions?" The Monarchy as well as the island elders looked at each other and scratched their heads." They would need a moment to think and discuss this," the island priest said. My father was led out of the building. After the elders huddled together arguing back and forth they finally came to a conclusion and motioned for my father to come back in. "We have come to a decision" the island priest said. "One of the things that a king must be able to do is overcome and or adapt to his surroundings. You must use the canoe and the tools. We can make no exceptions in this matter for this has been our custom and will not change." Although Bart did not like their decision, he knew in order to stay on the island he would have to go along with it.

He had already decided that when he caught and killed the shark he would put the shark in the canoe and he would hold on to the canoe and float it back to shore. Bart was confident in his abilities and plus the thought of being a king really sweetened the deal. He grabbed the canoe, the spear and the rock and headed for the beach. Time was wasting and he had a date with a shark. Bart paddled out into the glassy lagoon. The water was so clear he could see all the way to the ocean floor. This was in his favor he thought because the shark would not be able to sneak up on him. He took the dull spear and repeatedly jabbed his finger, he wanted to see how sharp it was. After four tries and a very sore finger, he finally penetrated his skin. "This is really pathetic," he thought to himself. He had finally drawn blood and decided he had better not waste it. He began squeezing his finger until there was a steady drip of blood entering the water. As he sat there watching his blood tinge the blue water it dawned on him that he had seen the natives that fished the shoreline use the rocks on the beach to sharpen their spears. He reasoned that he would not be breaking the rules. He was still only using the items that he brought. He had nothing to lose and he was getting extremely bored so he attempted it. He had to have something to do to pass the time. While he was busy sharpening the spear he was also straddling the canoe as if he were riding a horse. He was dangling his legs from the knees down in the water and kicking them back and forth. He was so busy working the rock across the prongs of the spear that he did not notice the fin that broke the surface of the glassy water and slowly made its way over to him. Distractedly he thought to himself that the islanders make this look much easier than it really is. As he struggled with the rock and the spear, he was still not aware of the open gaping mouth with razor sharp teeth that was now headed straight for his leg. Bart suddenly became very aware of the shark when he felt it graze his calf. Instinctively he tried to pull his leg into the canoe but this set the flimsy canoe off balance and it started rocking back and forth until he lost his balance and plunged into the sea with the shark that now had tasted his blood and wanted more. Luckily, he never let go of the spear but the silly blessed stone quickly sank to the bottom. When he plunged into the ocean, the momentum caused him to sink a bit. As he got his bearings and kicked his feet this caused his head to break the surface. As his head broke the surface, he whipped it from side to side nervously looking for the shark. He had not realized how big a shark actually was until now. He was not so sure that jumping in to get one let alone being in the water with one was the smartest thing to do. He scanned the surface and did not see it anywhere. He dared not look under the water. Not at all, he wanted nothing more than to get back in that cursed canoe. He tried repeatedly to get in the canoe, every time he started to pull himself up, it would dip into the water and roll on its side dumping Bart right back in the water with the shark. Minutes seemed like hours as he nervously looked around for the creature. He had one arm now securely over the canoe and in the other hand, he held on to the spear as tight as he could as if his life depended on it. He saw the fin break the surface not even 15 feet away from him. He turned to face his adversary and knew that this would be a fight to the death. He vowed to himself that he did not intend to die that day.

    The shark was upon him. He desperately tried to avoid the sharp end of the creature. He had heard once that if you punch them in the nose they go away. He was desperate at this point and would try anything. He took a deep breath, reared his arm back, clenched his fist said a prayer and punched the animal in the nose as hard as he could. He would have never believed you if you told him that a shark's skin feels like sand paper but he has the scars to prove it. Miraculously though it worked! The shark made a thrashing noise, whipped his tail around, and propelled itself in the opposite direction of Bart. He sighed a breath of relief. He decided to inspect his hand because as he looked around to make sure that the shark was not coming back for seconds he realized that the water was turning a very deep red in color. He noticed that he did get pretty cut up in the process. You see, to get to the nose of a shark, you have to get past many very razor sharp jagged teeth. When he punched the fish in the nose, he sliced his hand wide open. With all the adrenaline racing through his body, he did not feel his wounds. He just prayed that not all this blood (his blood) in the water attracted any other sharks. He swore under his breath that he would wear this shark's teeth around his neck before the day was through. Bart figured that after the shark recovered from being punched in the nose he would be back for more. He continued to try to get back in the canoe to no avail. This fight was going to be in open water and the only thing he had to fight with was a half- sharpened spear. Those were not very good odds on his part. He had underestimated the size, strength and agility of his opponent. Bart knew one thing in such close quarters this spear as it was is useless. Thinking quickly he broke the shaft of the spear basically creating a long knife, A little more confident now he once again looked around for any movement in the water that would give the sharks location away. He spied a large ripple in the water and got ready for what he knew would be a fight to the death.

The water became still again, "Where did it go he wondered nervously?" The shark had dove down and unbeknownst to Bart came straight up from the ocean bottom and clamped its jaws down on his calf. He thrust the spear into the water down towards the pressure he felt on his calf. The shark started thrashing and jerked Bart free from the canoe. Bart was under the water now with the shark. He continued to jab the shark anywhere his make shift knife would hit him. His blind stabbing finally landed a good blow to the shark's gills on the left side of the animal and it immediately released its jaws from his calf. Bart knew he was in trouble if he did not think quickly. The shark spun around in the water and was coming straight for him with its mouth gaping open. Bart steeled himself for the impact and as the shark was about to attack Bart took the crude makeshift knife and plunged his entire arm straight down the shark's throat. Bart could hear his flesh tearing and adrenaline or not he felt a hot searing pain as his flesh was being torn from the bone. His knife hit its mark though. Somehow, Bart had penetrated the soft tissue that surrounded the shark's brain and the animal instantly stopped moving. Bart could not believe that he had actually killed the shark. He ripped the spear out of its flesh. Now it was his and the shark's blood that colored the ocean water. He looked down at his leg and it had a large gash in it. He knew that all the blood and thrashing in the water had probably attracted more sharks that would be there sooner rather than later. He had to somehow get this big fish onto that canoe and paddle both of the back to shore. There was no way he could just drag the animal to shore because he was out in the middle of the lagoon and that would be like ringing the dinner bell. He tried to lift the animal onto the boat but he was too exhausted. It had to be done though and as fast as possible, the sea gulls were already starting to circle and plunge thinking that there were injured fish in the water. This meant that the sharks were not far behind. With all his might, he found the strength and he launched the shark over his head and landed it in the boat. He looked at the dead bleeding shark and could not believe. he actually did it. The shark may have had sharper teeth but Bart had a harder bite. He had a new respect for the creature, it fought hard for a meal, and the difference was that Bart had fought hard for his life. "It is amazing what you can do when you have no other choice but to do it." Bart thought as he wearily started the long paddle towards the shoreline. He dared not look back because he was sure that there were probably more sharks there now looking around for whatever had bled so much and caused such a commotion in the water. Although Bart was triumphant he did not walk away unscathed from this encounter. The shark had caused quite a bit of damage. For as long as Bart would live, he would bear the battle wounds and walk with a slight limp. As Bart battled his way through the surf and finally made it to shore he collapsed on the sand from shear exhaustion. He made it, he was alive and he realized at that moment that every muscle in his body hurt. With that, his eyes rolled back in his head and he was out.

When Bart awoke, he was in the infirmary and all the nurses were fussing over him. At that moment, he was very popular. He attempted to sit up but his arms felt like limp spaghetti noodles. He had no strength to pull himself up so instead of fighting it he just let his body sink back into the bed. Doctor Tenjin came over to him and said, "Do not push yourself too hard Your Highness, during the battle with the shark you strained a lot of muscles and they need time to repair themselves. The more you try to use them the longer it is going to take them to heal. You fought quite a battle from the injuries you sustained. When you were brought here from the beach, you were unconscious and your vital signs were quite erratic. Had it not been for your injuries it would have been quite comical though." Bart gave the doctor a very puzzled look. Dr. Tenjin continued, "Oh ok, let me explain…. As you know, you are quite a bit larger and outweigh everyone on the island. We heard you rather than saw you at first. There were ten adult men straining to carrying you up the path to the infirmary.

Four had your left side, four had your right side one was holding your head and the last one had your feet. It could have been a scene right out of Gulliver's Travels or Snow White and the 7 Dwarfs." "All we heard was heavy grunting and a lot of cursing. It really was the funniest sight I have ever seen, I kept waiting for them to breakout in song." Bart and the doctor started laughing at the images that appeared in their minds. When the laughing subsided, the doctor looked at Bart with a very grim look on his face. He began, "Your Highness, one thing you will learn about me is that I am a very straight shooter. I will not sugarcoat anything for you. I would rather you know exactly what is going on. When we did our medical examination on you, the outcome was not good. I am sure you realized how badly you were hurt on the outside.

Unfortunately, the damage was far greater on the inside. Your wounds were quite extensive. The damage that was done to all the nerves in your hand is pretty much going to render it useless. Aesthetically it will look normal except for some scarring, As far as functionality goes you cannot bend your fingers and you are unable to make a fist. This is not something that can be relearned through Physical Therapy because of the irreparable nerve damage that was done. Your calf did not fair too well either. The only way I can describe it was that it resembled raw hamburger meat. We had to scrape out most of the meat and most of your calf muscle. A shark's mouth and teeth are full of disease and bacteria. In the case of your calf, I could see that infection was already starting to set in. We were able to save your leg and you will still be able to walk. For the rest of your life you will walk with a very pronounced limp. You also had a few superficial gashes we sewed up." As Bart took a few minutes to let what the doctor said to him process, Dr. Tenjin continued, Ha, I would hate to see the other person but I have seen him and I must say you brought in quite a prize." Bart absent-mindedly said, "Yeah….I guess he was pretty big." Dr. Tenjin looked at him in disbelief and asked, "Do you even know what type of shark you killed?" Still reeling from everything that Dr. Tenjin just laid on him Bart shook his head no. The doctor went on…."You killed an adolescent Tiger shark. This shark is considered one of the deadliest, if not the deadliest sharks in these waters. When the anglers on the island get wind that one of these monsters is hanging around; they do not dare go in the water until it moves on. You my friend are being hailed quite the hero. I even hear the word "invincible" thrown around. Kudos to you…. If you want my opinion, I have a feeling that once you quit waging your internal battle against yourself, life will be easier for you and you will make a great king.

By the way, I thought you would be pleased to hear that the entire island has fallen in love with little Yana. She is quite a beauty and is recovering nicely. I am sure when you are rested you will want to see her. "With that, the doctor turned around and headed to the door. As an after- thought, the doctor paused and once more looking at Bart, he nonchalantly said, "I will have one of the nurses bathe her and get her ready to see her very brave Papa." Dr. Tenjin then walked out. Was that a promise or a threat?" Bart thought to himself, "Damn I guess I have to fake it until I make it and become a doting loving dad to Justine's brat." There are worse fates I guess….like being put to death for murder."

An older nurse came in to see if he needed anything and he pretended to be asleep, she was old enough to be his grandma and besides….He needed time to think and plan his next move. After the old maid of a nurse left the room though he saw a younger and much cuter nurse walking the hall right outside of his room. "Honey can you come in here for a moment please." He said in the sweetest most sincere voice he could muster up. She came right in. "Is there something I can do for you your highness?" He smiled at her, "Can you fluff my pillow for me please? I am afraid if I move too much I'll rip the stitches, not to mention all my muscles hurt." She thought for a moment and smiled as she said, "I'll be right back don't move." When she returned, she had some oils and a towel. "I'm going to give you a deep tissue massage and these oils are amazing, you will feel like a new man ready to take on the world!" Bart closed his eyes and laid back to enjoy the massage he thought to himself, "It's good to be the king." Normally the trials for the "would-be" kings lasted 6 days. Due to the wounds, that Bart sustained during his battle with the Tiger shark the Elders and the Monarchy decided that it was only fair to give this young prince time to recover. They decided that the trials would resume in one months' time. The next test was as dangerous and deadly as the shark hunt and this one was to take place on land. They had not told Bart what the test would be because they did not want him to prepare for it. Some of the other princes that were in the trials were still attempting to either capture a shark or well into the fourth test already. Oh yes, unbeknownst to Bart there were other able-bodied princes that wanted to be the king of Zanzi. During his recovery, Bart had been spending time with the pretty little nurse. He was attracted to her but had no ideas of taking it further than a mere fling. She could in no way better his chances and she was just a little above a servant and would not make a fitting queen. Of course, he never told her that. He was a smooth talker and spent many nights on a secluded beach having his way with her. He liked it rough and she never complained. She figured that once she was queen he could turn his advances towards any maiden in the kingdom and she would be spared his violent and sometimes painful affections. She would have to be present to bear the king's children but after that, he could do as he wished with whomever he wished. Unbeknownst to her Bart had other ideas for sweet little Chennai. He did not intend to let anyone find out about his tryst with this maiden. He was supposed to be in mourning for his wife. When he had enough of her, she would simply disappear. No one knew they had been meeting he made sure of that. He knew how and where to do it. He had been studying the island. First, though, he smiled and thought to himself, I am going to have a little fun. On the night he had intended to get rid of her she let a bit of news slip that through him into quite a rage. They were sitting on their secluded beach enjoying a drink and Chennai said to Bart, "One of the princes did not return from the sea today. The other nine candidates are afraid to try. They think maybe that you angered the gods because you completed your task so brutally quick. What do you think your Highness?" Bart dropped his drink and before Chennai could say another word, he had his hands around her throat, "What do you mean other candidates? How many are there? You better tell me now!" He growled at her. At that point, he realized what he was doing and removed his hands from around her throat. Chennai backed away from him. "You are crazy! What is wrong with you she shrieked?" She stood and started to run She was no match for Bart and he caught up to her quickly. He quickly strangled her and made his way to a deep gully that he had found while scouting the island. He snapped her neck to make sure she was dead and threw her into the gully. It was so deep in the side of the mountain that he never heard her hit the bottom. "She'll make good crab food." He thought as he walked back to the beach to collect any evidence that they had been there. No one ever asked him about Chennai because no one had known about him and her. Bart had gotten away with yet another cold- blooded murder. Now that Bart knew that he had competition, it was time to stop fooling around. He wondered to himself if it would be smart to try to follow the rules and beat them fairly or just get rid of them.

    He knew some were afraid to go in the ocean; A few drownings could easily be blamed on the sharks. Whatever he did, he would have to be smart about it. "Maybe he would thin out the herd before resuming the challenges." Bart thought to himself, "Chennai would have come in very handy right now had she not freaked out on him. Damn neurotic woman!" He had to find out which prince was next to hunt a shark, but how he wondered. As quickly as that, it dawned on him how and where he could get the answers he wanted. He would have to play doting daddy and keep his ear to the wall. "Nurses are just as gossipy as the servants are." He reasoned that since Chennai knew he was sure the others would probably know too. Ask the right questions in the right way and you will always get the answers you seek. Bart smiled….It was turning out to be a great evening. He was excited now, "I love when a plan comes together!" He headed off to his room to get high and finish off the Rum that Chennai had brought. "Perfect ending to a perfect night." Bart had all but forgotten that about an hour ago he had strangled and snapped someone's neck. She was inconsequential to him therefore she just did not matter.

The next morning he got good and high and headed over to the infirmary. He was not sure how easy it was going to be to pretend to care about this baby. In the past, he never had time for kids. He always felt that they were too needy and since they could do nothing for themselves, they were of no use to him. However, little Yana was turning out to be quite useful after all. Maybe if she continued to help his cause he might try to like her just a little bit. He took a deep breath and entered her room. What he saw actually astounded him. She was still asleep so he had time to study her. She was actually quite exquisite. She had thick jet-black hair and her skin was like that of a porcelain doll. She was not fat…he hated fat babies. Dare he say she was actually perfect? Suddenly (he was not sure where it came from) he found that he wanted to get to know her. He had never loved anyone or anything except drugs, alcohol and money so this feeling was unnatural to him. He was proud to say that this small little being was his flesh and blood. This was his daughter. He suddenly had the urge to wake her up….he desperately wanted to see her eyes. Tentatively he walked over to her crib and gently touched the hair on her head. He abruptly pulled his hand back, it felt as if he had been burned; he had never felt anything so soft. He carefully touched her again. Her skin was amazingly soft and warm. He gingerly picked her up from the crib where she slept. For a quick moment, he felt a pang of remorse and sadness that Justine had never been able to see her child. As quick as the feelings came they left just as fast.

This was his child and no one else's. He was not going to share this amazing little person with anyone. She was his and his alone.

He was going to provide her a kingdom and a palace to grow up in. This little girl was going to love him and yes, Bart already loved her. He was lost in thought when Yana stretched and yawned and opened her eyes. Bart let out a gasp because she had the most beautiful green eyes he had ever seen. Try as he might he could not remember what color Justine's eyes were. Honestly, he had never really looked at her that closely. He never loved her; she was simply just a means to an end. However, this little one astounded him. Yana contently laid in his arms and just stared up into his face. It is as if she was always meant to be his. "Big Bad Bart" found himself grinning from ear-to-ear, this was his daughter. They just gazed at each other and Bart found himself telling her, "Do not worry sweet Yana your daddy is here and will always be here for you no matter what." Dr. Tenjin had been watching most of the exchange and was very pleased with what he saw. He had started to worry that perhaps losing his wife was too hard for the prince. The doctor thought that maybe he stayed away because this precious little girl reminded Prince Rayno of everything he lost while on the Este Star just a month ago. He wondered if father and daughter would ever bond. What he saw this morning quelled those fears and put his mind at ease. This little angel had her daddy back. Now hopefully he would make it through the last three challenges. They were hard if not harder and more dangerous than killing the shark. Doctor Tenjin slowly backed out of the room giving the father and daughter time to bond. Yana reached her little hand up and touched Bart's face and he found himself nibbling on her fingers. He did not know how to do the "dad thing" but he was ready to learn. He was more determined than ever now to win all the challenges no matter what he had to do. A nurse came into the room with a bottle for little Yana. Bart had never fed a baby but he found that he wanted to do everything for her. He took the bottle from the nurse and gave her a questioning look. She smiled and told him exactly what to do. He thanked her and soon Yana was sucking away on her bottle and gazing into Bart's eyes. He felt like the Grinch when his heart swelled three times its normal size. As he was feeding her, two nurses stood in the hallway next to the nurse's desk. Bart was paying attention to Yana but also listening to the nurses' talk.

He was right on the money as usual they were talking about how the elder's finally talked one of the candidate prince's into trying to complete the challenge and capture a shark. He heard…."Poor thing was shaking like a leaf…I'm not sure he'll be able to do it…He's only 19 years old…I agree, he's much too young to rule a kingdom…I heard he's trying it tomorrow." With that, the nurses moved away from the desk and their voices became fainter and fainter until he could no longer hear them. Bart knew exactly what he was going to do. "Yana my girl, I am going to make you a princess…you watch and see." Soon Yana's eyes were getting heavy and as soon as she fell asleep Bart laid her in her crib, he promised he would be back in a little while kissed her little forehead and set about his task. He had not realized that he had spent the entire day with his daughter. Perfect timing though because as he made his way down to the beach to the line of canoes there was no one on the beach to see him. He knew exactly which canoe the young prince was going to use because it already carried the blessed stone and the useless spear. He took out his knife and slightly shredded the cord that held the rigging on the canoe. He knew that the prince would attempt to hold the rigging for support when trying to spear the shark, it will break and he will fall in the ocean. Then it is up to fate as to who survives. If he is small and sinewy then Bart's bet was on the shark. Now he stealthily made his way back to his room. He wanted to be up at sunrise to watch the prince cast off the beach.

    The next morning at sunrise, Bart was perched on a boulder far enough away as to be unobtrusive but close enough that he could still see what was going on. He watched the priest pray over the prince and he watched the prince shove off into the water. He would also be on his perch off and on throughout the day and especially at sunset to see if the prince returned. He checked off and on all day long and there was no sign of the prince. Sunset came and went and once again no prince. Later that evening as he was visiting with Yana he could once again hear the nurses gossiping at the desk. "It was awful…When the guardsman brought the mangled canoe…I know, no there was no sign of…I hate to be the one that has to tell that king…Yes, he was an only child…Do you blame them? No, I wouldn't get in the water either." Then the nurses walked away to start their rounds. Hmmm Bart thought, "I might win by default because all the challenges have to be completed there are no exceptions to that rule." He smiled down at his daughter, "We're almost home Yana, there are just a few more to go." Bart looked down at his daughter and realized at that moment that she was perfect for him. He had now spent almost two entire days with her and he had yet to hear her cry. Earlier he heard her whimper as he was making his way down the hall to her room. The mean old nurse was taking her blood. As soon as Bart walked over to her and she heard his voice she turned her head towards him and stopped sniffling. It is as if she knew that I was never going to let anything or anyone hurt a hair on her sweet head. Doctor Tenjin had a rocking chair brought into the room and soon father and daughter were fast asleep in it.

The nurse decided that the rest of the tests could wait. She covered them up, shut off the light and quietly shut the door. If she had a camera that would be a perfect picture. Chennai had been the shutterbug here at the infirmary…. I still wonder where she went off to. Maybe she would question her mother and friends again. It was unlike Chennai to just leave. I do not care what these lecherous rich tourists promise…They just end up using and hurting the naïve island girls. I hope Chennai has not fallen for that old trick.

Little Yana shivered a little bit which woke Bart up right away. He protectively covered her up with the blanket that the nurse had laid atop them before she shut the door. He had not slept this good in so long. He felt much rested and completely at peace. The only light in the room was the moonlight that peaked through the blinds. He looked down at his sleeping daughter and his heart filled up with so much love for her. He knew that he would protect her with his life if it ever came to that. He had never felt that for anyone, not even his brothers and sisters or parents. This little girl was his life now. Suddenly it dawned on him that since meeting the tiny person he had not done any of his drugs he had stashed in his room, what was even more astounding to him is that he had not even thought about it until now. He did not want any and he knew that he would never let little Yana know about her daddy's deep dark past. He was going to be the best dad he could. He had no idea what that meant or how to go about it and that scared him a bit because Bart always had everything planned out. He never left anything to chance.

He took a deep breath and told his tiny sleeping princess that they would have to learn what it was to be a family together. He knew he needed to put her in the crib and get busy on his next victim. He promised Yana a kingdom and he intended to deliver. He carefully stood up and gingerly placed her in the crib. He covered her up and placed a quick kiss on her forehead. He whispered that he loved her and left the room. He decided to stop at the nurses station to let them know he was leaving and he asked them to please check on her and call him if she needed him for any reason. One of the nurses smiled and said, "Your highness we can have a bed moved into her room if you want us to. You are welcome to stay here in the infirmary with Yana if that would please you." Bart did not think twice, nodded, and smiled in agreement. With that, he left the infirmary promising to return first thing in the morning so that he could feed her.

He had heard that the princes all got together at the Pub so that is where he was heading tonight. Drinks tend to loosen up the tightest of lips and he intended to get them all very drunk and find out exactly who is doing what and when they are doing it. As he neared the Pub, he could hear quite a bit of drunken laughter. "This is going to be easier than I originally thought," Bart said to himself. "It will be like taking candy away from a baby." Once inside the Pub he looked around and quickly picked out the table with the very drunk princes at it. He walked up to them and during the introduction; he almost used his real name. As drunk as they were they probably would not have noticed but he would have to be more careful in the future. He had to remember that Bart Randolph was dead and gone forever and he was now Prince Amir Rayno. He shrugged it off and sat down. When the Bar Maiden came by, he ordered a round of beers for all his new friends at his table. Sadly, he was beginning to like these people. Another time and another place they could have been genuine friends. He had to keep reminding himself that these people were his competition at least for now. He also had little Yana to think about. She was completely dependent on him and he was not going to let her down. Bart put on his "Poker face" when the Bar Maid brought over the round of Beers that he had purchased for the table. "Drinks for everyone! My name is Amir Rayno I'm guessing that we are all competing for the position of the king of Zanzi?" After that, one of the other princes stood up and said, "I am Prince Jyn Malaki nice to meet you Amir." Then another stood and introduced himself, "I am Prince Antara Tula, thanks for the Beer!" The last prince stood up and eyed Bart, he laughed and said…"You are the biggest man I have ever seen! It was really quite funny watching you paddle out in the little bitty canoe!" With that he stuck out his hand, "Prince Minho Brunei; nice to meet you Amir." Bart quickly shook Minho's hand and replied," Well boys tonight we are just comrades enjoying a beer together. Cheers!" Bart decided that he really liked these people and for once, he was going to play fair and let the best man win. They laughed and enjoyed each other's company late into the night. They closed down the Pub that night and made plans to do it again soon.

    As Bart was making his way back to his room, he was extremely shocked by his own actions. Why didn't he go through with his plan? There was so much riding on taking the king's place. He had a daughter to take care of and he knew he would not be able to do that from death row. "What was he doing"….He did not have a clue but for once he felt good about his decision. There would be no lies to tell to cover anything up. "Maybe this truth thing was not all that bad?" He muttered aloud to himself. He was changing, he was not sure he liked it all that much. This was a foreign feeling to him….he asked himself, "Do I tread lightly or jump in and hope for the best?" He had never allowed himself to be vulnerable. He had always steeled his heart against everyone so that he never took the chance of being hurt. Now though, now he was leaving himself wide open. Nervous and apprehensive, his first impulse was to run and never look back. His gut though was telling him it would be all right and he was making the right decision…This time he was going with his gut. "Go big or go home!" All of a sudden, he realized how important what people really thought about him was to him. He never wanted anyone to say anything negative about him to his daughter. He wanted her to be proud of the man and the father that he was becoming. His hope was that if by chance she ever found out about his past she would love him enough to let him explain how he turned it all around the day she looked up at him from her hospital crib. With that thought in his mind he entered his room and pulled out his drug stash and walked down to the sea shore, opened the bag and with no hesitation he let the wind carry the white powder and spread it over the sea. As he watched the white powder dissolve into the break of the waves of the shoreline he thought to himself, "Not long ago I would have killed for that as a matter of a fact I have killed for less than that." As he walked back into his room, he was very pleased with himself.

Normally it takes a good woman to change a bad man so how can a little girl that cannot even utter a word yet have that big of an impact on me? He looked up into the sky and thanked god for bringing little Yana into his life, he promised he would always put her first no matter what. He showered and knew that now he would have to be on his toes….Playing by the rules is a completely new concept to Bart, he was not sure what to expect but he was excited about it nonetheless. Tomorrow the tests were starting again for him. The doctor had checked him over today and said that he had healed sufficiently and could return to the challenges. Before Bart left the Infirmary, the doctor pulled him aside and told him that he had a very comfortable bed moved into Yana's room if he were so inclined. Bart smiled and said, "A stampede of wild hogs could not keep me away!" Both he and the doctor laughed at that. Bart knew what the next challenge would be. The doctor now knew that his new friend knew what was in store for him as well. Doctor Tenjin patted Bart on the back and said, "Son you are shaping up to be an excellent king. That little girl in there is a very lucky young lady." Bart stopped the doctor and said, "Dr. Tenjin I am the one who is lucky. That little girl in there has saved my life. She (and I'm still not sure how), has taken a very bad man and made him want to be good." Doctor Tenjin replied with, "If you ever need to talk I'm here to listen. Maybe we will go have a beer sometime. But right now you need to get some rest tomorrow is a big day and I know a little girl that would love to wake up with her daddy." Doctor Tenjin opened up Yana's door and lightly pushed Bart in, turned off the light and told Bart that one of the nursing staff would make sure he was up in time in the morning to take a shower, feed Yana and eat a good breakfast himself before the Challenge was to begin. Bart looked at the doctor and smiled gratefully.

He carefully scooped his daughter out of her crib and laid down with her on his chest. Soon they were fast asleep. There was a slight tap on his shoulder, which woke Bart up with a start. A little disorientated he sat up, rubbed the sleep from his eyes and looked around. He looked down at Yana who was still asleep. The nurse handed him a towel and some soap. "I thought you might want to wash up before your daughter wakes up and demands her bottle," the nurse said with a smile. Bart took the towel, bar of soap, and said, "Lead the way." She told him where the showers were and turned, carefully placed Yana in her crib and busied herself making the mussed up bed. By the time, Bart returned there was a tray on the bed filled with eggs, bacon and toast and some very much needed coffee. As Bart sat down and began to eat his breakfast little Yana began to stir. He smiled and asked his impatient little daughter…"I guess a hot breakfast is out of the question?" Yana started to whimper…."Ok, ok I'm coming." He said happily." He was becoming quite adept at feeding his daughter. He was also getting used to either eating while she slept or enjoying all of his meals cold "whatever they may be." Either way, he did not mind. As Yana snuged herself into Bart's arms with her bottle, Bart marveled at how this tiny little girl changed his entire life. His end goal was still to be the king of Zanzi that had not changed. Now though it was not just for selfish reasons. He wanted to make sure no matter what happened to him his daughter would never pay the price for his previous indiscretions.

As the king, he would have the respect and love from his subjects. This also meant that Yana would never go hungry and she would always have the best that life had to offer. Bart thought back, he wondered if what you experience as a child molds you into the person you will be when you reach adulthood. He tried never to think about his childhood. As he watched, Yana hungrily sucked on her bottle his childhood came flooding back to him. When he thought about all the things that happened to him it made him very angry. He swore under his breath that Yana would never experience anything like what he had to go through.

CHAPTER NINE

BART'S CHILDHOOD

At first, Bart had more love than he knew what to do with. Oh, never from the sorry excuse of a mother he had. She was too busy taking care of her needs to worry about him. He smiled fondly when he remembered his Grandfather. He was named after him. He was sure though that if Grandpa Bart ever looked down from heaven to check on him, he would have been so very disappointed in the man that Bart had become.

Bart was bad. However, not at first, with Grandpa Bart he learned manners and how to be kind. Everyone always told Grandpa what a sweet boy Bart was. They fished, they hunted; Grandpa always knew just what to do when he saw life becoming too much for his grandson.

Bart's mom Alice (his daughter) would go on drunken benders or end up shacked up with God knows who in some flop house. Grandpa always knew when that happened because in the middle of the night, he would hear a soft knock on his door and standing before him would be a sad, cold and always hungry little boy that was probably sporting a new black eye or fat lip. Without saying a word, Grandpa would guide his grandson into the kitchen and set him in his favorite chair. He would then stand up, put his hand on his chin and then as if he just thought of the most brilliant idea he would smile real big, point his finger in the air and say, "I know exactly what we are going to do Bart my boy!" Bart would forget he was sad, he would forget about the beating he had just gotten from his mother, he forgot about everything except whatever Grandpa had planned for them to do.

Sometimes they went on treasure hunts in Grandpa's house; it was fun to be a Pirate. Sometimes they were cowboys and they camped out in the living room. Grandpa always had time for him. Grandpa was his life. He taught him to be good, sweet, and kind. One day, when his mom returned from wherever it was that she went to him up Bart did not want to go. He looked at his mom and said, "Why can't I live with Grandpa? Why do I have to go with you? I don't want to go with you." Alice dropped the coat she was trying to get her son's arms into and slowly stood up, she looked at her father and then she looked down at Bart. Bart thought for a moment that she was going to let him stay with his Grandpa. He started to cross the room to stand next to him until a steel grip grabbed his shoulder and stopped him in his tracks. His mom looked down at him and gave him a very icy glare, she handed him his coat and in a very low stern voice she said, "Get it on and get in the car now boy…John is waiting for you. (John was mom's latest boyfriend.) Bart started to protest and without missing a beat Alice raised her hand and soundly slapped Bart across the face. Alice's father stood up and looking at his daughter he said, "Alice, there is no need to hit the boy. He is a good boy. If you wanted, that might not be a bad idea….let Bart stay here with me. I will not turn you in; I will not ask you for a dime to keep him. He will go to school, get an education, get the hell out of this place, and make something of himself. Let him stay here, no one will know. You can go do whatever you want and not have to worry about him. What do you think Alice?" She looked at her dad and said, "You think you are better than I am? You are trying to turn him against me. You are making him soft and sweet and it disgusts me. I came here today to tell you that John and I are getting married and we are taking Bart and moving away. You, you silly old man will never see your grandson again. In addition, I promise you, this, I will beat the sweet out of him. He is going to be mean and tough and do whatever I want him to. He is going to be my dog not yours! Got it old man?" My mom turned around, walked out my grandfather's door and got in the car. Grandpa and I locked eyes as I stared at him from the back window of the station wagon that John drove. As we pulled away, Grandpa put his hand on the cold glass back door of his house and I put my hand on the back window of the station wagon. That is the last time Bart saw his Grandpa alive.

Alice was true to her word; Bart was beat on a daily basis. Soon there was no more laughter or smiles, it started slow but Alice saw the change. The sweet boy was getting a hard look in his eyes. He argued at school, got sent home on many occasion for fighting. He skipped school whenever he wanted. It was not unusual to see Bart walking around town with a six-pack or more of beer. He threw rocks through storefront windows, he broke into people's houses when they were either home asleep or away on vacation (he did not care.) He beat people up to gain their fear or just for fun. He stole cars and motor cycles just to drive them into the river or over a cliff for fun. He trusted no one but his mom. She told him she was the only one that loved him. Together he and his mom plotted and planned the heists that Bart would pull off. She was pretty happy with her protégé; she was grooming and preparing him for bigger things. She feigned interest in him to show him attention. Alice was good at getting what she wanted, even if that meant using her son in the process. Bart ate up the attention. He found that the worse he was the happier mom was. Bad Bart in his mind equaled mom's love and affection. It was not a hard decision for him to make. Happy mom meant no beatings and not being screamed at. Besides, he rather liked the way everyone looked at him and did whatever he wanted them to do. One night for fun, he made a kid cluck like a chicken and hop on one foot for almost an hour. Then to add humiliation to the mix, he had the boy tell him how much he enjoyed doing it for him. "Poor stupid sucker" Bart thought.

He never considered his mom a mom. She always insisted that he call her Alice. She did not cook and she did not clean. She would always tell him, "I'm good at making babies….not raising them. If you want clean clothes then go steal them" she continued, "If you are hungry too bad you figure it out". It is because of her, his mother that he learned women were only a tool to get what you wanted in life. You could use them to do the domestic things, satisfy your needs and if they had money, ha, then a few heart-felt lies and they were your dog. She was never "Suzy Homemaker" so he knew firsthand what it felt like to go to bed hungry for he had done it more times than not growing up. His mom well, if you want to call her that. She had children for one reason and one reason only….She stumbled on something she did well and she was paid to do it, she was a great "baby-making machine." Honestly, he was not sure how many brothers and sisters he had; she started having babies at eighteen, she sold quite a few of us. The ones that were lucky enough to stay with her really should have been adopted.

She ended up keeping five of her children. She kept two of the boys and three of the girls. His other brother ran her errands, as a matter of a fact I do not even know what his name was…he was just "Errand Boy." Bart never saw much of him and at sixteen, he never saw him again. Errand Boy was just gone one day. His oldest sister watched all the brats mom had until someone would buy them. His youngest sister was supposed to keep the house presentable when people would come to buy babies from mom. We were never close; I think mom did that on purpose. We were all there for a reason and as he grew older Bart wondered what his purpose would be.

They lived in the worst part of town. His moms reasoning was, number one it is dirt-cheap and number two, no one ever-wanted trouble so they kept their mouth shut and mom could do as she pleased. Bart remembered that one of the first things his mom taught him to do was roll her joints for her. It was about the only time she ever paid him any positive attention. When he was 12, she got him high for the first time. That is when Bart found his "happy place." After that, he was high whenever he could steal some weed from his mom. Sometimes she even had him go get it for her. That is usually when he pilfered as much as he wanted. When he would get back with it, she would complain aloud that it was short to Bart but never to her dope man. Growing up with Alice for a mom had been hard on him.

His mom beat the "sweet boy" out of him. She told him, "A cute smile will get you beat or killed on the streets. Get hard and mean and take what you want, never ask?" She then grabbed his hands and told him to make a fist...."Do you see these?" Bart nodded, "These are fear, when people fear you then you have power and control over them. They will do anything you want. Being nice gets you nowhere in this life."

When Bart turned 16, he dropped out of school and became a dealer. His mom was once again proud of him. He liked when he made his mom happy. "I taught you well Bart, now go out and don't come back until you have something for your mommy and a wad of cash in your pocket." Bart was gone for three days. On the third day, Alice (Bart's mom) got a phone call from the police stating that Bart had been brought into the hospital in bad shape. She pretended to be worried and upset when she spoke with the police officer on the other end of the line. Alice explained, "Bart is sixteen now and does not need my permission to drop out of school because by law he is allowed to. He hangs with such a rough crowd, I am almost sure there are drugs involved. Whenever I say anything to him about it, he tells me to mind my own business. I am honestly afraid he will lash out at me one of these days he is a very big boy for his age. His father, rest his soul was Russian and Bart takes after his side of the family. I have been dreading receiving your phone call but I knew it would come sooner or later, I am just thankful that he is not dead." She continued to explain, "He came home from school today and told me that he had quit school. We got into a very intense argument. I probably should have never given him an ultimatum but I did she cried. When Bart refused to back down, I had no choice but to tell him he needed to leave. The younger children look up to him. What kind of an example is that to follow?" She went on, "I decided to use tough love on him." The officer bought her made up sob story hook line and sinker. She then proceeded to tell the officer that she had no transportation to get to the hospital, of course the nice officer offered to come get her. When Alice got off the phone, she smiled and thought to herself how easy it was for her to manipulate people into doing whatever she wanted them to do, especially men, "The damsel in distress scenario works every time." She had once again averted trouble. She would make sure that whatever trouble Bart had gotten into it would not fall back on her. She shook her head in disgust as she thought about Bart. She was strong and experienced enough to handle the streets but now she knew it was time to really toughen him up, after all, he was her meal ticket. True to his word, the kind young officer showed up at Alice's Trailer within half an hour to escort her to the hospital where her injured son was being treated. Trying to make small talk on the ride there Officer Cain said, "You have quite a few kids Alice. That must be hard on a single mom." Alice smiled big and responded, "I love children, and I feel that women were put on this earth to be mothers." Officer Cain smiled at that response. "Looks like we are here, do you want me to go inside with you? I heard he was beat pretty badly." "No, my boy needs his momma now....Can I call and bother you for a ride back home later though? Say around 8:30?" Officer Cain told her she could call on him anytime she needed him. With that, Bart's mom entered the hospital to feign concern over her very stupid and very weak son. She shook her head at what a disappointment Bart had turned out to be. At least she smiled to herself Ian was a chip off the old block and he was showing promise. She put her shoulders back, her head up, time to play the game that she was really good at....

Alice went up to the desk and demanded to see her son. "My name is Alice Randolph and my boy Bart needs me, where is my boy?" The nurse tried to explain that they had no insurance information on Bart and could she fill these out? Alice pushed the forms away from her face....She then sneered at the nurse, "My boy is injured and you are worried about forms? Let me see your Supervisor now!" "There is no need for all of that; we can get the paperwork done after you see your son. Please follow me and I'll take you to his room." Alice had a smug look on her face as she followed the nurse down the hall. She was supposed to keep insurance on the kids and the state paid her to do it, there was just always something she wanted or needed and the insurance could wait." She always got away with everything and came out on top.

Bart remembered he was awake when his mom entered his room, he remembered her concerned look. He started to tell her that he did everything she said to do and Alice quickly shushed him up by placing her hand over his mouth…."Poor baby, don't talk honey mommy is here. I do not care what you did, the main thing is that you are safe….shhh. When the nurse turned her back, she shot him a warning glare and squeezed his arm until she got his attention. Even in his groggy state, Bart knew that was a warning to shut up, so he did. When the nurse left the room, Alice turned all her attention once more on her son. "What in the hell did you do?" Bart tried to explain but Alice was having none of it. She impatiently told him what was going to happen now, "You are going to tell the police officer that comes to talk to you tonight that you were making a delivery for the Sandman and some punks jumped you and took everything you had plus all the money you had already collected. The officer is going to recommend a Boys Home to me and I'm going to agree." Bart looked shocked and started to protest. Alice put her hand up, "You screwed up and the only way to keep this out of the courts (because they drug tested you I'm sure) is to spend a few months being rehabilitated. Once you get out I'll take care of everything." Bart put his head down. Son she said, "You played in the big boys game and sometimes you have to pay the price." Bart started to cry…"Those better not be tears or I will give you something to cry about. Now I have to go make a phone call, remember what I said." With that, Bart remembered his mother gave him a stern look, got up off the side of the bed and left the room. Never once did she ask if he was ok, if he hurt anywhere. She was only concerned about how this was going to affect her. As he looked down at Yana who was now asleep, he vowed to always put her first. Bart remembered spending time in the Boys home. He toughened up there and became hard. He learned to fight there to keep what was his. He beat up the younger boys so that they would fear him and do his bidding. About the only thing, his mom was right about was that if people fear you, then you own them. They do not question they just blindly obey your every command. That is how Bart lived his life, until now that is. A few months in the Boys home ended up lasting two years. Bart could never seem to stay out of trouble. Fighting and gambling were the big ones but he did other things as well. By the time he left, he ruled that place. He had gotten a taste of power over others and he really found it to be his liking. His mother never came to visit him, no one did. He had not seen his mother or siblings in two years so, on his eighteenth birthday he was released and went straight home. When he got to the trailer he found it abandoned. He went from having a brother, three sisters and a mother to being an orphan with no one. Bart turned to what he knew best, he began slinging dope again and this time he was really hooked really quickly. The rest of the story did not matter until about fifteen years later when he was making a delivery at a high mucky-muck party and he spied Justine. She batted her eyes and smiled real big at him. He saw an easy mark and went after her. He looked down at Yana just then and said to her, "I'm not sure the way we got here was the best, but I am your daddy and I love you. I pray you never find out about the terrible things I have done. If you do please know that, I now regret every one of them. But I would do them all again if it meant by not doing them I would not have you." He glanced at the clock on the wall above Yana's door…"I have to go baby girl, I have some bacon to cook!" He laid her in her crib, kissed her forehead and made his exit forgetting about the coffee that was cold by now and the breakfast that remained un eaten. As he passed the nurses station, he waved and off he went.

CHAPTER TEN

HERE PIGGY PIGGY PIGGY

One more challenge after this one and I am home free Bart thought to himself. He had underestimated his opponent from his last challenge. He did not intend to make the same mistake this time. He listened intently as the island elder explained what he was up against and what he was to do. He inspected the tools he was allowed to use. He was given a 10-foot cord, a dull spear and a bushel of wooden 4-foot spikes. He listened closely as the elder said that he could possibly dig a pit using the bamboo that grew wild all over the island. The instructions were pretty clear; he was to capture or snare a wild boar and humanely kill it then return to this spot with the prize. If he were successful, he would move onto the last challenge, if he were not able to complete this challenge then his bid for the kingdom would be lost. Bart understood what was at stake more than the elders or anyone else did.

Becoming king for him meant freedom, his daughter and his life. If he failed then for once in his life there was no backup plan. It was all or nothing and he meant to have it all. He had only lost once in his life and he did not mean for that to happen again. Definitely not here and not now. He thought of little Yana and he knew beyond doubt that he owed it and his life to her. He took a deep breath, grabbed his shabby equipment and headed into the sticker-filled bushes to find his boar. In his youth, the only time he could escape his mother's abuse and his life was to sneak out to the woods by his house and teach himself how to make snares and traps. He was poor and had no weapon but hunger breeds desperation and he learned quick how to satisfy his belly when it growled at him. He sometimes stole hunting magazines and imagined another life while reading through the pages. He read a lot about hunting trapping and killing different types of game. He had read quite a bit about hunting wild boars and sows, at least this animal he knew a little bit about. He felt a sudden excitement about this hunt. He looked around when he entered a clearing that had a small water source. He saw rub marks on the trees and the telltale hoof marks by the small fresh water inlet. He also spied under a tree a worn out place where he assumed they bedded down. He knew from reading about them that they are extremely dangerous and if you do not kill them on the first blow or if there are piglets in the vicinity they will charge and maul you with their tusks. They also have a very keen sense of smell. He grinned at that because he was sure he smelled of Yana's milk and soap and not hog. He made his way down to the watering hole and dipped his hands into the lukewarm rather smelly water, he was about to douse himself with the water when he decided the quicker way to do it. He waded into the water and crouched down in it until he was completely drenched in the stagnant water. Then he waded back out of the water and rolled around in what he was sure was pig feces and dirt and god knows what else. He laughed when he imagined what he looked like at that moment. He thought to himself….six months ago if you had told me that I would be rolling around in pig shit because some 5'3" old man told you to, I would have told you, "Not in a million years!" Yet, here he was doing just that. Funny how life changes.

 He was lost in thought and almost missed the rumbling noises in the distance. He quickly climbed the tree above the water line. He wanted to see how many boars there were and whether or not there were any piglets. He had to plan his attack by first sizing up his prey. He knew that while ferocious they spooked easy and the one advantage they had over him (besides their tusks) was that they had four legs while he had two, this meant they could cover more ground at a higher rate of speed. They are also opportunistic eaters and somewhat lazy. If they have to work hard for their food or water, they will just go somewhere else. Bart hoped he had disguised his scent enough as not to draw attention to himself. From his perch in the tree, he spied something moving in the dense brush. They are not very quiet animals so he could tell how close they were by the incessant grunting and squealing. There they were in the clearing above the brush. The large male looked to be between 200-300 pounds and his tusks were probably 6 inches in length from one side to the other. He was a big boy and Bart intended on giving him a wide girth. There were three adolescent males, maybe four females, he also spied six piglets. He was sure that the big boar was the leader and protector of the herd. He decided if for some reason the big boy decided to rush him he was going to use the very dull spear and stab it in the ribs. After the boars left, he took the 4-foot sticks. He was alone on this hunt and did not want to end up as the hunted. He had a semi plan and for the life of him, he hoped it would work. He found a pretty solid rock by the shoreline. The constant splashing of the water and being ground down by the sandy beach surrounding the small watering hole had smoothed one side. That looked promising as it would not damage or cut his hand that was still healing. In addition, the stone was large enough for him to maneuver and hold with his damaged dominant hand as well. As he started to make progress, Bart smiled to himself and imagined Dr. Tenjin's nod of approval. After he had all the stakes sharpened to his satisfaction, he decided to create a barrier that would herd the animals where he wanted them. He then grabbed the flimsy spear he had been provided, disgusted he through it back down. "That will never penetrate a boar's tough skin," He said with a disapproving tone in his voice. He would have to look around and see what he could substitute in its stead. A ways back on the trail he remembered seeing a thick patch of mature bamboo. He decided it could not hurt to take a quick stroll over there and see what he could find. As he neared the bamboo patch, he heard a deep guttural growl. He had no clue what had made that sound and he definitely did not want to find out. Slowly he backed away never shifting his gaze from the bamboo patch. He had to admit he did not like this situation at all. The only weapon he had on his person was one stake and the rock that he had used for sharpening. He heard the growl again and this time it was much louder and much closer. He nervously looked around trying to see the animal that was most likely about to attack him. All at once there was a loud crashing noise, it almost sounded like what he imagined a herd of elephants would sound like. Charging straight at him was "Big Boy" whom he had sworn to give a large girth to. Bart realized that he had not bothered to watch which way the herd had left the watering hole. He stumbled right into their lair and the "Head Honcho" was not happy at all. This was the largest animal he had ever seen and he knew he only had seconds to think of something before he would feel those deadly tusks rip through him like melted butter. He quickly looked around, the trees were too far away but there were some large boulders that he might be able to fit between. It was the only chance he had. The boulders would buy him time to come up with a plan. He turned and ran as hard, as fast as he could towards the boulders. He lost his footing and went down hard on his knee. He did not bother to look back he just got up and sprinted as fast as he could to the safety of the boulders. He forced himself to slide between them and he barely fit. A few seconds later he felt the ground shake beneath his feet and braced for impact. He prayed the boulders would not crumble due to the pending impact of this mammoth pissed off boar. His weight and enormous size hindered the boar and could not stop his charge and hit the boulders that Bart was squeezed in between with such force he can only describe as feeling as if he was being hit head on by a freight train. Bart closed his eyes as the animal was about to hit. "Please hold, please hold…oh god, I beg you please hold!" Bart let out a loud fearful yell as the boar plowed into the boulder. After the animal smashed into the rock, it stumbled back as if it were in a drunken stupor. Bart quickly sprang to action because this would be his one and only chance to best the beast. He leapt from his hiding place, charged the dazed and bewildered animal, and started running around it as the animal swung its head from side-to- side trying to maul him with his tusks. Bart easily dodged the deadly tusks. He continued to circle the beast and jab it with the very sharp stake whenever he could. Some of the lunges penetrated the hide and some did not. Then by sheer luck, he thrust the stake behind the boar's front leg and it went down to the ground. He likened it to slicing through someone's Achilles tendon. The beast tried and tried but could not lift itself off the ground. Bart knew that at that moment he was once again the victor. He dispatched the animal quickly by slicing through its throat and letting it bleed out.

He inspected himself for battle wounds. He had a pretty good gash below his knee where he had fallen and his chest was scraped up from fitting between the boulders…all in all he came out unscathed. After he calmed down a bit and had counted all ten fingers and toes to make sure he was still intact. He glanced over at Big Boy. It is then that he realized exactly how big he was. How in the world am I going to drag you out of the bush? My God, you have to be at least 500 pounds. I'm strong but not that strong." He looked around and decided to make a type of lean-to out of bamboo and use the stakes and cord to secure the animal to it and then drag him to the clearing where he was supposed to meet the elders. Bart busied himself in chopping down bamboo stalks. Once he had about six that were approximately 5-feet long he tied them together with the 10-foot cord he was provided for the challenge. He then ran back to the watering hole and pulled up the rest of his spikes. He stabbed the animal and wedged the spikes through his lean-to so that "Big Boy" would not slide off and end up down in one of the gulley's along the path. It took him about three hours to bring his prize out of the bush. The elders were getting ready to leave and retire for the night when all of a sudden they saw a remarkable sight. In front of them stood, Bart covered in not only mud but by the smell of him some type of poop and lots of blood. He was brown from head-to-toe, the only time you could tell he was not an island native was when he smiled. That was not a problem though because he was grinning from ear-to-ear. Bart then moved to the side and said, "I would like you to meet Big Boy. He put up a hell of a fight and deserves your utmost respect. Say your blessings and prayers over him (or whatever you do.) Take whatever part of him you deem necessary; feed the entire island if you must…. But (Bart said with a very serious, no questioned asked, just obey tone) His tusks are mine." and Bart eyed them all as if to say, "Try me, I dare you to." The elders quickly agreed, with that Bart dropped the handles to his lean-to turned and walked the path back to the village. He went straight to the infirmary and when the nurses smelled him, they marched him right back outside. The Head Nurse said, "Your Highness, you have a choice, you may either jump in the surf at the beach or there is a water well with a bucket around the back of the building. Whichever method you choose does not matter to me, however, and I mean this with the most respect, you are not coming back in the infirmary until you are clean and do not smell like…well, I am not exactly sure what you smell like other than really bad. This is after-all a hospital." Bart nodded and laughed and said, "Point well made, I will go clean up." With that, Bart marched off to the beach to wash off. When he returned to the infirmary, he was immediately whisked away to Dr. Tenjin. Bart grinned as the doctor continued to look him over. "Your Highness, you must have an angel on your side because after I saw the boar I was sure you would be sporting some horrendous wounds. Everything I'm seeing is extremely superficial." Bart crossed his arms across his chest and waited patiently until the doctor was done. "I'm thinking a few stitches and you should heal just fine. Boars carry a lot of germs so we are going to scrub those wounds clean, apply some antiseptics, give your muscles a few days to heal and you will be ready for the last challenge." The doctor put his head down and Bart noticed he looked troubled. "Doc Tenjin, what is the matter?" Bart asked with genuine concern in his voice. Dr. Tenjin looked up at Bart and said, "By telling you this, I am breaking the rules. I cannot in good conscious keep this from you. You are not just competing for yourself as most of the Princes are you are trying to make a good life for little Yana. Against my better judgement, I am going to tell you what you are battling in your next challenge. The doc looked up at Bart with a very sad look in his eyes. "Not many people survive this challenge. It is worse than the shark and the Boar put together. Your Highness, you are going to battle a Saltwater Crocodile." Bart quickly looked up at the doctor in utter shock and disbelief, "Say that again please? I am not sure I heard you correctly. You said that I-I am battling a what? I think you said saltwater crocodile. I am sure that cannot be right. ARE YOU PEOPLE INSANE?" he bellowed. Doc please tell me that I am Rip Van Winkle and slept until April fool's Day. You are joking right. Ha Ha, jokes on me....not funny. There is no way I can defeat a Saltwater croc. The shark was risky; the wild boar was sheer luck....A saltwater croc? Nope, I am not doing it!" Dr. Tenjin ignored Bart's outburst and continued, "These animals are so strong and can fight on both the land and in the sea. I wanted to you to know, Although, I'm not sure why other than to possibly relieve my own consciousness....It is not as if you can prepare for this challenge." Bart looked at the doctor quite perplexed. The doctor ignored him once more, "This challenge is not the simple stalk, hunt and trap the animal." Dr. Tenjin looked across the lagoon and said, "Do you see that island about a mile away?" Bart scanned the horizon until he saw the island and nodded his head.

"That island is called Manu Island and before you ask, yes it is uninhabited. Oh, not because it lacks resources to sustain a community of people. Actually, it is quite the opposite; it over-flows with fresh water, fruit trees, excellent soil for planting and lots of wild game. We have tried to cultivate that island many times throughout the years. The problem is in traveling to the island itself. A natural reef lies just under the surf. I believe it stretches the entire expanse of the island. This makes it impossible to access the island by canoe." Bart shielded his eyes with his hand and squinted to see if he could see the reef the doctor was talking about but he was unable to make it out. Dr. Tenjin realizing what Bart was trying to do continued, "It is very hard to see as it disguises itself quite well in the rough breaking of the surf. The only way to access, the island is to abandon your canoe and swim over the reef and through the lagoon to the shore. If you want to leave the island, you have no canoe. There is nothing to tether the canoe in the middle of the ocean. Anglers have tried securing them to the reef but that did not work either. By the time, they went to retrieve their canoes they were battered and broken." Bart was about to suggest something but the doctor continued without pause. "They tried to carry the canoe over the reef to continue the journey to the shore but the surf is so strong that the fishermen get swept off their feet into shark and crocodile infested water and that my friend is never a very good outcome. Now if they are planning a fishing trip to Manu it is usually just for the day and someone remains in the canoe as the others tempt fate and try to make it to the island. If they are successful, it is well worth it because the fish, the lobsters, the turtles etc. are quite abundant. The reef is always teaming with oceanic marine life. The island anglers have no idea about the tide tables so sadly most do not make it to the shore. You see Prince Amir, because of the tide tables high tide lasts about six to seven hours but low tide lasts anywhere from three to four days.

The reef is so vibrant and enticing; it attracts quite a bevy of sea creatures. It offers something for even the fussiest palate. Different species of shark frequent the reef during high tide to feed and are stuck there during low tide. The water is deep enough to sustain them but the reef blocks their escape." Bart shook his head and then furrowed his brow, "Basically, you are saying that going to Manu is like playing Russian roulette. Are the Elders mad? Do they really want a king at the end of this challenge or is this all just sport to them? Wasn't the shark challenge and the wild boar enough to prove prowess, strength, bravery and whatever else a king needs to possess?" Dr. Tenjin agreed with Bart, this did seem foolhardy and a bit over the top. Although…. The Dr. began, "Some do survive, after I put them back together they rule until they cannot and then we do it all over again." Bart asked, "As the king, am I not allowed to change any rule I want and make up my own?" Tenjin responded, "Yes, as the ruling monarch you have the right to do that." Incredulously Bart threw his hands in the air and said, "Then why has it never been changed? I do not understand." "Either the posing king forgets about it or maybe figures if he had to endure it then every candidate that vies for the Kingship should have to do it as well. I really do not have an answer for that," Dr. Tenjin said. "Either way, you have to do it. With my help though, you will conquer it." Bart looked at the doctor and asked him, "Why are you helping me? Is that not against the rules? What kind of trouble are you facing if you are found out?" Tenjin responded, "I know the consequences of my actions and I alone will accept the responsibility if I get caught. That is my crux to bear Prince Amir. You just need to absorb everything

I am telling you like a sponge and follow my instructions to the letter." Bart was very confused; he had never in his life met anyone that helped without expecting any type of compensation or reward at the end. He had mad respect for this person and felt that they would be lifelong friends if he survived this. "Ok doc, what else do I need to know? Before the doctor had time to answer him, Bart quickly asked another question. "Oh, one more thing, once I kill the croc, how am I supposed to get it off the island and back to Zanzi without attracting every other hungry mouth and with no canoe? That is a very long swim after what I am sure will be a very arduous and tiring fight. I am not Superman and do not possess superhuman strength by any means." "Do not worry Your Highness, I have that all figured out as well. Now if you don't mind, we need to talk about the different types of sharks you will encounter and then the Crocodile." Bart nodded and gave the doctor his undivided attention once more. The doctor began again, "The least aggressive and most docile of the bunch is the Lemon shark. This one is more of a nuisance than anything else is. They rarely pose any type of threat to man. They are very fussy eaters and you my friend, are not on their menu. They remind me of a child that refuses to try anything new. Prince Amir, the Lemon shark, well honestly any shark looks scary but the worst a Lemon shark can do is take a bite at you. You still have to respect them but not really fear them.

The next type of shark that has a presence off the shores of Manu is the Tiger shark." Bart looked at the doctor and said, "Really, you mean I have to fight with one of those again? The last time I tangled with a Tiger I was almost killed. This is crazy! If I did not have, Yana to think about I would throw in the towel and walk away. This is ludicrous." Dr. Tenjin with a show of support put his arm around Bart's shoulder and said, "You have something that none of the other candidates have my boy" Bart looked in the doctor's direction. "This is a deadly challenge. However, you have 35 years of experience on your side." Bart looked confused again. The doctor continued, "You have me. While I will not be on the island with you my words and wisdom will be your guide."

This time all you will be supplied with is a long knife. You will have to make your own weapons. As I said, very few survive it." Bart who was flabbergasted at this point did not know what to say. He desperately looked at Dr. Tenjin, "What am I supposed to do doc? How am I going to survive with just a long knife against sharks and crocs and god knows what else?" "Prince Amir, I am going to tell you exactly what you need to do to not only survive this challenge but to conquer it. I ask one thing in return." Bart looked at him and said, "Anything doc, anything that I have is yours…just not my first born." With that, they both laughed. They found themselves sitting on the beach and Bart was listening intently as Dr. Tenjin explained how high tide and low tide worked on Manu Island. As he drew the tide table onto the sand to illustrate to him how important, it was to get to the reef in time. He went on to explain the different characteristics of each of the shark species that were present there at the reef. He learned which ones hugged the reef and which ones stayed deep and never came up unless there was excessive splashing or blood present in the water. Bart listened and took mental notes.

When the doc was done explaining, he looked at Bart, "Prince Amir Do you understand everything I have explained to you?" Bart regaled the important points. He repeated what the shark behavior was and he explained the tide table to the doc. He stressed how important it was to cross the reef at a certain time. When he was done, Bart looked at Dr. Tenjin and smiled, "Am I right doc?" A nod of approval met Bart's question, "I wish I had more students like you Your Highness. Some of my nurses think just having a pretty smile and a cute little touché is all they need. When it comes to following instructions and actually caring for the patients the quote unquote elevator has stopped a floor short, if you know what I mean." Bart grinned and agreed.

Bart understood all about the sharks now and reef and the tides, what about the Saltwater Crocodile he wondered. He decided that he would bite the bullet and ask the doc, "Dr. Tenjin, you have explained everything to me except the part about the crocodile. Do you mind telling me what I'm up against?" Dr. Tenjin thought for a moment and said, "Prince Amir, the Saltwater Crocodile is an extremely deadly opponent, it is called a man-eater. They fear nothing and will charge prey four times their size. Their hide is as tough as chain mail. If one attacks you and you are lucky enough to survive then there is a good chance that the infection from the bite or bites will kill you. So do me a favor….Try not to be bitten! Saltwater Crocodiles are opportunistic eaters and will eat anything that they think they can kill quickly and easily. The males are also territorial and sometimes their territory is miles long. If there are eggs present, the females can be more aggressive than the males. If the male sees you as a threat, he will charge and attack you. They can run as fast as they can swim. If one happens to lock its jaws onto you then you are pretty much done. Their jaw muscles are so strong that I have seen one completely crush the rudder and the side of the deck of a Supply boat that got in his way. After that, I did some research on them and found that saltwater crocodiles slam their jaws shut with 3,700 pounds per square inch of bite force. Prince Amir, a saltwater crocodile can drag a full-grown water buffalo into the water and rip chunks off it while it is still alive. It can bite through the body of a car as if it were melted butter on a piece of toasted bread." Bart started to look worried and asked, "How am I supposed to kill one with just a long knife then?" Doctor Tenjin smiled, "Your Highness, yes, the crocs are very strong but they have a one-track mind….The only thing they think about is eating. You need to take your knife and kill a sea turtle or two, not in the water because that will attract the sharks. Make the kill after it lays its eggs and is headed back to the sea. Dig a pit (about five to six feet deep and about four feet wide.) When you dig your pit, make some grooves in the side of the pit that will let you climb in and out of it fairly easily. Proceed to gut your turtle or turtles and make some blood trails from the shore to your pit. One is okay but at least two coming from different directions is better. Go find a Bamboo thatch and chop down some stalks, you need at least ten. Take your knife, and sharpen the bamboo stalks into stakes. Bury the stakes about three to four feet into the bottom of your pit use your foot and knock the stakes around to make sure they are secure. To ensure that the croc falls in the pit take the turtle carcass and set it right on the edge of the pit. It has to be half over the opening so that the slightest breeze or even a sneeze would knock it in. There are two reasons for this, number one, hopefully the animal will take the bait and fall in. With this being such a fresh kill, the smell of death has not been triggered for the croc as of yet. If the croc sees the turtle go into the hole, there is a good possibility that the croc will give chase and follow what it thinks is a living turtle. Bam! You got him! Anyways, after you line the bottom of the pit with stakes, make your blood trail, place the turtle and cover your pit then climb your tree and take a nap. I suggest getting rest whenever you can because for most of this challenge you are awake. This wait should not take too long. A wounded or dead turtle is an easy meal and trust me; the crocs are all about easy." Bart was getting excited now. "Once the croc follows the blood trail and falls onto the stakes puncturing his soft underbelly then you are almost home free. Wait until it quits thrashing about and throw some rocks at it to make sure that it has lost enough blood that it is going in and out of consciousness. Take your shirt off, and remove your shoelaces. Carefully climb down into the pit, throw your shirt over its head, and jump on its back (in front of its front legs.) Quickly grab its snout (right at the front.) You can use one hand to hold the mouth shut and the other to wrap your shoelaces over your shirt and around its jaws. Once secure, take your long knife and drive it through the animal's eye into its skull. The croc will expire in about 30 seconds. Just make sure that it has had time to bleed out a while from the stakes that have punctured the soft underbelly of the beast. I would give it maybe an hour. Hang out in your tree and take a nap." Bart liked what he was hearing. Prince Amir, it is very important that you pay attention to the tide tables. It is going to take you almost a day to make it to the reef and then you will have to wait for low tide to climb onto the reef. Do not jump into the other side and attempt to swim through the lagoon to the shore. I can almost guarantee that you will not make it. Instead, walk the length of the reef (which will take most of the night.) Keep in mind the only light you will have to walk the length of the reef with is the moonlight. Check your footing each time you take a step. The reef is quite slippery and if you fall in the splash will attract the hungry predators.

Do me a favor please, do not fall in!

Towards the north end of the island the reef is about four feet from the shore and during low tide, only two pockets contain water. Be quick and get to shore. Spend the next day scouting the island for the best place to dig your pit. Find a spot about ten feet from shore and in the open but with a tree in the vicinity. Find a smooth rock, dig your pit, and kill a turtle. The digging will be slow since you will be using a rock. This should take you most of the second night. Towards morning (after your pit is dug) find and kill the turtle. Make sure that your blood trail is fresh by the morning. Climb your tree and wait patiently for your prey. If it takes more than two hours then kill another turtle and make another fresh blood trail or two." Bart could see how this could actually work. Doctor Tenjin continued, "Make sure your stakes are secure because once stabbed the animal is going to thrash and try to climb out of the pit. Make sure your pit is deep and wide enough that he cannot get out. Lastly make sure your pit is covered with coconut leaves so that he cannot see it as he follows the blood trail. When the croc quits thrashing take your rocks and test it to see how much fight he still has. You will know when the time is right to make the kill."

Bart understood all of this and yes, he could see it working but he still had a question, "How do I get the croc back to Zanzi?" Tenjin smiled and said, "There is nothing in the rules that says you need to bring the entire croc back. Take your long knife and chop it up. Fashion a basket with large handles similar to a backpack and put the crocs head in it. This one you keep and provide to the elders as proof of the kill. Trust me, they have seen enough of them to be able to tell that it is a fresh kill and what type of instrument killed it. Now, make some cord (at least ten feet long) out of the coconut leaves and then fashion another basket. Tie this basket to your waist so you do not lose it on your walk back across the reef. Walk the length of the reef again and before you exit the side of the reef to swim back to Zanzi, throw the basket with the cutup body of the croc on the side of the reef closest to Manu. This does a few things for you. Number one it brings the bigger deadlier sharks from the deep up to the surface and trust me a feeding frenzy will ensue. Once the croc has been completely eaten, the bigger sharks will attack the smaller sharks, which will give you enough time to vacate the area.

Any other sharks in the area will sense the blood and commotion and leave you alone to go check it out. You my friend are home free to swim your prize back to Zanzi." After Dr. Tenjin finished his explanation and instructions, he had a "cat that ate the canary look on his face." Bart was really quite impressed. This could actually work....Take that back, this is the only plan he had so it would work or he would die trying.

Dr. Tenjin?" Bart asked tentatively. Tenjin looked at him, "What is it Your Highness? Bart nervously cleared his throat and continued, "If something happens to me, you will take care of Yana won't you?" Bart held his breath waiting for the good doctor's answer. With absolutely no hesitation Dr. Tenjin said, "Of course Your Highness....Of course, but nothing is going to happen to you except that you will be very sore and very tired and very triumphant." Bart liked the sound of that. He was a little hesitant to believe that it was all going to be that easy though.

The doctor-sensed doubt starting to creep into Bart's thoughts and he knew that the last thing the prince needed was to doubt himself. He tried to distract and redirect his thought process...."Your Highness, you are going to have quite a trophy selection when this is all over." Bart looked at him confused and said, "How so? What trophies are you talking about?" Tenjin smiled and said, "Well let's see, hmm, seems to me that your Tiger shark teeth will be ready for you when you return. Oh, yes, there are the tusks from the boar. Although personally I would have just mounted the entire, boars head on the wall in your Great Hall. You call him Big Boy I think. Is that correct?" Bart smiled big now, "Yes, I named him Big Boy…Were you able to access his actual weight for me?" The doctor laughed, "You do know that it took 10 islanders to bring him down from the bush right? It was really was not nice what you did to the elders the other day." Bart furrowed his brow puzzled, "How so? What are you talking about?" The doctor started really laughing then, "You came out of the bushes with Big Boy all covered in, well anyway you were quite a sight. You introduced the boar to the elders, barked your demands and just left the boar there and walked away. They assumed that since you, just one man drug him by yourself out of the bush, well….Suffice to say, they ended up having to call for help and did not retire to their homes until almost midnight. They are quite perplexed by your strength and stamina." Bart was rolling out deep belly laughs now. The doctor continued, "The nurses, especially the head nurse was none too happy with you either. Oh my, it took her almost an hour to scrub the hallway that you entered when you walked straight into the Infirmary." Bart said, "My intention was to go to the showers first thing, the head nurse was having no part of that ha ha!" "Your Highness, do you have any idea how bad you smelled? My office as you know is all the way across the building and I smelled you as you came up the walkway even before you entered. It took me two days to calm that nurse down." Bart was laughing so hard now he was doubled over clutching his sides because it hurt. "Doc, doc, enough….I cannot take anymore! Please man stop already he laughed." The doc put his hand up and said, "All I am saying is that you are creating quite a reputation for yourself. They are curious to see what you do next."

The doctor looked at his watch and then looked at Bart who was quite pleased with himself and said, "Well Your Highness, it is getting pretty late and you have only one day to let your muscles rest before you once again assault them with the last challenge. Tomorrow, your doctor orders are to relax and spend the day with your daughter. You should take her to the market place or the beach. I think she has been cooped up in the Infirmary far too long. Fresh air and a day with her daddy will do her wonders and I think the break will be good for you too. I can have one of the nurses pack you a lunch and a few bottles and nappies for the little miss." Bart happily agreed, that sounded like an excellent plan." He felt like a huge weight had been lifted from his shoulders. He thanked the doc, stood up, brushed the sand off his shorts, and started to make his way up the beach back towards the infirmary. All of a sudden, he remembered something the doc had said…He only wanted one thing in return for helping him. Alarm bells went off and he spun around in time to see Dr. Tenjin get up from his sitting position. "Doc"

Bart said. The doctor turned towards him with a questioning look. "Your Highness?" He responded. Bart changed his mind because that was a conversation for another time. He smiled at the doc and said, "Good night, see you tomorrow." They waved at each other and both turned in opposite directions, Dr. Tenjin was going home, his wife had promised him fresh fish stew and he was already late. Bart was headed to the Infirmary, he had wanted to get there in time to give Yana a bath but he feared she was probably already asleep by now. He figured he would just scoop her up and let her sleep on his chest. His days were no longer complete if he did not begin and end them in the presence of his baby girl.

When he got to her floor in the infirmary, he was met with a disapproving look from the head nurse. He walked straight up to the nursing station and pulled a bunch of flowers from behind his back, "Am I forgiven now? I wanted to apologize to you for the other day. Honestly, all I wanted to do was shower and hold my daughter. I gave no mind to my appearance, my smell and everything I was tracking in." The nurse smiled real big and took the flowers from Bart. She blushed, waived her hands at him and said, "Your Excellency, you are forgiven. Honestly, we were more afraid of the germs that you um, rolled in. There are many sick children here and their immune systems are not 100% so even the slightest germ, especially from what you were rutting around in could have made them very ill. Oh, and then there was the mess all over the floor. I can imagine what the bathroom and shower would have looked like had you gotten that far." She brought the back of her hand up to her forehead and shook her head back and forth. Then she looked up at Bart, "We headed you off at the pass and avoided the catastrophe. No harm, no foul. I will say this though, royalty or not…If you ever and I mean ever make a mess like the one it took me an hour to clean up the other day, I will hand you the broom, mop and mop bucket myself!" Bart laughed, blew her a kiss and spun around to go to Yana's room. He looked in her crib and there she was sound asleep. He went into the bathroom and took a quick shower. When he came back out he carefully scooped his sleeping daughter out of her crib and sat down in the rocking chair. He had a lot to tell her about his crazy busy day.

As Bart started quietly telling Yana about everything that happened on that day. The next thing he knew the room was light and Yana was fussing about her bottle and probably needed to be changed. All he remembered was sitting down, covering them both up and now this. Wow, he thought, I really must have been tired. Right them Yana let out a very irritated whimper. Bart looked down at her, "Ok, ok, I get the message loud and clear! I'll go fetch your bottle." He laid her in the crib, which she let out a protest to, and out the door, he went to get her a bottle.

After Bart, bathed and changed his daughter he let the nurses pick out something for her to wear. Bart was in awe at the generosity of the island people. Yana went from having nothing to having more clothes, blankets and anything else she needed. He had never met people like this. They are just like the doc; they give and help because it is needed. They do not expect anything in return. This entire island works together in everything they do. I understand now why the young boys are in charge of capturing and killing the coconut crab. They are conditioning them to always put the needs of the people first above all else. It made Bart feel good to know that these are the people Yana will grow up with. These are exactly the values that he wants instilled in her. If something happened to him his heart eased a bit because now he could see what type of person she would turn out to be because you are whom you associate with.

At that moment, the nurse brought Yana in. She was gorgeous in her little pink dress. Up until that moment, the only thing he had seen her in was the standard hospital white onesie and little socks. To make the nurses happy he picked her up and began admiring her outfit. Yana opened her eyes and Bart sucked his breath in. With her deep piercing green eyes it was almost as if she could look all the way into your soul. Bart knew that he had many deep dark black places in his soul but he was trying to be better. This was the first time in his life he actually wanted to be better. There were no ulterior motives. When he looked at Yana, he knew she deserved only the best.

Bart had never really been one to "Stop and Smell the Flowers" so to speak. As he pushed Yana in her stroller around the Marketplace, he was quite impressed. He had never watched anyone make an honest dollar so watching the Merchants in action was amazing. A Merchant haggled with someone for twenty minutes in regards to a pair of cheap earrings. The shopper offered the Merchant quite a bit less than what was listed on the price. The Merchant raised the price a little arguing that this was in pristine condition…blah, blah, blah. After the back and forth bartering between the Merchant and the Shopper it was finally decided that, the Shopper would pay 10% less than the original price. Bart walked up to the Merchant and before he even said anything the merchant turned on his biggest smile and started trying to sell Bart anything and everything. Bart said, "Please stop, I just have a question for you. At the end of your last sale you only gained a few dollars, was it worth working that hard for just a few dollars?" The man paused and looked at Bart, "This is how I make a living. Honestly, I actually made about ten more dollars than the earrings were worth. I mark everything up and I get the shopper to think they are getting a great buy when actually I am guiding them exactly where I want them. The next time they come to the marketplace they will come to me because they think they got a great deal. They will also tell whomever they are with so I will get even more business that way. The ends justify the means." Bart thanked him for his candor and he and Yana left the merchant's tent. Bart was very impressed with this man and made a mental note about him. When he became king, this man was going to run the treasury department. He was a swindler by nature but he was honest. Bart understood how this man's thought process worked. He wanted people working for him that he could relate to. He knew what motivated this man. This would be used to Bart's advantage. Looking down at Yana in her stroller, he smiled and told her that this visit to the marketplace was becoming very valuable.

    Nothing else really stood out so they left and headed to the park. Yana was starting to complain and squirm so Bart figured it was around lunchtime. "Do we eat at the park or on the beach little princess?" Yana started to cry a little and get fussy. "The park it is!" Bart found a spot a little bit off to the side. He liked being able to hear and see everything without being right dab in the middle of it. He spread out the blanket and got Yana's bottle out of the bag.

He released his squirming daughter from her stroller and propped her on his chest. When she saw her bottle, she started cooing and kicking her legs. Bart smiled, "All that for a silly bottle? Ha ha, wait until I put a steak in front of you," he laughed to himself. He got out his sandwiches and ate them while Yana finished off her bottle. He burped her, changed her, and propped her up on a pillow. For what seemed like a long time father and daughter just laid on the blanket, enjoyed the sights, and sounds the park offered. Bart looked down at his daughter and she was sound asleep. He was very content.

Could life get any better….

CHAPTER ELEVEN

PROMISED

At this moment in time he did not think so. Soon his eyes too grew heavy and he was asleep. He thought he was dreaming because he heard a familiar voice. Bart woke with a start and realized that standing over him was Prince Branoi, Prince Malaki & Prince Tula. He smiled and jumped up shaking all the extended hands. He had not seen these guys since the night in the Pub. When all the back slaps were done, Bart motioned for them to sit with him, "The blanket is big enough for all of us and I'm sure Yana will not mind the company." That is when the three princes got a look at little Yana. Prince Branoi said, "Wow Amir, the rumors are definitely true, she is quite a beauty." Bart thanked him for the compliment. "Being a single father is not easy but I love every minute I get to spend with her." It was as if Yana knew she was the center of attention because she chose at that moment to wake up and open her eyes. All three of the princes gasped, Malaki was the first to speak, "Look at those beautiful eyes…if only I had a son." Tula was next, "Well hello there little princess, you are stunning and your dad better watch out when you get older ha ha." Bart shot him a desperate look. Branoi then said, "Rayno, we need to talk, I. do have a son that is just now two years old and as of yet is not promised to anyone." Bart was a bit confused at first but soon understood where this conversation was going. "Branoi my friend, what do you have to offer this kingdom if I am the victor? Pratcha thought for a moment, "I have a great army and sea worthy vessels. My group of islands are bountiful in food, fresh water and live game. One of my islands has a gold suppository that has only just been tapped and well as crude oil to warm the coldest nights. This makes my monarchy the wealthiest in the chain. I have another son who is already promised to another princess and will assume my throne when I can no longer rule. You my dear Amir have no sons. No one to assume your throne. If we promise Yana and Micho to each other, per the island customs he will travel here on Yana's eighteenth birthday to go through your island's challenges. If he bests them then we will wed them. When the time comes that, you can no longer rule he will step up and assume the role of king for Zanzi. Amir if we are able to join our families through this marriage we will be the strongest and wealthiest monarchy in the chain." Bart thought for a moment, this was all very foreign to him. Arranged marriages, wow, this is the twentieth century right? He had to remember where he was and what he supposedly was….a prince. This was the common practice here in these islands. This is how the monarchy survived. The bloodlines remained pure. He smiled and looked at Prince Branoi, "I think our two monarchies together will make an unstoppable power house. If I succeed and win the kingship here on Zanzi then, yes, Pratcha, I agree to the betrothal of our children. Micho will travel here when Yana turns eighteen. He will go through the challenges; if he is successful then they will be wed. Pratcha interjected, "If he fails he will be put to death as per the ancient customs. I am well aware of what is expected of him, as he will be as well. We have all gone through it." With that, the men shook hands and Prince Branoi said he would get the wheels in motion for the Promising Ceremony. Of course, everything depended on whether or not Prince Amir Rayno could come out the victor in the last challenge, which was to begin tomorrow. Tula looked over at Bart and said, "We are going to the Pub later on tonight, if you care to join us you are very welcome." Bart shook his head no, "Thank you for the offer but this last challenge is deadly and I need to have my wits about me. I also want to spend the evening with Yana just in case it is to be my last." The other princes were still attempting to capture the shark. If Bart were victorious then the challenges would stop for he would be the successor and assume the crown of Zanzi as their ruling king. Branoi, Tula and Malaki accepted and more than understood his reasoning for declining their invitation. Bart said, "I need to get Yana back to her room. Good luck in your upcoming challenges. I hope to see each and every one of you at the Promising Ceremony." They all said their goodnights, Bart headed off alone and the other three headed to the Pub to see what trouble they could get into. Each of the three were so lost in their own thoughts none of them noticed the figure in the dark leaning against the street lamp pole that had listened intently to every word they had said. No one saw him back away and disappear into the night.

 Each was secretly hoping that Amir would be triumphant so these challenges would be over. If there is a successor then the rest of the candidates wait to rule their own kingdoms or if another throne comes open, they will compete in those challenges. None will lose their lives except Amir. If he loses and survives or quits then per ancient customs he will forfeit his life. Was he aware of that part of the custom? Branoi piped up then and broke the silence, "Do any of you know what the last challenge is? I can't get anyone to talk." Malaki laughed and elbowed him in the ribs, "Maybe you are losing your touch old man. Your big brown eyes are not having the same effect on the maidens as it did before Amir got here." They all laughed at that. Prince Tula remarked, "Do you see how oblivious

Amir is to all the maidens' advances. It is crazy; if he did not have a baby daughter, I would think he was gay. Although, I would never tell him that. Prince Branoi put his hand up, "Really guys? Not a month ago the man lost his wife, became a single father and if that is not bad enough has had to go through these challenges while still morning his losses and worrying about his daughter." The other two put their heads down in shame. Prince Branoi continued…."If something happens to Amir prior to the Promising Ceremony then I will take Yana and raise her as my own. When she turns eighteen, I will still wed her to Micho and send them here to rule Zanzi. I would do that to honor her father. You do realize it is because of him that none of us are dead yet. Have any of you ever been in the water with a shark? Let alone killed one. I think not.

Have you, any of you looked at the wounds that Rayno sustained from that beast? Then there is the boar. Have any of you even ever hunted?" Pratcha jumped up from the table and grabbed Malaki's hand and turned it over inspecting it…."Just as I thought" Branoi said. "You do not have even one callous. You have never worked a day in your life. What about you Tula, have you ever broken a sweat in anything other than chasing the skirts of the servant girls or palace maidens?" Both Prince Tula and Prince Malaki hung their heads once more. Malaki mumbled, "We were only teasing. I really do like Amir." Prince Tula agreed…."Yeah, me too."

Prince Branoi was still angry with the other two princes. He stood up and said, "I lost my appetite for beer tonight." Then he sneered at them, "Maybe it's just the company that I do not have the stomach for." He got up, went over to the Bar Maid and paid his tab. He looked over at Tula and Malaki, turned around, and exited the Pub. As he walked along the path to his room in the palace, he shook his head in disbelief at how Tula and Malaki talked about Amir. He hoped that what he said to them in the Pub sank into their young, immature idiot heads. If they had gone through just one of the things Amir has gone through in the past month, he did not think that they could handle it. Prince Branoi decided that before he went to his room he was going to walk over to the Infirmary and talk to Prince Amir. Bart was sitting in the rocking chair with Yana. He had bathed, fed and changed her and now she was very contently snuggled up on his chest. As he rocked her gently, he talked to her about their day. "Yana, I want you to know that if today was my last day on earth then there was never a more perfect day. There is nowhere else I would rather be then in your company. Thank you sweet daughter for coming into my life and giving it meaning. Thank you for making me a better man today then I was yesterday. I pray I beat this challenge and give you the life you deserve. If I am bested and do not survive the challenge that they have set before me. I want you to know that my life did not begin until the day you reached your little hand up from your crib and stole my heart. I never thought I was capable of love and selflessness. I never felt anything even remotely similar to those feelings for anyone until you. How is it possible that one so little that has never uttered a word has that kind of power of me? How did you do it little Yana? You have given me a reason to best every challenge and obstacle that is ever put in my path if only to keep you safe. Then he giggled a little, "You my little one have also had quite a day. You cannot talk, walk, or even sit up and yet you are now promised to a prince on your eighteenth birthday.

Talk about growing up quickly ha ha!" He was about to turn off the light and snuggle up with his baby daughter when he heard a slight tap on the door. "That's odd he thought, the nurses never knock. Come in, the door is open." Bart was very surprised and slightly alarmed when it was not a nurse but Pratcha that stuck his head in the door. "Amir Can we speak? It will be very brief as I know you have to rest for the last challenge tomorrow." Bart motioned him in, "What is wrong? Are Tula and Malaki alright?" Prince Branoi continued, "No, no, I'm sorry if I gave you the wrong impression, everyone is fine. I just came here tonight to give you some peace of mind. I wanted you to know that if you do not survive this last challenge, if you allow it, I would take Yana to my island and raise her as one of my own. On her eighteenth birthday, she and Micho would be wed and then sent here to Zanzi to rule as we agreed on. I do this to honor and show you respect my brave friend." Bart was speechless, "Branoi, you have no idea how much that means to me. I am grateful to you for what you have offered as well as your friendship. I have honestly never met anyone like you. So yes, on behalf of Yana and myself I accept. Thank you my friend." Prince Branoi smiled down at little sleeping Yana and bid Bart goodnight, gently closed the door and left to go to his own room in the palace. Bart looked at Yana, "We can have a very good life here little girl, I think I have a friend." Suddenly it dawned on Bart that he had never had anyone that he thought of or called a friend; this was his very first ever. Prince Branoi was the first real friend he has ever had. His eyes drooped and soon he was asleep.

The sun rose early but try as he might Bart had a very restless sleep the night before. So many thoughts raced through his head. "Was this to be his last day? Would he ever again lay eyes on his little daughter? Was this to be the day he would have to atone for all his sins?" He hoped not, he had so much more left to do in this life. He knew he could never wash away all the horrible things he had done in his life. He knew that one day he would have to answer for every one of them. He vowed that he was going to do right by Yana and make sure her life was as perfect as he could make it. She was going to be an amazing Queen someday. He just prayed that his past would not come back to haunt her.

A nurse poked her head in the door, "Prince Amir, excuse me for interrupting you." Bart looked up at her and motioned for her to come in. She still stood in the doorway nervously looking at him. "What is it nurse? What can I help you with?" She then said, "Your Highness, all the nurses got together last night and asked the Priest at the Infirmary if he would say a prayer over you this morning before you head out." She stopped and looked up, "With your permission of course." Bart stood up and walked over to her, "Thank you, I would be honored and very grateful for that." She smiled big then and said, "I'll go get the Priest…Be right back." Bart looked at Yana after the nurse left, "These are wonderful people, how did we ever get so lucky little one?" A little while later they were all standing (well Bart was kneeling because of his height) in front of Father Ka'ba as he said a blessing over Bart.

When the blessing was concluded, Bart took Yana back to her room. He wanted what might be his last moments with her to be special. He unclasped the necklace from around his neck and gave her the only thing that meant anything to him. "Baby Girl" he began, "If I never see you again I want you to keep this and know that you saved me. This was my grandfather's and we were very close before he died. He taught me about the person I wanted to be. He instilled good values in me. The day before he passed away, he gave me this necklace. He got it in the war. He is the only person that ever loved me and I loved in return. If he had lived, I know I would have been a good person. Just like that, he was gone and my mother saw an easy mark in me and . beat the love out of me little Yana. When I cried she beat me harder. She replaced all the love in my heart with hate. She made me feel that everyone was out to get me or use me in some way. She taught me to use them before they had a chance. No one mattered to me. There was no joy in my life. Your mom tried, but I had no use for her. I only wanted her money. She was so gullible and naïve, it was really too damn easy. Then out of nowhere, you came along. You looked at me and it was all over....The fat lady sang her song. I love you little one. If I don't return from this challenge please, no matter what you ever hear about me....just know that I love you." Bart placed Yana in her crib and quickly turned and walked out the door. Rushing down the hall, he had his head down so no one could see the tears that were streaming down his face. Unbeknownst to Bart, someone had indeed listened to his heartfelt confession and had witnessed this display of emotion. This stranger watched Bart exit the building.

CHAPTER TWELVE

MANU ISLAND

The sun was already peaking its head over the horizon as Bart made his way down to the beach. Waiting for him were three island elders and the current royal monarchy. They all watched Bart with very somber looks on their faces as he came, stood before them, and then kneeled down onto the sand. The island priest was the first to speak, "Good morning Prince Amir, are you well rested and ready for the final challenge today?" Bart nodded and slowly raised his head until he was able to look each one of them in the eyes as if he were reading their minds. They shuffled from one foot to the other very uncomfortably under his intense gaze. The priest cleared his throat and continued, "The only weapon you will have on this challenge is this long knife that I have already blessed for you my son." Bart took the knife from the priest and turned it over and over in his hand inspecting each side of it. One of the other elders then spoke, "The challenge that is set before you on this day is the deadliest of all the challenges that you have faced. We are going to take you by canoe out past the point where the waves crest and break so that you do not have to tire yourself battling the surf. When we let you out of the canoe, you must swim to that island (the elder pointed to Manu Island.) That island is called Manu Island. Once you get to Manu you must capture and kill a (the elder paused a moment) saltwater crocodile." Then the elders watched Bart carefully to see what his reaction would be. Right on cue, Bart jumped up and started yelling, "Hold the phone, now wait just a minute, I don't think I heard you right, You want, I mean I have, you want me to capture a what? Kill a what? A saltwater crocodile? Now I know there really is such a thing as Island fever because you people must have it (he pointed at every one of the elders.) You do realize that is a suicide mission right? Especially with this dull thing, (Bart looked down at the sorry excuse for a long knife and threw it on the sand.) You may as well ring the dinner bell and tell him to come get me now. He started to pace back and forth muttering to himself…."There is no way, even seasoned professional hunters stay away from those things. Have you seen the teeth on them?" He stopped pacing and pointed at the elder that had been talking to him, "You do realize how close to it I have to get to one with this, what you called it? Oh, yeah…a long knife. Ha, it is more like a rusted piece of useless metal." The elders waited until his tirade was over and impatiently asked, "Are you through throwing your temper tantrum Your Highness? You honestly did not think we were just going to hand the kingdom over to you did you. You have to be worthy; you have to have the favor of the gods. If you complete this challenge then no one will ever doubt or question you again. Your word will be law and people will fear you yet worship your strength, endurance and prowess. They will blindly obey because they know that you are able to protect the kingdom and all that dwell in it. Your mere presence will demand respect and going through these challenges, you will have earned it. If you think for one moment that we are a bunch of uneducated, savage native islanders you are sorely mistaken. I myself can read and write five different languages. Not because I have to, no, it is because I have a thirst for knowledge and I want to. Ka'ba (the priest that blessed you this morning) Yes my son, we may not say a lot but we know everything that goes on here. Anyways, the priest that blessed you created the Wind Turbine Electrical system on this island. No books, just common sense, a bit of electrical engineering and now we are self-sufficient and have been for a very long time." He stopped and looked at Bart who was staring at him now. He pointed towards the canoe and said to Bart with a bite of sarcasm in his voice, "The day is waning and we be away lest you will be swimming in the dead of night with only the moonlight as your guide. Lucky me, I am your guide today….whoop-ee."

Bart followed the elder into the canoe, looked up at the sun, and smiled. He sent a mental message to Dr. Tenjin, "Right on time doc, if we follow the tide tables then I wasted just the right amount of time with my outburst." Damn he chuckled to himself; I should have been an actor because the elders and the monarchy bought that little show hook-line-and- sinker. "Right on schedule they shoved off in the sea for what was to be the hardest thing that Bart was ever to do in his entire life. Nervous did not begin to describe how Bart was feeling; he was scared, actually, he was downright petrified. Oh, he did believe the Dr. Tenjin's plan would work but he was sure that it was not going to be as easy as they had originally thought. Nothing is ever that easy he sighed to himself. As they neared the edge of the crests," the elder looked at Bart and said, "Here, this is where you are getting out Your Highness. We will be waiting at the beach on Zanzi every day from the third day on. Either the way the tide works around here you will swim to the beach or the tide will carry what is left of you to us. He laughed when he said…. "We have never lost one yet, dead or alive." Bart just shook his head at the strange little man and slipped into the deep blue water. He was really starting to dislike the ocean he thought as he shoved off the canoe with his feet and propelled himself out into the water. He had never felt so utterly alone in all his life. He looked once more at the canoe that was paddling away and then looked towards his destination Manu Island.

No time like the present, he thought to himself as he turned and swam towards the island. As he swam closer to the island, he was able to see the reef. Dr. Tenjin had been right it really does sneak up on you and he was right about another thing, wow this reef was an eruption of beautiful bright colors and my god, he had never seen so many fish. No wonder the anglers risk their lives to come here. Just looking at it, you could not sense any danger, it just looked very serene. Just then, there was a commotion in the water just off the other side of the reef. Two sharks were circling something in the water. Bart could barely make out what it was....some kind of bird and it was wounded. He treaded water on the other side of the reef in safety and watched as one shark lunged out of the water to claim the bird as his and then the other launched right into the side of it knocking it back into the water. The victor then took his prize and swam away. Then as if nothing happened, the water was once again calm and serene. The marine life that had disappeared when the sharks showed up were back in full force and it was as if the incident had never taken place. Remarkable, Bart thought to himself, absolutely remarkable.

He waited a few more minutes and feeling a bit nervous and exposed, he put both of his hands on the reef and pulled himself up. Doc was right, he thought as he looked up at the receding sun in the distance. The tide was going down and low tide was setting in. He knelt down and peered over the side of the reef that led to Manu Island. He was trying to see if he could spot the monsters that lurked just below the surface. He wondered to himself if he jumped in, exactly how long it would take the silent killers to surface. He was not about to find out, he stood once more and started walking the length of the reef towards the shoreline. Every once in a while he would hear some commotion and look out over the lagoon in time to see a female sea turtle attempting her sojourn to shore only to witness the tell tail dorsal fin appear a few feet from its intended prey. The shark would lazily trail the female turtle as she tried to make it to shore to lay her eggs....then just like that, the fin disappears as quickly as it appeared and the turtle is gone. All that remains from the encounter is a ripple in the water. Sharks were a force to be reckoned with but what was a tangle with a saltwater crocodile going to be like? That was the question he was going to get the answer to in a few short hours. "Was he insane? What was he doing here? How in the world did he end up here in this situation? Life was strange that was for sure." Bart could almost make out the shoreline….Almost ShowTime he said aloud. As he got closer to the shore, he saw the four feet of water that separated him from the safety of the shore. "What in the world? Ah shit"…in the deep- water pockets that he had to be passed, he saw not one but two dorsal fins. "Thanks Doc" Bart mumbled. He stopped walking and tried to access this new situation. He is over six foot tall, maybe a run and jump. He looked around, nope, no way to go around this. Here goes nothing, he backed up about twenty feet and took off towards the shoreline in a hard run going full speed. He reached the edge of the reef, let out a yell, closed his eyes and leapt throwing all his momentum forward. He dared not open his eyes, he was either going to be eaten and definitely did not want to see that coming or he was going to land on the beach. Either way it was a crapshoot. It felt like it took an eternity until he thankfully felt sand under his feet. He opened his eyes, he made it! He could not believe it but yes, he had cleared the two water pockets and was standing on the sand. He turned around and realized that he had just barely made it, but dammit he did and that was all that mattered. One hurdle down, time to get busy now. What part of the salty was he going to keep? Ah hell, I think this time I will keep the whole damn skull! He recited in his head everything that Tenjin had told him. Croc pit, ten feet from shore, kill two turtles, find bamboo and sharpen the stalks, flat rock for digging…he smiled to himself, I got this. He scouted around for a good hour or two to find the perfect place for his death pit; there was also a tree about five feet from where he was going to dig. The digging was hard work, who in their right mind uses a rock to dig? Without a lot of time to waste though, he continued to dig. Many hours later, he was finished and quite pleased with how the pit turned out. It ended up being about five feet deep and approximately four feet wide. He made grooves in the side closest to the tree so that he could get in and out easily. Now what, oh yes.... Bamboo. Where the beach ended and the brush began, he saw a large thicket of bamboo. He made his way there (he had a hog flashback but nothing came running at him ha ha!) He got busy cutting down the bamboo stalks he would need for the pit. Ten ought to do it he thought. He set about sharpening them. He had to admit that he was actually getting a little bit excited and could feel the adrenaline start to flow when he thought about catching and killing one of man's apex predators. He, Bart Ran....Oh no....He, Amir Rayno, no.... He, Prince Amir Rayno was about to conquer a saltwater crocodile. How many people can say that? He smiled and thought to himself. Not many, not many at all. Okay, bamboo stakes in hand, it was time to head back down to the pit. He jumped in the pit and strategically placed his stakes. He remembered what the doc said and tried to kick them loose with his feet, good....They did not budge. Next, next were the turtles. He scoured the break line on the shore, oh wait, not the ones in the water....Find the ones that have just laid their eggs and grab two of those. That was easy enough, soon he spied his prize. He grabbed them and made quick work of dispatching and gutting them. He made two blood trails and threw the rest of the carcasses in the pit. He was forgetting something...What was, oh yeah, banana leaves, I have to cover the pit and damn, one of the turtle carcasses has to rest on the edge of the pit. He gathered his banana leaves and quickly scrambled down into the pit and retrieved one of the dead turtles. He covered and placed the turtle on the edge. Now what? Nap, take a nap and wait. With knife in hand, he scurried up his tree and climbed into his perch, took in a long gulp of air and hunkered down to wait. As he laid in the tree, Bart mentally went over everything to make sure nothing was left out. Before he knew it, he was asleep. He did not think he would actually fall asleep but surprisingly he did and rather quickly.

    Bart woke with a start and almost toppled out of the tree. He sat up and glanced over at the pit. Everything still looked as he had left it so what was all the commotion that had woken him up? He shielded his eyes with his hand and scanned the surrounding area. Bart followed his first blood trail and saw that he had a rather large crocodile headed his way. He knew that soon it would be time to implement the doc's plan, but wait a minute, out of the corner of his eye he noticed some movement coming from the other direction. "Oh my god, are you serious? He said to himself. Incredulously, coming from the other direction (his second blood trail) there was an even larger crocodile also headed for the pit. Stunned he sat back in his perch. "Ok doc, we never figured this scenario into the equation. What in the hell do I do now?" He could see that this was not a good turn of events, not good at all. Bart thought to himself, "Best case scenario is that the crocodiles will see each other and fight for the prize (the turtle carcasses.) Maybe one will kill the other and get mortally injured in the melee? Worst case scenario is that the first croc falls into the pit and gets impaled by the bamboo stakes, the second croc falls on top of the first one and does not get impaled at all." He got an idea but it was not a very good one and a little on the dangerous side. He did not see any alternative because he knew he could not jump in the pit with a fully healthy and very pissed off croc. That would be suicide, although, what he was about to do ranked right up there with it. Bart mumbled, "No choice, here goes nothing." Bart jumped out of the tree, ran full speed to the pit, grabbed the dead turtle, and then in full sprint, he headed straight for the tree line by the bamboo thicket. Once he got to the Bamboo, he turned to see which croc was chasing him. Neither one of them were, they were stilled both headed for his death pit. Frustrated by this chain of events he remembered something the doc had said, "Your Highness, they are opportunistic eaters and very lazy. If a meal is too much work they will find an easier dinner." Damn, he had forgotten that. He looked back at the Pit; the crocs were both almost to the Pit. He knelt down and waited to see how this was going to play out. He did not have to wait long, he watched one croc fall in and the other one followed shortly afterwards. Tentatively he started walking back towards the Pit. He heard a lot of growling, hissing and thrashing about, as he got closer. When he peered down into the Pit he was shocked at what he saw, somehow both crocs were staked. Neither one was dead but the fight was going to be a little bit easier. Visibly he saw that the croc that went in first was mortally injured. The second had one stake through the meaty part of his left back leg and he saw another stake sticking out of his shoulder on the right. Bart sighed and thought at least he is immobile and I have a fighting chance. He had to be patient though and let nature do her job. He climbed the tree and decided to take a quick nap. He woke about an hour later and the croc on the bottom was dead. The highly pissed off Salty that was pinned on the top was still hanging in there. He tested the doc's theory and threw a rock at it, all he heard was hissing and growling as it reared its head and started thrashing around. Bart gauged that he still had a lot of fight in him. He was about to climb down in the Pit but stopped as an idea popped into his head, "he needed longer stakes," climbing into the Pit was stupid and foolhardy. He was not going to kill the beast in the Pit; he was going to drive as many long stakes into it from outside of the Pit. Bart was excited, he did not think he would have survived the Pit, this idea was pure genius! He just hoped that the sorry excuse for a long knife held out for him, he inspected it and had his doubts. He swore that once this was over and he became the king the challenges were definitely going to change. He would talk to Tenjin about this when he got back. Now back to the task at hand, he made quick work of cutting and sharping at least twenty bamboo stakes. Booty collected he carefully ran back to the Pit. He looked over the side of the Pit, yep, he is still there and he is still really pissed. The croc must have heard him come up because he whipped his head in Bart's direction, snarled, snapped his jaws open, and shut. Thank god, I am up here and you are down there. "Here goes nothing, open wide big guy." He threw the first spear and it bounced off the animals head. "Ok Bart my boy you have to concentrate, you got this, deep breath, slow and easy." Bart threw a second spear and it stuck. "Yes!" The croc swung around trying to get to the spear that was wedged in his shoulder. He could not reach it and he could not go into a roll to dislodge it. He sure could thrash around though, he threw another and then another. His plan was working he sighed with relief. After about ten minutes of what Bart called "foreplay" he landed a mortal blow. Sheer luck, dumb desperation or hard work and perseverance, he was not sure which. He hit the croc right by the base of the skull; it was a kill shot but not the kill shot. He mused this is one tough croc and continued to chuck spears at it. One more good shot and it should be over, right at that moment Old Salty (as Bart affectionately named him) swung his head around and Bart's spear found its mark, it pierced the left eye socket and planted itself in the beast's brain. The croc instantly stopped moving, it was over, Salty would hunt no more. Realizing what he did, Bart started jumping up and down and took off running up and down the deserted beach. He was flailing his arms and singing, "Ding Dong the Witch is Dead" repeatedly. If anyone had been watching, they would have thought he had lost his mind. When he could run no more he collapsed and sank down in the warm welcoming sand up to his knees. After he rested a bit it was time to get back to work. He wondered aloud if he should chop them both up or make the baskets to hold them first. He opted for the baskets. Up the coconut tree, he scampered to collect the material he needed. He was still singing as his big clumsy hands attempted to weave two baskets. After an hour he came up with something, they were definitely not quite baskets but with a few well-placed knots, here and there they would hold the croc heads quite nicely. He was still reeling in complete utter shock that he pulled this off. He not only bagged one he bagged two crocs. How many people had been able to do that he wondered quite pleased with himself. He laughed aloud when he pictured the doc's face when he brought these two heads back to Zanzi.

He looked up at the sky, "These heads are not going to cut themselves off and I need to get the rest chopped up for fish food." He tried to lift the croc on the top up out of the Pit and that was not going to happen. He never realized how massive these animals were before now. He had to think for a minute, he decided that they were going to be dissected down in the pit and then brought up and stuffed in his, well they were not really baskets he laughed. The more he looked at the more he looked at the ones that he had to make the long swim with the more he realized that they would never make it. Bart decided that he would have remove on eye on each beast and use his extra strength shoelaces to make an extremely strong fishing stringer. He was bringing both of them back on his back the manly way (over his shoulder and on his back) and not in some "stinkin girlie baskets!" It took Bart hours of hacking and sawing with this thing they provided him with to use as a weapon to get these crocs into "Shark size bitable morsels." By the he was done he was covered in croc blood and body parts, he could even feel it squishing between his toes. He looked down at himself, "What would the elders think if they saw me now?" When he was finally finished, he was just going to jump in the surf and enjoy the cool water while being cleaned up. He got up and started making his way to the water when something caught his eye. Right past the break of the waves were three shark fins gliding back and forth. "What the….why are they that close to shore?" He looked around and realized what had happened, once he finished chopping up the crocs, he tossed them all up out of Pit. He was not that far from shore and when he looked he saw a steady blood trail of croc blood leading directly into the sea. "Ding Ding Ding, Bart had unknowingly rung the dinner bell. He scolded himself, "You have to pay attention to everything you do Bart Old Boy, you almost became a Bart-ala-mode dessert." If you lived on this island, there would be no need in having an Army to protect you that is for sure. He looked around, he did not want to leave the croc meat here unattended but he really wanted to clean up. He felt slimy, sticky and just all around gross. A few yards away quite a ways from the shoreline he saw a small pool of water. He walked over to investigate, hmm, about four feet wide and maybe four to five feet deep. He could see most of the bottom, there were a few blind spots but they were definitely no big enough to hide a shark. He closed his eyes and jumped in; he was enjoying the cool water and relaxing for just a second. "Damn, what was that? Ouch,, what the?" Bart jumped up and got out of that wading pool. His legs and the bottom of his feet felt like they were on fire. As he rubbed his legs he peered down closer into the pool and he saw what he thought might be jellyfish only they were really tiny. Small but mighty and pack a hell of a punch. He learned his lesson real quick, look before you leap. His body was starting to ache all over and he was getting nauseous. He went back over by the Pit and sat in the sand with his head in his hands trying desperately to quell his stomach. He reminded himself to ask Dr. Tenjin about those little jellyfish things.

Bart knew that sick or not the tide tables wait for no man and he was ready to get off this island. Someday soon though, he was going to come back here and explore everything. He had big plans for the Isle of Manu, he planned to tame it and learning all the secrets, the island hid so well. After resting about twenty minutes, he got up and started loading up the croc heads and the chopped up meat, he looked up at the sky, it was time to go home. With the (we will call them baskets) tied around his waist and his two makeshift fish stringers securely over his shoulder he headed back towards the reef. He came, he endured and he conquered, Bart was a happy man. Happiness is fleeting, he had all but forgotten about the two water pockets that he had barely jumped over to get to shore. There they were staring him in the face, his ego deflated and he was at a loss as far as what to do. He reasoned that he alone had barely made it and that was when he was completely rested and not packing all this extra weight. Then it hit him, the extra weight! The two sharks have most definitely exhausted all their food sources in the pockets and he had an overflowing bounty of their most favorite snack. He looked at the pools of water, he figured if he threw some croc at the other end and hugged the side he would be in and out in less than two minutes. How much croc would he have to sacrifice to make his plan work? Maybe an entire croc tail would suffice. He had nothing to lose at this point except possibly his life and it was the only plan he could come up with. Besides, just maybe these were the nuisance ones. Lemon sharks if his memory served him correctly. The water was a little too murky to be able to tell. Bart knelt by the edge of the pocket opposite the shark and unknotted one of his baskets. He threw the first chunk and it landed close to the other side of the shark. There was movement and thrashing as the shark ripped into the tough croc meat. Bart silently slipped his leg in the water and slowly lowered it until he touched sand. He stood as still as a statue. Never taking his eyes off the commotion at the other end. The shark made quick work of that piece and started to look for more, Bart threw another chunk a little bigger than the first and the shark immediately stopped his hunt and zeroed in on it. That was Bart's cue to move, in went the other leg. To be safe he threw in another large hunk of meat. As fast and quiet as possible he got to the other side of the pocket. As he was pulling his leg out he felt a ripple in the water and saw teeth, come up that barely missed his calf. His heart was racing, he made it by the skin of his teeth, damn he thought, I did it! Now on to the second pool. A little more confident this time he knelt by the edge of the second pool and threw in a chunk of croc. Same reaction, he threw in two more and got in the pool. He started to make his way over to the other side when all his hair on his arms stood up. Something was wrong, he glanced at the spot that the shark had been but saw nothing. He frantically tried to climb out of the pool but the sides were too slick and slimy. Now he was starting to panic, he looked around to see where the animal was and felt something brush the side of his leg. When he looked down all he saw was the dorsal fin. This thing had to be five or six feet long. He thought he was done for until he felt a tugging at his waist. He looked down and saw nothing, he looked back and saw the shark come out of the water and completely engulf one of his baskets in its jaws. He quickly loosen the cord that securely tethered the basket to him and got to the other side and out of the pool as fast as he could. His entire body was shaking as he stood and looked into the pool of water. He never wanted to experience anything like this again. He collected his remaining basket and started his trek home. It took him most of the night to make it to the spot on the reef where he would once again get into the ocean. He threw his remaining basket as far into the middle of the lagoon as his tired aching muscles would allow. He waited and watched for a moment until he saw at least ten or more sharks circling and going to battle for the basket. Bart wanted so badly to start the long swim home already, but he knew he had to wait for high tide.

    He was stuck here on the reef until about sunrise. He had a lot of time to think while he sat and waited. He thought about everything that he went through to be here today. His life had been one crazy chain of events after another. He went from being someone that everyone avoided to someone that people actually admired. He did not understand it all, but he was holding on tight and getting ready to take the ride of his life. All he had to do now was make it back home, back to Zanzi and most of all back to little Yana. Listening to the lull of the waves crashing against the reef sort of put him into a daze and pretty soon he was asleep. He awoke to seagull's dive-bombing him; they were trying to get to the croc heads that were still strapped on his back. He shooed them away and stood up to stretch. As Bart looked around him, he could see that high tide was setting in. That was his cue to start swimming. He made sure the pack was secure and dove into the sea. Accept for almost swimming head on into a school of jellyfish and some nosy bottle-nosed dolphins it was an uneventful swim. It took Bart about three maybe three and a half hours to make it back to Zanzi. He saw a beach full of spectators as he drug himself through the surf and finally collapsed from pure exhaustion onto the sand. Before he closed his eyes he mumbled, "Yana, daddy is home." One of the little island boys ran to get Doc Tenjin and the elders.

"News spread quickly that prince Amir had returned. It seemed though that he had failed the last challenge. He had no type of dead animal with him and he swam in from the sea. That rumor was spreading like wild fire. As Dr. Tenjin made his way to the beach he could hear people whispering, "That poor little girl, first she lost her mother and now she is going to lose her father….I heard that he tried to escape but got too tired…No I heard that they are already planning…He is to be executed at first light." Dr. Tenjin hoped that these rumors held no merit. He prayed they were all wrong. He scolded himself for getting close to Bart. He tried to avoid the princes that competed in the challenges because it hurt less when he pronounced them dead either by dropping out or failing the challenge." Sadly, he really thought Bart had what it took. As he reached the beach, he saw a crowd of people and in the crowd were two familiar faces trying desperately to get through the mob and to their friend. The doc took charge, "Get out of the way and let the man breathe. " He heard someone say, "He's already dead." Finally, the doc laid his eyes on Bart. "You idiots, the man is exhausted and has passed out. But he will die if he cannot breathe, now move back!" The crowd relented and moved back. "That's better! Does anyone have anything cold to drink? Preferably water?" A young child walked up and handed the doc a glass of cold water. He thanked her and then threw it in Bart's face. Bart woke up with a start, "What the, who threw water on me? Don't you people think I am water logged enough? Where are the damn elders, I have something I hope they choke on!" Tenjin started laughing robustly, "The show is over everyone, ha ha, prince Amir is perfectly fine." Three of the elders walked up, the shock at seeing prince Amir was very apparent on the faces. Bart looked at them and said, "Honey, I'm home!" Tenjin and Amir were rolling in laughter then. Impatiently one of the elders said, "Well? Did you just give up and swim back?" Bart looked at the doc and then at the elders and said, "Hardly." He took his makeshift backpack off and eyed Tenjin, "Don't judge me old man, I am not Suzy Homemaker. It served its purpose and that is all I cared about." He ripped open the leaves and out on the sand poured not one croc head but two. Doc stood up, "Well now prince Amir, do you always have to show everyone up?" The two started laughing again. The elders walked over to the heads to inspect them. One of them said, "Where are the rest of their bodies?" Bart said, one of the bodies was split between two tide pools that blocked my way to the reef, ya know a distraction. The other body I think I counted maybe twelve or thirteen sharks fighting over it. I used it as another distraction. There was nothing that said I had to bring back the entire croc, I just needed proof of the kill. Here is your proof doubled!" Then he rose from the sand and said, "I am extremely exhausted and I want to see my daughter if you don't mind?" The elders moved out of his way. Bart nodded to the doc, turned, and walked away. The elders turned to the doc, "We are not sure this qualifies Dr. Tenjin." Dr. Tenjin looked at all three and said…."Gentlemen, everyone knows that you get to choose what challenge the princes will do. You people gave prince Amir the most dangerous and deadly challenges we have. You are angry, he is arrogant and pompous, and will not bow down to you. I am sorry, but as custom dictates, I the Chief Doctor am the one to determine if these are valid kills. From what I see, you have a new king. All hail King Amir Rayno." With that, Dr. Tenjin got up, bowed to the elders and started to walk off the beach. One of the elders stood up and said, "We will see tomorrow whether or not he passes the last most important challenge doctor, we will see whether he passes that one." All the elders started cackling. A worried look crossed the features, he was not so sure himself, and there were many things about prince Amir that did not quite add up. Unless he failed, Tenjin knew that Bart was going to be an excellent king (with his help) and make major changes for the betterment of the people. He was not out to please either the monarchy or the elders, Bart was for the people, Tenjin knew this even before Bart realized it himself. Yes, Tenjin thought, we are going to be an unstoppable team.. He never let on to the elders though who were very sure he would fail. Tenjin turned to them and said, "You will have a new king tomorrow not a mindless thing that you control, mark my words." With that, doc left the beach, his wife made steamed clams for dinner and they never quite tasted the same cold. He smiled when he thought of Bart, he was very proud of his protégé and, wow, he got two crocs. That is a story I have to hear…. tomorrow.

CHAPTER THIRTEEN

A NEW KING

Bart was so angry he did not remember the walk to the Infirmary. What in the hell did he ever do to the elders? Even if you were blind and deaf, you would be able to tell that they absolutely hated him. He didn't treat them any better or worse than he treated anyone else, what gives he wondered? He said aloud to himself, "I guess this is another question for the doc." Peace once again washed over him as he peaked in Yana's room. He expected her to be asleep but he was quite surprised because as soon as she saw him she started kicking her little legs and flapping her arms up and down. The best thing though that melted his heart is that she was smiling at him. He almost teared up when he realized she was happy to see him. It felt good to know that somebody loved him. He turned away for a moment to put his shirt on the rocking chair and she started to cry a little. As soon as he was back in her line of sight, again she got so excited and broke out in another big toothless smile. It was the most beautiful thing he had ever seen. "Yana," he said, "I would fight a whole sea of crocs and sharks for you if you asked me to. You have your daddy wrapped tight around your little finger." He scooped her up and moved over to the rocking chair. He tried to lay her across his chest but she shocked him, straightened her legs, and was in a standing position on his lap. Her little legs were not very strong yet so when she bent her knees it was as if she was bouncing on his lap. He started laughing, "Slow down little girl, I just got the feeding, bathing, burping and changing thing down. Looks to me like you are ready to start running, forget walking. I'm not ready for that yet." He realized that the more he talked to her the more she was bouncing, smiling, and waving her arms up and down. The facial expressions are what really got him though, and her crazy little tongue. "Stop growing up so fast, that's an order from your king." That is when it hit Bart, he made it, and he was going to be the new king of Zanzi. He looked at his little ball of energy, "Yana, I did it for us, I'm going to give you the keys to a kingdom little princess. We are royalty now baby girl. No one will ever snub his or her nose at you for being Bart Randolph's daughter, you are Princess Yana Rayno. Always be proud, yet be humble and show empathy for your fellow man. However, I promise you no harm will ever come to you as long as there is breath in my body. I will kill them and not think twice about it. I love you my sweet girl. I honestly do." He smiled and scooped Yana into his arms and ran out of her bedroom door. All the way down the hall he was yelling, "Hey, Hey," All the nurses came running, the head nurse asked, "Your Highness, what's wrong? Is there something wrong with the little princess? Are you hurt?" Bart got a stitch in his side and was doubled over unable to speak now. Dr. Tenjin (who was coming down the hall with his nose in his clipboard) glanced up to see what all the commotion was. All he saw was Bart doubled over and a bunch of nurses around him. Very worried, he dropped the clipboard and ran over to Bart, "Prince Amir, where are you hurting? When did it start, what are your symptoms, is it the baby?" Bart finally able to catch his breath and get his side to stop hurting stood up laughing robustly, "Please, Please he laughed, stop fussing (he pushes hands away,) there is nothing wrong, no one is hurt, (he looked at doc,) and there are no symptoms. I just wanted to show you what Yana could do now. That is all (he said sheepishly.) I am sorry; I never meant to cause such an uproar." Then beaming he looked at all of them and held her out in front of him and said, "See, she smiled at me. She can actually recognize me and smiled just for me....I just wanted to share it with all of you. Still holding Yana out for all to see, she chose that moment to give them all a great big sloppy toothless grin." He put his head down, he was sincerely apologetic for worry them all like that. One of the nurses smiled at him, took baby Yana from her daddy's arms, and sat her on the counter. They were all fussing over her now, tickling her and talking to her....Her little smile was contagious.. Bart leaned against the nurse's station; he was on top of the world as he watched them with his daughter These people genuinely cared for not only little Yana, these wonderful little island people had also taken him into their hearts as well.. As their king he was going to make sure, they are treated fairly and never taken for granted. As the king, he decided that he would never ask someone to do something he would not do himself. He figured that would be a good way to give merit to his judgements. Dr. Tenjin took that moment to stand next to Bart, "Your Highness, when you have a few moments come find me, we need to talk a bit. It's not pressing; when Yana falls asleep we can do it then." He patted Bart's shoulder affectionately, bent and gave the baby a quick kiss on her forehead and went down the hall to collect the clipboard he had thrown down. Bart turned back to his daughter; he told the nurses how she insisted on standing up on his lap. The head nurse looked at him and said, "They grow up so fast, make sure you do not miss a second with her if you can help it. Every day she will shock you and start doing more and more. It is amazing how fast they grow. One minute they need you for everything and then (she looked off a little sad.) Then they do not need you at all. Your Highness, all I can say is enjoy that miracle of yours. Bart surprised even himself as he walked over to the head nurse and gave her a hug, "I am here if you ever need a shoulder. I'm learning to be a good listener." Yana let out a big yawn, Bart reclaimed his daughter and said, Looks like someone needs a bottle, then a bath and then bedtime." Bart yawned too, "Ha ha, I guess the same will go for me, well, minus the bottle." They all laughed at that. One of the nurses said, "Your Highness, I can bathe the baby while you take a shower if you like. We also made you a plate of food from dinner. We can heat it up for you. I am sure you did not have much to eat these past few days." Bart thought for a moment, "Thank you so much, I think I will take you up on that offer." He looked at all of the nurses then, "Unless it is too much trouble or unless you are all busy?" They told him to go bathe and that this was their pleasure. They all parted ways, Bart off to the shower and nurses to take care of Yana. Wonderful people he thought as he opened up the door to the shower room. Tomorrow a completely new world was about to open up for Bart and Yana, it was to be King Amir Rayno's coronation day. Good-bye Bart Randolph, good-bye Prince Amir....All Hail King Rayno, ruler of the Isle of Zanzi. Long live the king.

After his shower and dinner, he and Yana passed out in the rocking chair (that was their favorite spot.) Morning came too soon, today was a big day. Bart remembered he was supposed to talk to Doc Tenjin last night. With Yana in his arms, he got up to go find him. He stopped at the nurse's station and asked after him. No, they did not know where he was. He walked to his office, hmm that was empty too. Where could the doc be Bart thought. Oh well, he had to get Yana back to the nurses. They apparently have a special dress for her to wear today. He did not understand what the big deal was, yes, he passed the challenges and yes, he is the new king. What did that mean exactly, he was not sure? He had never ruled a kingdom before. He assumed it would mean that he and Yana would have a roof over their heads and maybe he would get the deciding vote when there were disputes. Other than that, he was not sure. He was certain though that it would be nothing like the cartoons (Cinderella & Snow White) came to mind. He would just wait and see. When he got to Yana's floor, the nurse impatiently took her from him and looked at her watch, tapping her foot in irritation she looked at Bart and said, "Your Highness, where have you been? You have a fitting to attend and I have to get the little princess ready as well. Now off with you, the seamstresses are waiting for you." She started to walk away but Bart stopped her, um nurse, excuse me, where am I supposed to go?" She stopped and giggled, "Oh my, I'm sorry, I forgot that you are not from the island. I am so used to seeing you now; it must have slipped my mind." She quickly gave him directions to the tailors and told him to hurry because they hate tardiness (even from the king.) Bart followed her directions and found himself at the edge of town. He had never been this far out, it was quite another world.

Apparently, the seamstress was also the village medicine woman. It actually rather gave him the creeps out here. He had the feeling that not something but some things were watching him. He walked up a long dark overgrown path and finally found her house. It was exactly what he expected it to look like. It was spooky and he was just waiting for a black cat to run out in front of him. He nervously chuckled, "She must be Zanzi's best kept secret." He took a deep breath and was about to knock on the door when he heard a voice from inside, "Do not knock on my door, it makes my pets nervous. We prefer them calm, as you will too. Your Highness just come in." Bart entered and started to walk towards her, she bellowed, "STOP," she stood up slowly, astonishing he thought, she was taller than he was and much bigger. She pointed to his shoes, "It upsets my pets, we want them calm, you will too. Remove those and put them out the door." She turned and soothed something behind her back. Bart obeyed and quickly but very quietly he placed his shoes on the front porch.

He stood in the doorway, she motioned for him to come into the sitting room, and pointed to the floor by her feet, "You may sit here." With that, she sat in her chair. Bart never questioned her or reminded her that he was now the king; somehow, he did not think that she cared and he knew it would not make a difference. He looked up at this very large woman, "May I ask a question?" She turned and looked behind her back and then turned back, "Pet says you may ask, if Pet does not like your question then be warned you will anger him. We like him calm; you will prefer that as well. Ask your question." She crossed her arms on her chest and looked down at him impatiently. Bart quickly said, "Actually I have two questions if that is permitted." Once more, she turned and spoke some strange language and turned back, "Pet says you may ask two questions but that you have been warned." Her arms crossed and this time she bent down, pursed her lips, rolled her eyes at him and said, "Ask your two questions." Then she straightened back upright in her chair and waited. Bart felt very small and uncomfortable at that moment, "I do not know what to call you Madame so excuse me if I seem rude. (He cleared his throat.) My first question is more of an observation if you will; somehow, I do not think you are the tailor, is this correct? She laughed (she had a very deep almost manly laugh.) She looked him in the eye and said, "You sir are very observant, Brava I applaud you! You see, you have the favor of the gods and you have the approval from the people but, there is always a but is there not? You do not have the approval of the island elders so they came to me. You may call me Mama Samedi, I have a third eye you see and I can see a lie form in your head before you ever speak i.e. can see everything that happened and will happen in the future. Bart shifted uncomfortably. Mama Samedi noticed Bart's angst and continued, "You have acquired this name, and you were born another." Now Bart was really alarmed and uneasy. Mama Samedi turned towards whatever was behind her again, it seemed to Bart, although he could not understand anything she was saying that she and "her pet" were quarreling.

 He thought to himself that this was turning into a very strange morning. Mama Samedi whipped back around as he was finishing his thought and said, "Yes, this is indeed a very strange morning Your Highness." Bart almost jumped off the floor but Mama put a hand out to stop him, she laughed and said, "Do you believe now… hmmm I'm thinking yes. You were also correct, my pet wanted to eat you but I see good in you and the things you will do for the people, well we can overlook your lost days. As I said, you cannot lie to me; it would not be wise if you did." Bart heard something rustling around behind her back; he also thought he heard a distinct hiss. Mama looked at him once more, "Your second question if you please?" Bart had all but forgotten what it was, he asked another instead, "Mama

Samedi, my Yana, she will be happy and have a good life won't she?" Mama uncrossed her arms and looked down at him once more, "You are wise, my pet did not like the question you were previously going to ask.

He approves of this one, therefore I will answer and you sir, will keep your head for another day. Yes, your Yana will be very happy and will never regret being made of you." Bart smiled and relaxed a bit. Mama Samedi continued, "You angered the elders, this is why you have been sent here to me. I am your judge and your jury,." She laughed the deep guttural laugh again, "My pet is disappointed because he would have been your executioner." Bart looked alarmed at the thought of being whatever was behind her back's dinner. Mama then said, "The only eyes that see pet are the ones he is going to devour." "I am fine right where I am, I do not need to see it. I am good really," Bart said quickly. She turned to her pet again, some strange parl'e of conversation began again, and she turned back towards Bart. Mama leaned in real close to Bart, she began to speak in a very low tone, "Pet wants to give you a glimpse ahead in your life as the king.

I never think it wise to tell, some stories are best left untold. You must close your eyes because you will hear my voice and see what unfolds." Bart obeyed and closed his eyes, he now felt as if he were very drunk in a dim lit room. He no longer saw the strange dwelling of Mama Samedi, he was definitely somewhere else. He heard her voice as if in a dream state. "Your Highness, you must quell your thoughts there is only room for one of us in here (she was inside his mind.) You must trust in Mama, relax, that's better, now just watch and follow my voice." She showed him what he could only describe as a home movie that had not yet been filmed. He watched bits and pieces of Yana growing up. He saw some of the things he would accomplish as the ruling monarchy. Then everything went black. This frightened Bart. He heard Mama's voice again. "That I am afraid is the end of your rule Your Highness. Just remember that things are not always as they seem" Just like that Bart's eyes were once again open and he was standing at the doorway that led into a sitting room.

A very tall and very large woman was watching him. She stood and asked, "Have you lost your way? Where are you trying to go Your Highness?" Bart looked stunned, she seemed familiar to him but for the life of him, he could not remember her name. "I am sorry; I am supposed to see the seamstress for a fitting of some kind. Are you the seamstress by chance? She laughed (she had a very deep laugh, almost manly,) "Oh my, Your Highness, you should have zigged when you zagged. I am afraid you turned the wrong way at the fork in the road. Go back to the fork and make a right, you will find the seamstress there waiting for you. You must hurry though, she hates tardiness." With that, Bart apologized for bothering her, wished her a good day and left the strange house. As he walked away, he had the strangest feeling that something had happened to him but he could not put a finger on what it was. This had turned out to be a very strange morning indeed.

He found the Seamstress just as that odd woman had said he would. He could have sworn though that there was no fork in the road when he began his trek. Oh well, he had other things to think about so he put it out of his mind for now. He looked at the young woman that was busy pinning material here and there, "Can you tell me what exactly I am being fitted for miss?" Bart asked. She laughed and looked at him with her hands on her hips, "Your Highness, I cannot tell you that. If I did, it would not be a surprise anymore now would it. What fun would that be?" The seamstress was humming as she flitted around him pinning and measuring, "Please lift your arm, thank you, ok, now stand up straight, ah, good, I think I have it all now." Bart smiled, "Can I ask you a question?" She stopped what she was doing and eyed him questionably, "As long as it has nothing to do with your clothes, sure ask away." Bart then said, "Who is the, um, wait I, hmm, never mind, my mind went blank, I guess it wasn't important." Not missing a beat, the seamstress said, "Your Highness, somethings are best left unknown." Then she laughed, it was a deep guttural laugh that sounded very manly in nature." She stood up, she was facing Bart's back and he did not see her reflection in the mirror. (if he had seen her reflection he would have been staring at Mama Samedi.) The seamstress faced him then and said, "You are all finished your Highness, when you return from the beach your garment will be waiting for you in little princess's room. Have a wonderful day." He thanked her and left her establishment and found himself headed for the beach, although he was not sure why.

As he stood at the edge of the sand where land meets sea, he reflected back to his time here on Zanzi. Lost in thought he did not hear the doc walk up to him. Doc looked very relieved to see his friend standing there; he was not sure how this morning would play out. "Your Highness, Your Highness, yoo hoo, Your Highness?" Bart snapped back to reality, "Oh wow doc, I did not see you come up, I have been looking for you, sorry man I fell asleep last night, and we were supposed to talk?" Doc smiled and said, "No worries, you are here now, we have a few moments, let's sit a bit shall we? Bart sat and stretched out his long legs. He put his hands behind him into the sand, looked at the doc and waited patiently. Doc began, "You know that I am your biggest supporter and I will back you right or wrong, I have to know who I am backing though (he took a deep breath and paused.) Your secrets are safe with me. I just need to know that it is King Rayno I am supporting or Bart Randolph looking for an easy mark?" Bart stood up and started pacing, "How did you find out? I have tried to be so careful. Who else knows? What does this mean for me, for Yana?" Doc also stood, not sure, whether Bart would try to harm him, which did not happen thankfully. "Amir, first of all, had I wanted to tell anyone I would have. I am coming to you with what I know. Oh, I have to admit, my first instinct was to turn you in, but-but then I watched you slowly bond with your daughter and I saw Bart Randolph start to ebb into the past and I saw Amir Rayno appear before my eyes. Your priorities changed, you changed. So, I watched, just to make sure you were genuine. You are either an expert liar or you have found something or someone that you trust enough to show the real you to." Bart stopped pacing and looked down at the sand, "I am so ashamed of the person I was, the things I did are too horrible to mention. I never want to be that person again. I cannot erase the past, it scares me though to think that if I did it once, I can easily fall back into it and become him again. "He desperately looked at the doc, "What happens if I turn into what I hate the most because of all the power I am about to have over these wonderful little people?" Doc thought for a moment, "I have all the newspaper clippings and I, well I have acquired your wife's journal." Bart looked up at him, "How, where, how did you get Jus, Justine's journal?" Doc said, "I have my ways, what I want you to do with these things, Amir are you listening?" Bart numbly nodded and kept his eyes glued to the sea." Doc continued, "I want you to put all of this stuff in a box that we will store, it is to be marked Personal / Private. When you feel yourself slipping, I want you to go to that box and see what hell and destruction Bart Randolph caused. Then, look around at your kingdom and see the good that King Rayno created." Humbly Bart lowered his head so that the doc could not see his eyes fill with tears. Then doc said with a very excited voice, "Your Highness, you passed the last challenge with flying colors, come on, we have a coronation to get you to." Bart smiled when he thought of the two crocs, "Yes I bagged two of them and not one, I bet the elders were surprised." Doc (knowing that Bart did not remember his meeting with Mama Samedi) said, "Yes you did, that is one for the ancient records, now come on, not a minute to lose, you don't want to make the natives restless. I will help you don your garment and wait until you see little princess Yana. She is going to take your breath away." Bart smiled then at the thought of his daughter, "Doc she does that to me every day." They walked off the beach together towards the Infirmary and into a bright new future.

    The doc was not lying, oh, my god Yana was beautiful, her dress brought out the green in her eyes and her jet-black hair, and she looked like a porcelain doll. Bart was almost afraid to touch her lest she might shatter into a million pieces.

    Doc would not let him look in the mirror until he had everything in place, "There that should do it as he placed a prince's crown on his head." Bart was as anxious as a poodle on the Fourth of July, "Can I see it now, can I see what…" When Bart stood up and looked in the mirror, he no longer saw Bart Randolph, before his stood a king. "How did the seamstress get all this done this morning? That is not possible." Doc said, "Your Highness, the island has many secrets she has left to unfold for you. Let us go before we are late. The islanders."

Bart and the doc then said in unison "Hate tardiness!" They both broke out in laughter as they left the Infirmary. "Oh hey Doc, one of the things I did learn as a kid, ya know another way to escape life, anyways, I used to draw, and do you mind if I show you something I sketched last night before I fell asleep?" Bart asked. Doc smiled and said, "Why Prince Amir, you my boy are full of surprises. I would love to see it." Bart nervously pulled a piece of paper from his pocket, "I'm not sure what the Coat of Arms is for Zanzi, but I thought this might be fitting, it needs a bit of work, ha ha I haven't drawn in a long time." He held it out for the doc to see. Doc Tenjin looked at it and said, I am quite impressed, and yes, this is perfect for Zanzi's new Coat of Arms. May I keep this so I can have it touched up and added to all uniforms and the banner over the palace door?" Bart sheepishly said with a boyish grin, "You really like it? Of course you may have it." Doc Tenjin took the drawing and put it in his pocket as they entered the palace.

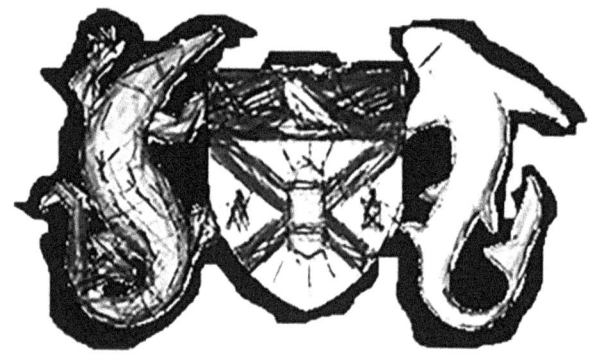

When Bart entered the palace it was a remarkable sight, someone came over and took Yana from his arms to get her all ready. Bart looked around and turned to Tenjin, "This is all for me?" The doc smiled really big and said, "You deserve this and more. You better get used to it because this is your new home." Bart marveling at everything and yet afraid to touch anything lest it break. "Am I dreaming doc, maybe you should pinch me?" The doc just kept pushing him along, "Come on Amir, your people are waiting for their new king to address them." Tenjin led Bart into the throne room. There were so many people it was standing room only.

Tenjin motioned for Bart to take a knee and kneel in front of the Chief Elder. When he was in place Somas (the chief elder) began, "People of the Isle of Zanzi, before you is Prince Amir Rayno, he came to us as a foreigner from a faraway land… He accepted our Rite of Passage and competed in the challenges that were set before him. Having no knowledge of the island ways he not only completed them, he conquered them…In many millennia I have not had the honor of placing this coveted title, he is now and will be until his death "Keeper of the Challenges. Rise now King Rayno and assume your role." The little man raised his arms up over his head, as he did this Bart slowly stood up. When he looked around the room everyone from the very young to the very old were bowing in his honor. He glanced out the window and was quite astonished, everywhere he looked people had stopped what they were doing, and they were all facing the palace bowing for him. He looked at Tenjin and found that he was also kneeling to show homage and obedience to his new King. Bart did not know what to do as he stood there in awe. Somas began to speak again, "Please welcome the foreigner who became the brother and is now the King, all hail King Amir Rayno. (Somas motioned Bart to come near him) I hereby retire the headdress worn by a mere prince and in its place bequeath you the crown to be worn by a king." Somas then placed the crown on Bart's head. "King Rayno, please address your people." Somas bowed to Bart, turned and left the palace. Bart looked at Tenjin as if to ask, "What now?" Then he remembered that he was the king and as such, he needed to assume the role. Bart stood and said, "Great people of Zanzi, I am honored on behalf of myself and Princess Yana to accept the role as your king. We will make many changes in the near future that will not only benefit the people but the Isle of Zanzi as well. Please, if I am out where you see me and you have a problem, a question, or even a suggestion just ask. I will always have time for my people. You are what makes everything work here. Without you, the building would be empty and the monarchy would not exist. I am your king; I am the king for the people." The entire island erupted in shouts of welcome and clapping. Tenjin knew that he had chosen well in King Amir Rayno. "Your Highness, "Bart looked at Tenjin, "I want to introduce you to a few people if you please." Tenjin turned and showed Bart a small group of people. "This is Mana and his family and they are going to be yours and Yana's personal house servants. Mana has a son and he is almost two (Doc Tenjin patted the small boy on the head.) "Your Highness," This is Nahuel Kimo and he will protect and watch after Yana as they grow up. Bart smiled; this would be Yana's first friend. Tenjin then introduced Bart to the rest of the family, "This young girl Honi will be Yana's head maiden. Honi will see to the princess's every need." Bart looked at him a bit perplexed. Tenjin assured Bart that Honi would never interfere or try to take his place in his daughter's life, "She will just make it easier for you, and you are going to be busy ruling a kingdom after all." Tenjin looked down at his watch, "I have to go take care of a few things and check in at the Infirmary, I am still the doctor here you know. It will find you later after you are settled in." Tenjin turned to leave, "By the way Your Highness, we will miss you two at the Infirmary. I was such a pleasure having you and little Yana stay with us." Bart looked at his friend, "We will miss it to old man." Tenjin smiled and walked out. He hated lying to Bart but he had to get to the cave on the beach, there was a bit of unfinished business to take care of that could not wait.

Tenjin walked into the cave and was greeted by all the elders and Mama Samedi. He bowed to the elders. Tenjin looked at the rather large pod next to a very deep pit in the middle of the cave, "Can we get on with this. It is time to dispose of that thing (he pointed towards the pulsing slimy green grotesque pod.) The chief elder looked at Mama Samedi, "Mama, it is still not too late, we can replace them, no one would be the wiser, (he looked at Doctor Tenjin,) those that did know would never say a word." Tenjin started to protest but was stopped when Mama put her hand up, "Somas, you just gave the new king your blessing, were your words false? Think carefully before you answer, my pet has still not eaten and is ravenous." Somas mumbled something and said, "Yes my blessing was pure of heart, but this king he…." Mama looked at him, "We do not get to choose who challenges, and we put the task afore they, most times they fail and then we take the rule under the guise of the victor. We rule then for as long as it (she pointed towards the pod,) can sustain a life force. We were blessed this last one-lasted forty years. Our reign was grand but ancient custom dictates that if there is a real victor of flesh and bone that passes the challenges set before him then we must allocate the throne and bow to the new king. King Amir Rayno is made of flesh and bone and though he will rule for many turning of the tides. It is only a small moment in time that will pass. Somas, you and I have watched many rule and we have assumed the rule many times. Fret not my friend; this King Rayno has many deep dark secrets that still thirst for revenge. For now though, you must obey and the rule of King Rayno will stay the course. Now bless the pod and send it whence it came from until we summon it another time." Somas knelt before the pod and blessed it. Once the blessing was administered, he pushed it into the pit. Mama raised her hand and the pit disappeared and was once again a sandy floor. Doc doused the fire and they all exited the cave. As Doc, left he thought to himself, "thank god that nasty business is over. I hate when the elders hold the throne, it is always the worst for the people." Someday he would explain to Bart how a new King is really chosen. However, today he wanted to let him enjoy being the king. This story would be for another time and another place.

CHAPTER FOURTEEN

PROMISING CEREMONY

True to his word, Prince Branoi arranged the Promising Ceremony for our children. His wife brought Micho and of course, Yana was already here. It was quite an exciting time on Zanzi. Bart had been king now for six months and in that time little Princess Yana had discovered mobility. King Rayno could hardly keep up with her and Honi was exhausted. Although Yana could not, yet walk before you even set her down she was already poised in a crawling position and it was as if you put batteries in her like the Energizer Bunny. As soon as her little legs touched the floor, she was off like a rocket. If she ever go a hold of a cup of coffee, we would all be in trouble.

It was even funnier watching little Micho trying to take his "responsibility" seriously and keep up with her. He would catch her and try scolding her. He would stand in her path; Yana would stop and look at him. Micho put one hand on each shoulder and wag his finger at her speaking a very broken toddler talk. Yana would laugh at him and if she could not pass him then that head went down and she barreled right through him. Micho got up, put his hands on his hips, let out a big sigh and the chase was on again. With Micho, here at least Honi could take a well-deserved break (her eyes were always on Yana though.)

Bart had started to make some pretty important changes in his sixth month of rule. He finally learned that he had indeed been correct in his assumption that the elders did not like him. When he found out that, they personally chose the challenges that all participants had to complete in many things made sense to him at that point. The elders chose every challenge that Bart had to do. From what doc said, he got the ones that no one has ever beat all of. Some may pass catching and killing the shark and maybe the boar but not the shark, the boar and the croc. They expected Bart to die in the challenges. Every time Bart came out the victor, it seemed to make them dislike him that much more. They thought they had him with the croc fight….the looks on their faces when the bag he tore open had two heads instead of one. He still did not understand the animosity they had towards him and when he asked Tenjin, he skirted the issue. One of these days Bart would get him to talk, it is a waiting game. Since the end of his challenges, he has now had an Armory built. Now if there is a competition or a challenge of some sort the rules are a bit different. Why set the young men up to fail, at least give them a fighting chance. There are explicit instructions for how to defeat the challenges as well as useful weapons. For instance, if someone has to perform the shark challenge, they are given a spear and a day to catch fish to use for bait. They are provided a sharp knife and a sharp spear as well as a net. Sadly, some still fail and lose their life against such a worthy adversary but at least it is not pigs walking into the slaughter. That is just one of the changes he instituted. He implemented the changes slowly so that it was not such a shock. Change makes people overall get nervous so when someone all of a sudden implements a bunch of changes there is a lot of resistance and discord. If the changes are made slowly then people tend to accept it and may even find that it is better or in this case safer to do it the new way. Bart reasoned that even though he could change whatever he wanted does not always mean he should or at least not all at once. He meant it when he said he was the King for the people. At first when he was out in public such as the beach or the market place, his subjects were afraid to approach him. It was that way until a brave little girl came up to him one day and was tugging on his pants. He knelt down so he was on her level and asked her what he could do for her. The little girl responded, "Um, Mr. King, Your Highness, my name is Kea and my mommy made me cookies, and she said that they were only for me (she took her finger and with a very serious face pointed at her chest,) those other mean kids, well, um, they took all of them. They did not even leave me not one of my cookies, and my mommy said they were only mine. Can you make them give them back? Bart chuckled and thought for a moment, he put his hand on his chin, "This is very serious indeed," (the little girl crossed her arms on her chest and nodded in agreement vigorously.) He looked at her again and said, "What do you think we should do about this?" She copied him and put her hand on her chin, "I don't know, maybe they need a spanking or a timeout that is what my mommy does when I'm bad." Bart responded, "Your mommy is a very smart woman. I have an idea though, come with me Kea." He stood up, and took her hand in his and walked over to the group of kids. When they saw Kea coming over to them holding the king's hand they all froze. Bart addressed them, "Kea tells me that you took all of her cookies. Is this true (he slowly looked at each one of them.)" Nervously they all tried to talk at once...."She was teasing, she wouldn't, we wanted to teach, we didn't mean to eat all....We are sorry Kea, we really are." They all hung their heads down. Bart looked at Kea, "Do you accept their apologies Kea?" Kea thought for a moment, "Yes, yes I do, I don't think they will take cookies from me anymore. (She looked up at him and motioned for him to bend down.) Bart a bit puzzled bent down and kea put her arms around his neck and gave him a kiss on the cheek. Bart hugged her back and said thank you. As he got up to leave, he noticed that he had drawn quite a crowd of onlookers. He quickly bowed and smiled while saying that this was a very serious matter. Bart turned to leave the area and applause broke out. Unknowingly, Bart had just won the trust of the people. After that people would just come up to him to chat or ask his opinion on a certain matter, oh hell, sometimes they just wanted to say hi. Either way they now knew they could come to him and they did all the time. This was the first time in a long time they had a king that did not act like a mindless robot with no heart. Zanzi was a very happy place.

Bart did something that had never been done; he invited the entire Island to Yana and Micho's Promising Ceremony. The elders were not happy because they felt that common folk should not be allowed to attend royal events. The islanders were extremely excited about this turn of events. Prince Branoi was afraid there would not be enough food etc. Tenjin spread word that everyone needed to bring a covered dish. The day chosen for the ceremony was fast approaching and nothing was ready. Bart was a nervous wreck. Tenjin was in his room trying to calm him down when suddenly Doc broke out in deep belly laughs. Bart stopped pacing and asked what was so funny? Doc Tenjin looked at him and said, "Old Boy you are hilarious." Bart was getting a little angry now, "Why Doc, why do you say that?" Doc stopped laughing and looked at him, "Your Highness, this is just a Promising Ceremony….I'm wondering what you are going to be like on Yana's first day of school or her Prom? I would love to be a fly on the wall for one of these events." With that, he laughed some more. Bart thought about it and then started laughing himself, "You are right Old Man, it is not a huge deal and Yana will not remember any of it anyway. School and Prom are ions away; I am not going to worry over those right now." Just like that, all the tension left He smiled and thought, "Leave it up to my trusted advisor to save the day." They left the palace to get some fresh air and to just chat a bit about mostly nothing. Neither one of them had done that in a long time. Doc asked what new things Yana had shown her daddy and Bart asked about the patients and nurses from the hospital. "I bet things are calm and back to normal now huh Old Man? Tenjin laughed and said, "Your Highness, normal is very over-rated trust me. However, there is something we do need to discuss. Bart rolled his eyes and sighed, "Work, work, work….Man you are a slave driver Doc." Tenjin looked at him with a very serious expression, "Bart, oh I mean Amir, sorry it slipped." Bart looked at him and said, "You have to call me Amir, if someone hears you that is going to cause a lot of questions that we do not need asked." Doc hung his head, "I know, I know, it won't happen again scouts honor.

Back to the topic at hand, you went to the market place today did you not?" Bart responded, "Doc, you know I try to go every day. I think it is important for everyone to see me, I think it makes me approachable." Doc nodded in agreement, "There is no problem with you frequenting the market place or anywhere else on the island. The problem is that, well, how do I say this without offending you?" Bart (getting a little impatient) looked at Tenjin, "Just spit it out Old Man, what am I doing wrong now? Either it seems to me, that no matter what I do, someone has something to say about it or someone is unhappy or better yet, someone can do it better than I can. To tell you the truth, I am getting a little fed up with it and I am about to go off. I feel sorry for whoever is in my way when that happens. I did not grow up royal; I am not sure how to act or what to say most of the time." Tenjin understood Bart's frustration, "You are exactly right when you say you don't know what is expected of you. From small on up a child born of royal blood is taught what a royal does and does not do. There is a code of etiquette that is followed. At this point, you are guessing you are doing and acting correctly and at the same time you are hoping that if you screw up, it will not be blatantly obvious. Does that sound about right?" Bart's shoulders slumped, "I am trying, and it's just that I have no one to ask or follow the lead of. I am so afraid someone is going to put to and two together and then what happens to Yana? I do not care what happens to me I care how this would affect her. She does not deserve to pay the price for the things that I did. "Tenjin thought for a moment and then it hit him. His wife has worked in the palace longer than they have been married." He looked at Bart and smiled, "Do not worry Boss, I got this. We are going to make a king out of you yet. Let's get through the Promising Ceremony tomorrow and then I'll put my plan into action." Bart, who a moment ago felt like he had the entire world resting on his shoulders, looked at his royal advisor, "What would I ever do without you Old Man? You have saved my bacon so many times now I have lost count. All I can say is thank you my friend.

Thank you for myself and especially for little Yana." Doc (a little embarrassed now) shrugged it off, "Ok, now down to business, I need you to be a sponge again and absorb everything I say. All of the royals have at one time or another attended a Promising Ceremony. I am going to tell you what you should as a royal already know." He then got busy explaining the entire ceremony to Bart and making sure to tell him exactly what role he was to play tomorrow. When he was done, he looked at Bart, "Did you get all of that? Do you understand the part you are to play in the ceremony? If not, I'll go through it one more time." Bart smiled and relayed everything the doc told back to him verbatim. Tenjin shocked said, "Amir you really do amaze me. You must have an idyllic memory. There is no other explanation. That is really quite impressive." Bart felt quite a bit more confident now, "Thank you, I mean it, thank you for telling me all of that." Tenjin looked up at the sky, "Wow, the sun must have a set a while ago. I bet my wife is fit to be tied. I had better get home or she will send out the dogs to track me down. He got up, bowed slightly and left Bart who was still sitting on the sandy shore. He was still nervous about tomorrow but with Tenjin's help he will get through it, he always does. He looked around and chuckled to himself. He was very glad that the elders and the monarchy had finally agreed that he did not need a bodyguard. Bart was the tallest man on the island and probably the strongest one too. He rose and made his way back to the palace and went straight to little Yana's room. When he opened her door her saw her all curled up in Honi's arms. At first that used to make him feel very jealous but now it made him feel good. He figured that the more people that loved his baby girl the better she would turn out as an adult. He knew that Honi genuinely loved her and would never let any harm come to her. Softly he tapped Honi on the shoulder and told her to retire to her room and get some sleep. She thanked him and quietly got up off the bed and made her way to her room (which was adjacent to Yana's room.) Bart slipped in next to the little sleeping girl and brushed her hair out of her face with his fingers, "I have had quite a day little one. Getting ready for your Promising Ceremony is very tiring. But, it will all be worth it in the end. As long as you are looked after, it is all worth it. Bart yawned and snuggled up to his sleeping daughter and soon he was sleep.

In the morning, Honi went to Yana's room to get her up and ready for her big day. She was quite surprised to see that Yana had already been fed and bathed and was sitting up on her bed all wrapped up in a towel while Bart sat next to her reading her a story. He looked up, smiled, and said, "Right on time, she is all yours. I would have dressed her but I have no idea what she is supposed to wear." Honi giggled at him, scooped the little princess up in her arms, and said to her, "Your daddy is strange, I have never seen a daddy that takes care of his daughter the way he does. He must really, really love you." She kissed her and walked off to get her dressed. That was Bart's cue to go to his own room and get himself ready. He loved spending time with Yana; she had quite the personality, and was starting to voice her opinion when she was unhappy with something. He was not so nervous around her now. She was a lot tougher than she looked. Now she was able to sit up all by herself but still did not have her balance completely down pat so she has taken a few tumbles. He laughed to himself, at first when she got even the smallest bump or bruise Bart would rush her down to the Doc's house. Now at least he would assess the situation before panicking. He still gets nervous but he lets Yana experience things, Doctor Tenjin told him that he needed to let Yana do things for herself so she could learn to depend on herself. He could hear Doc's voice, "Amir, you don't want her to be dependent on someone to do everything for her. She needs to have the confidence in herself to know that she can overcome any situation. That starts when they are young. If you make a big deal out of it when she falls or gets a superficial scratch, she will be afraid to do anything on her own. You can make sure she is not badly hurt, then though you need to shrug it off. Never let her see you worry because she will mirror your actions and learn from you. She will look to you and your reaction will dictate hers." Bart smiled when he thought of the Old Man. He was very wise and had Bart's back, He respected him because he was not afraid to put Bart in check when it is needed. His relationship with Doc is how he imagined his relationship would have been with Grandpa Bart. Being around Doc was almost like having his Grandpa around. For the first time in a long time Bart felt whole, he had what he considered a family. He knew he did not deserve it, but Yana did. Whatever happens in the future, he would hold on to this feeling of love. He would use it to make the bad days bearable, the good days the best and the so –so days comfortable.

Right now, though he had a ceremony to prepare for. He quickly showered and shaved. As he attempted but failing miserably at putting on his wardrobe for the day. "Hell," I think I'll really shock everyone and show up in my birthday suit." He heard a familiar tap-a-tap-tap on his door, right on cue Doc appeared. He laughed, "Thank God Old Man, I was about to find the nearest window and chuck this damn thing out! How in the world do you put this on and where does this part go? This, I think I'm supposed to tuck in but it has a mind of its own and won't stay." Bart stopped talking and looked at Doc, "What is so funny about this? Really look (he held up some kind of braided belt.) Does this go across my chest or around my waist? I was just about to tie it around my forehead. Why are you laughing?" Bart happened to look towards the large floor length mirror, he realized how ridiculous he looked and started laughing himself. "Ok Doc, we, which means you, have to fix this. You seriously cannot tell me that royals dress themselves. They must have had to go to school just to learn how to dress themselves. This shit should come with instructions!" Doc was doubled over laughing so hard he had tears streaming down his face and thought he was going to urinate on himself, "Please, Please Amir, I'm begging you, stop talking or there will be a puddle right here on your floor." Once the laughter subsided, Doc made quick work of helping Bart with his wardrobe. Occasionally he would start laughing and Bart would remind him they had no time for games, "This is serious stuff man, act straight." At that, they would both start laughing and crying. When he was finally all dressed and ready to go he looked over at Doc who was still wiping the tears off his face, "Is this as hard to get off as it is to put on? Am I going to be all ties up in knots before it is all said and done? Doc started laughing again and excused himself to the restroom. "Humph, at least he gets to go to the bathroom to relieve himself. If I try to take it off by myself, I will never get it back on again. I really do not understand why the clothing is so complicated."

When Doc was satisfied at the way Bart looked, they started walking to the Great Hall where the Promising Ceremony was to be held. Bart was reciting everything Doc had told him last night. "A slight bow to each elder as he passed them, if he ran into an islander or palace servant he was to hold his hand out and wait until they paid their respect by a slight bow or curtsey and a kiss on his big gaudy ring. He was to turn to Branoi his family and their entire entourage, make a slight bow, or just a lowering of his head would suffice. Once they bow in return, then he is to turn and walk up the steps, slowly, but not too slowly, turn one more time, make a slight bow to the entire congregation. Do not wait for a response, turn and stand with his back to his throne but do not sit. The servant knows that once the king is standing in front of his throne it is his cue to go remove his robe and place it over one of the armrests. When the robe has been placed on the throne then the king may sit. Once he has taken his seat on his throne, he turns his head towards Doc. When he gets Doc's attention, he is to nod his head towards him. Tenjin will raise his and bring them down in unison this is the signal for everyone to take their seats. Then he nods at Doc once more, turns and look forward over his people as if he is now watching over them. Doc will signal the ceremony to begin by two claps of his hands. After that, Doc will take his place standing to the left of the throne, approximately 4 feet away.

Everything went perfectly and the ceremony began. First the Island Elder Somas read aloud Micho's and Yana's horoscopes and blessed the union. Both of the children are brought before the king, Prince Branoi's servant holds squirming little Micho (Bart secretly agrees with Micho, these clothes are awful.) Honi was holding little Yana, who as usual looked like an angel in her pristine white gown (knowing Yana, Bart marveled that the gown was still white.) He was to lower his head in a nod of approval over the union. Not missing a beat he nodded his head, out of the corner of his eye he saw Doc make a sigh of relief. Bart thought, "Tsk, tsk Doc, have some faith in me ha ha." Little Micho is then adorned with a simple gold necklace that sported two solid gold teardrops. Doc had told Bart earlier what was behind the meaning of these two pieces of jewelry were. He was also informed that Micho would learn from a young age that it is never to be removed or played with. He will also know the seriousness of its meaning and the consequences if it is lost or removed. Bart then watched as a small anklet was placed on Yana. She would also be taught what the importance of the anklet stood for and how important it was to keep it on and never lose it. It too held two solid gold teardrops. The children were once again brought before the throne and Bart was to nod his approval. He did this per Tenjin's previous instructions. Now one of the Elders from Branoi's clan approached the throne. He never met Bart's gaze, and he never stood straight up. Bart held out the hand that held the big ring and the elder blessed the king and kissed his ring. Bart nodded approval and without standing up the elder proceeded back down the throne steps continuously making slight bows and blessing the king, the throne, the children and finally the Isle of Zanzi itself. When he had cleared the throne, he went over to the children being held by Honi and Branoi's servant, said a joint blessing for both kids, and blessed each one separately. Leis were placed around the children's necks (Bart smirked and wondered how long his little Firecracker would leave hers on?) Both Elders then turned towards the throne and bowed to Bart, in turn Bart slightly lowered his head in respect for them. That concluded the Promising Ceremony. Bart marveled at the idea that little Yana who was not even a year old was already engaged to be wed in seventeen years. Bart watched as Honi started to leave the Great Hall with Yana, he smiled as he saw those little curious hands pull at the lei, he guessed she wanted to taste it as everything good and bad went straight in her mouth. Bart remained on the throne until everyone had left the Great Hall so that the Kitchen staff could bring in and set up all the food. Once they were all gone, Tenjin came up to him and said, "You were perfect, every move was like clockwork, it was as if you do this every day. I am speechless, (Doc laughed,) well I'm more than impressed how's that?" Bart laughed and patted Doc on the back, "I don't care what anyone says about you old man, you are ok in my book."

CHAPTER FIFTEEN

IT'S NOT EASY BEING THE KING

I have to admit though, after reading my mother's journal, it is hard for me to believe that the man in those pages is my father. That man caused pain and suffering because he liked it. I have seen my father pass many judgements during his ruling years. As the king, he is the jury, the judge, and the sentence. The accused serves his sentence, endures his or her punishment and then it is over. My father, on the other hand deals with his conscious and many sleepless nights over his decisions.

Once he had a farmer flogged for stealing another man's sheep. The thief went so far as to place his brand over the existing brand that was already present on the sheep's backside. He probably would have gotten away with it had there not been a witness. When the sheep was inspected, you could still see the markings from the owner. Flogging causes some debilitating cuts and slashes. Because of the flogging, the farmer was not able to tend his animals or work his fields. Food and supplies were anonymously sent to his dwelling so that he and his family would not go hungry. That is not something the man my mother described would do.

Here on the island, the most heinous crime a person can commit is rape. Rape is considered worse than committing murder. Both are an automatic death sentence so you would think that it would be a deterrence but it is not so. When a murder is committed on the island, the offender or offenders are swiftly brought to justice. They are either decapitated with the Guillotine or thrown into the Pit with the Vipers and Black Mambas. Once they are dead and gone their human suffering ends. It is not so for their victim, because of what was done to them against their will they will suffer for the rest of their lives. Even though he or she was found innocent in front of the king and court; in everyone else's eyes, they are still guilty. When a woman is raped, it is not unusual for her to take her own life or just suffer in silence.

The island natives' believe women were only put on this earth to procreate and raise children. An unwed mother is a plague on society; no one will ever marry a maiden that has been raped. If she is unmarried, and is a victim of rape then from that moment on in society's eyes she is unclean, through no fault of her own she will be considered a whore. If a married woman is sexually assaulted, her husband will never again be intimate with her. It is then the husband's choice whether to divorce her or not. Married or not, she is now a disgrace to her family and is considered no better than the rapist that violated her; any children born of her after the attack will bear the same label. If she already had children prior to the attack, they will never again look upon her as their mother. Her entire family turn their backs and shun her because of the shame she has brought to the family name.

Most rape victims do not live long after an assault. They usually take their own lives in lieu of living out the rest of their days in the life that fate has cast for them. The locals believed that rape victims must have fallen out of the favor of the gods and angered them somehow; therefore, they deserved what happened to them. There is never pity or empathy shown to them, no kind words only vile accusations are hurled their way. Even the victims felt that they deserved the treatment they got. Rape was the god's way of punishing them.

If the women do not end up taking their own lives, then the rest of their days they will constantly look over their shoulder waiting for a friend or family member to kill them. The black mark they have bestowed on their families will only go away when they are no more. Many times their relatives volunteer to kill the victims. Feeling that they will forever be cursed the victims do not fight back and it is considered a mercy killing. This type of murder is celebrated as honorable and the murderer is deemed as a hero. The victims no longer suffer and the families' noble names are restored.

The violators (knowing that the families will never turn them in) to the king blackmail them. There are worse things than suffering the wrath of the king. The Rapists know the shame and disgrace they cause when they violate women. They also know that it is one of the easiest crimes to get away with. It is a crime that everyone knows about but no one tells.

That is very backwards, "Do the crime, do not pay the time." Rape is a very lucrative crime. They are paid to keep quiet; they also feel entitled to have sexual relations with the victims. They become very brazen and prey on the victims whenever they want. Who is going to tell? No one ever will. When someone is murdered, they are convict, friends and family mourn and then it is done. Rape on the other hand is a lifetime sentence for the victim. This is one crime that even having a royal title will not make a difference. A woman is a woman, whether she has royal "blue" blood running through her veins or the blood of a simple commoner. Rape victims are all treated the same. My father had to rule on a case that haunted him for many years.

A young girl named Magi had gone on a picnic with her Tutu named Nandia. They went where the wild strawberries grow in abundance. Nandia's boyfriend Kio was waiting for them when they got there. For an old man Kio did not have a very nice reputation. He said things to the young maidens that were inappropriate and had been caught many times grabbing and touching areas that he should not have. He was old; no one ever thought he could actually hurt anyone. Most women would just tell him to go away and shoo him off. They all saw of him as harmless, unfortunately that was not so. Kio was a time bomb waiting to go off. Nandia had heard all the rumors and gossip going around about Kio; she had never seen that side of him. She chose to ignore it. That was a mistake she lived to regret. He met Nandia and her granddaughter Magi for their picnic lunch. He chose a secluded spot for the rendezvous. He assured Magi that he knew a great place to pick strawberries and they would go after lunch. Everything was fine for a while. Magi dozed off almost immediately after she ate her lunch. Nandia thought it a bit strange, she voiced her concern to Kio, "She never sleeps during the day; she is always the one who wants to go, go, go. Maybe I should take her home. She might be coming down with a bug or something." Kio gave her hand a squeeze, "She is a growing girl. Kids sleep when they go through growth spurts. Maybe she is having one of those. She seems fine Nad, just let her nap for a bit. Besides, I have something I want to show you." They put a light throw over Magi and headed into the woods hand-in-hand. They did not expect to be gone very long. At least that is not what Nandia had planned.

A few hours later Kio came out of the woods….alone. He walked up to the blanket that still held sleeping beauty. He took his time with Nandia because he knew that the sleeping draught he had slipped in the chocolate milk he brought for Magi would keep her knocked out for most of the day. He smiled, he had time, and there was no rush. Everyone is always rushing around, no one takes time to stop and admire (he reached down and stroked Magi's soft curls) the beauty that life provides for us. He knelt a little closer and his knees popped, this was so much easier when I was younger he complained aloud. Slowly he pealed the blanket off the little girl and ran his fingers across her arm. "Exactly how I imagined it would feel, soft as a cotton white bunny." Magi started to stir a little bit. Kio smiled, "Shhh little one sleep it's ok." She settled down again, and Kio removed the rest of the blanket from her tender little nubile body. Ever so softly, he untied her shoelaces and slipped off her shoes. He marveled at her pink chubby little feet. He lifted her foot and rubbed it on his chest. He was starting to get a bit excited. "Slow down old man, enjoy her to the fullest. She may be your last. However, you had a good run throughout the years and will have a lifetime of memories to warm the cold nights.

Kio thought about Nandia, it excited him so he started mocking her aloud, "Kio, what are you doing? Kio? Kio? Kio that hurts…. Why are you…." He remembered what he told her and when she finally realized what she had done. The best part though, the part he has always loved the most was when they realized that they had just been pons in his sick twisted game. (His pulse started to quicken and he was vigorously rubbing his hands together,) Right before they die, knowing that they have delivered to me, their prized possession all tied up in a pretty bow. The guilt, the begging and then the hopeless look of despair, and then nothing….dead eyes.

A concerned bus driver caught Kio Nassi. When his home was, investigated evidence was found that linked him to approximately fifteen abductions spanning over at least the last five years. Most were tourists that authorities assumed had gotten lost in the woods.

When his box of "treasures' was brought out, Kio proud of all he had done started to tell his very sordid tale to the king. Kio began with…." When I was younger and stronger I kept the women alive long enough to see what they had done. "Delivered their precious lambs to me for slaughter.' Now though, I cannot handle the woman and the child at the same time. However (he grinned), I always made sure that the women know what I am going to do to their precious little ones before I snuffed out their miserable lives." He thought back, "When I was in my prime I always sought out the single women that had little girls. Island life is hard, husbands and fathers died all the time. There was always an abundance of women looking for husbands. I was quite handsome back then and a well-placed smile got me in the door pretty quickly. For a while, I was doing maybe two or three a month. The gods have not let me age gracefully though. First, I had heart problems and Doctor Tenjin said I would recover but would tire more easily and not be as strong as I was before. Then my damn knees started to bother me. I had a mother-daughter combo, and was just getting started when my knees buckled and I lost my balance. The little one was so pretty and I had come up with all kinds of delicious things to do to her. When I faltered, I saw the look in mom's eyes and I knew all things I had planned were for naught. Mom got loose; instead of fleeing, she was trying to untie her daughter. Silly, silly woman that was her demise. A quick blow to the head and it was done. The little one would not stop screaming so I had to made quick work of her too lest someone heard her incessant wailing." My father, shifted on his throne uncomfortably, "Continue." He said. Kio continued, "Now with my ticker and my knees I was lucky if I got one every couple of months. Anymore the only time I could get them was when there was a bad storm or some other freak of nature. Nandia had been different; she was a widow that was starved for attention. At first, I ignored her flirtatious advances (too old, way too old honey I thought to myself.) One day though I was strolling by the park (my favorite hangout) and I spied Nandia with a little girl. Curious, I walked over to her, "Hi pretty ladies, what has you two at the park today?" Nandia looked up, unsure if the question was meant for her. When she saw me, she smiled really big, "Oh hi Kio, I bring my granddaughter Magi to the park every Wednesday." I quickly said, "Well then I guess I know where I'll be on Wednesdays from now on. I looked at Magi and could feel my palm start to itch and my pulse quicken, "Hi sweetheart, my name is Kio, and I'm a friend of your grandma's. You look like you are having fun here today." Magi stopped digging in the sand and looked up at me, "Tutu and I always have fun here…wanna play in the sand with me?" I looked at Nandia; Nandia smiled and nodded her approval. For the rest of the afternoon I chatted with Nandia (finding out what her schedule was, how often she had company, what she liked to do, and most importantly how often she had Magi etc.) I also chatted with Magi, I found out her favorite color, her favorite things to do etc.) At the end of the day, I walked them to the bus stop (another good thing to know….no car.) I made all kinds of mental notes so I could plan the best day and way for the abduction. I went home that night and pulled a dusty box out from under my bed. My heart started to race as I opened it up to reveal all my perfect keepsakes from my past little lambs. A locket of hair (I brought it up to my cheek, so soft.) I put it back lest it get damaged, it is one of my favorites, the oldest one I have. I found what I was looking for, and fished out my notepad and pen. I put the tip of the pen to paper and started writing. Strawberries, chocolate milk, picnic….) I had a plan. Sweet, gullible and starved for attention, Nandia was going to take the bait and fall into my trap just like all the others had throughout the years.

When I nonchalantly suggested the picnic to Nad, I made sure it was on a day that she was scheduled to watch Magi. Nandia had jumped at the chance to spend some time with me away from all the gossipers. I remembered it quite well, I said to her, "Nad, I miss just being with you, how about we make a date and have a picnic lunch, just the two of us. I have Wednesday open. What does your schedule look like?" She smiled and then frowned. Playing dumb I asked her (already knowing,) "What is it Nad? Why the frown? Don't you want to have a picnic with me?" She looked at me, "Oh Kio, I would love nothing more, the problem is, I am watching Magi on Wednesday." I smiled (I knew I had her then) and patted her hand, "Is that all? Do not fret over that, I love Magi, we can bring her along. I remember Nandia's face lit up and she said to me, "You are wonderful, and Magi will love it." I quickly told her to keep it a secret, "Don't tell her, let's surprise her." My father stopped him then, he was told that Magi had something to say. Poor brave little girl, "Bring her in he told his guard." In walked a little girl with a very ugly scar across her left cheek. Bart saw the fear in her face when she saw Kio sitting there in front of him. He motioned for the guard to take Kio out of the room. Once Kio was gone, he smiled at Magi, "Honey can you tell me about the day of the picnic?" Magi hesitantly scanned the room, she saw her parents in the back with their heads down. She looked at the king, sighed and began her story…

"On the day of the picnic Tutu was like a busy bee in the garden, she was all over the place, (Magi giggled) it was funny and I just watched her wondering what was going on. I asked her, "What is going on Tutu?" She smiled at me, I remember her saying, "Nothing sweet girl, put your shoes on, we have some errands to run and we mustn't miss the bus. Hurry up honey, we have to go." The bus driver talked to Tutu a bit, he seemed worried about us. We walked a long ways and met Mr. Kio He had a picnic lunch for us and promised we would find strawberries. We ate and I guess I fell asleep. When I woke up he was, he was (she started to cry.)" Bart quickly told her that was enough, he understood. He told her she was a brave little girl and her mommy and daddy should be proud of her. Magi glanced over where her parents had been and saw an empty spot….Her heart fell, she was only ten but she knew what happened to rape victims. She got down off the chair and left the room. When she left, Bart asked to have the Bus driver brought in. The Bus driver nervously entered, he knew the story he was about to tell would destroy Magi's life. He also knew if he did not and Kio walked away from this he would go on to hurt more little girls. Sadly, he thought to himself, sometimes for the good of the many you have to destroy the one. The king interrupted his thought and brought him back to the present. "Excuse me, what is your name?" "My name is Tonga Your Highness." The king continued, "Thank you Tonga, can you please tell me the rest of the story so I do not have to see that wretched old man again?" Tonga looked at the king, "Your Highness I want you to know that I do not want to tell you this, it will hurt one to save many." That statement confused Bart, it would be many months before he knew the meaning of those words. "Please continue Tonga, "Bart said. Tonga cleared his throat, "I could not understand why that sweet old lady and little girl were getting off the bus by the woods on the outside of town. I asked her repeatedly why and she pretty much shrugged me off. I could not keep her on the bus, she is grown woman. It bothered me all day, when I got off work I drove back over there. I figured they would probably already be gone but I wanted to make sure. I remember driving slowly down the road, I almost hit the little girl when she staggered into the road and collapsed. Her clothes were torn and she was bleeding from a gash that had filleted her face open. I only saw her but I heard someone screaming, I thought maybe it was the old woman. I laid Magi in the back and ran down the hill following the screams. It was not the grandmother, it was Kio. Apparently, during the struggle with Magi she kicked his knee and broke it or something. He could not get up and was screaming in pain. I was not going to put him in the backseat, it was pretty apparent to me what he had done or attempted to do to Magi. I checked him for weapons, found a knife with blood on it (I assumed it was Magi's blood.) I grabbed him and threw him over my shoulder; he was begging me to take him to the hospital. I promised him I would, got him up the hill to my car, opened the trunk and threw him in it and shut the lid. I grabbed my flashlight and ran back down the hill; I had a sick feeling that Miss Nandia was probably dead. I called her name repeatedly and heard nothing. I found her, well I found her body. She was tied to a tree and she was dead. Your Highness, do you really need me to tell you more?" Bart looked over at Tenjin, "No, Tonga, I have heard enough to pass judgement. Thank you for being concerned enough to drive over there to check on them. Magi would probably be dead had you not." Tonga sadly looked at the king and mumbled that she would probably wish she were after this. Bart confused by that comment dismissed him. He looked at his guard, "Bring the accused back in please." Kio was returned to the throne room, forced to kneel before the king, "Mr. Nassi, I have listened to all the evidence against you, some from your own lips I might add. I have also seen the permanent damage you have inflicted on Magi. You have taken away her innocence and not only scarred her on the outside for everyone to see but you have scarred her on the inside. There is a place reserved in hell for people like you and today you will be there with all the other scum just like you. Misery loves company so I am sure you will fit right in. I am tired of looking at your face, is there anything you would like to say before sentence is carried out?" Kio looked up at Bart and said, "My lambs were beautiful, each and every one of them. I loved them then and I love them still. I watched them take their last breath as they looked into my eyes. They loved me too. There are more out there like me, you cannot catch us all. When one falls twenty rise up. You can lock your doors, you can bar your windows, we find a way in, and there are always Nandias that welcome us with open arms." Bart cut him off, he had heard enough, "Throw him in the Pit he bellowed, throw the snake in the Pit. He should enjoy that; his brothers are waiting for him." As the guards drug Kio from the room Bart could hear him yelling, "you can't stop us...we get in, we always get in...." Bart looked at Tenjin and said, I am glad that is over. That poor girl, Doc will her scar heal?" Tenjin (knowing Bart had no idea what rape victims go through) looked at his king (who thought it was over) and said, it won't matter Your Highness, unfortunately, it just won't matter." Bart thought he meant that she would learn to live with it and that is why it would not matter. He dropped it, he wanted to get back to Yana and hug her really tight.

Not being from the islands my father had no idea about the stigma that surrounds this crime. He listened to the case and passed judgement. Kio Nassi was thrown in the Pit and the king thought it was over. A few months later, Bart was strolling through the market place and saw a young child sitting on the curb just past the merchant tents. Looking at her, she could not have been more than maybe ten or eleven years old. She had no shoes and was filthy dirty. The king started to make his way over to her when he saw some people walk by her and randomly kick or spit on her. This made Bart angry, "Hey, hey, you need to stop that right now. If I see any more violence directed towards this girl, you will be punished. The girl had her head down, a very dirty and tattered rag covered most of her face. Bart knew he had to do something, "Girl he called to her (she looked up,) When he saw her eyes, shivers ran up and down his spine. He felt he knew her but for the life of him could not place where. He continued, "Come here to me right now." As she stood up, he noticed that one of her legs was grotesquely twisted behind her. As she started to walk over to him, she fell and could not get up. Bart quickly walked over and scooped her into his arms protectively. He knew she would die if he did nothing, "I am the king dammit and can do as I please "You are going to be ok, (the rag covering her face fell away) I have…. (Bart looked down at her and froze.)" That scar, he knew that scar. "Magi, why are you in this state? Did you run away from home? Does your family know you are out here?" Magi's eyes rolled back in her head and then her head just lolled from side-to-side against his arm. Bart knew she was in bad shape and whether Doc liked it or not he was going to have a new patient. "Let anyone mistreat you, I will make them wish they were dead." He growled to himself. Then he looked down at poor little Magi and his tone softened as he spoke, "Don't worry little one, I'm not sure what happened or why you look like this, but I am going to make it all better. Sleep sweet girl, gain your strength, I will watch over you, no one will harm you, I promise."

I remember a conversation I had with my dad about what made a good king. I watched him throughout the years and he had to make many hard decisions as the ruler of Zanzia. He told me about the changes he wanted to make for the people. His main concern was for the young princes that competed in the challenges (his challenges.) He told me how difficult and dangerous they had been for him and he decided he wanted to at least make them fair for the future competitors. The first thing he did was that he made them public knowledge. He had a wooden box made; each of the princes would draw five slips of paper from the box. When they unfolded their paper, they knew right away, what they were going to do. They had time to prepare if they so choose to. At first, there was a lot of resistance. No one wanted to stray too far from the old ways, they were afraid they would anger the gods. My father was the king and therefore they had to obey like it or not. Eventually when more and more competitors survived, they kind of started to listen. Father provided them weapons they could actually use. For the shark hunt, they were given the day before to fish and gather bait. The spears were sharpened and they were provided a knife. My father sent out a spotter when the princes went out to kill their sharks. The spotter was not allowed to interfere unless it was under threat of death. If the prince was in mortal danger, the spotter had the king's permission to kill the shark. This would give the prince a chance to hunt another day versus have his family weep and mourn over his dead body. For the wild boar hunt, my father had two challengers go out together. As a team, they were able to snare and kill the boars without being maimed or killed themselves. My father wanted the challenges to be just that challenges, he did not want them to be life or death struggles. He always told me, "Yana, you do not have to die to prove you can be a king and rule a kingdom. Most of the time ruling starts with your smarts not your strength.

Anytime you can resolve a situation with your brain rather than bully your way through with pain and suffering that is when you are a true king. Diplomacy over war and bloodshed, remember that sweet girl." Once he even grabbed her hands, "Yana, make a fist (she was confused but she did it.) He then said, "You see these, they represent fear. My mother taught me that and it got me to places I did not want to be. I'm going to teach you another way because ruling with fear is the cowardly way out. Anyone can do that, and you have an enemy for life. The first chance they get they are going to attack and retaliate against you. I looked at him, "But father, all the history books show great kings leading battles, do you not want to be a great king?" Bart smiled at her, "Honey, all those kings died to achieve their fame. Can you imagine how many more great things they could have done if they had made peace and signed a truce between the two kingdoms? They could have worked together and accomplished great things and both kingdoms would have benefited from it. Sometimes Yan, just because you are bigger and stronger does not mean you are better." I was never more proud of my father; he spoke that day as a true king.

CHAPTER SIXTEEN

GROWING UP ROYAL

JAX

Today is my sixteenth birthday. According to Island customs, I am no longer a little girl. Now I have to start learning how to become a queen and someday rule next to my future king. My father never remarried so I have no one here on the island to teach me what it is that I must know or do. My father is throwing a grand party for me this afternoon. After the gala event, I leave for O'Sangha to apprentice with Queen Lani for two years. Weather permitting I will travel to my home on Zanzi for most of the weekends. I am not to discuss anything that I am learning with anyone and that includes my father. I am excited and nervous at the same time. Having never been away from my father (except when he makes his solo trips to the Isle of Manu.) Those trips are brief maybe a day or two. He goes every couple of months and he always goes alone. I have asked about these trips but he is tight lipped. He says, "Yana, there will come a time that I will reveal all to you. Right now, you have to trust that I am looking out for the both of us. The less you know the safer you remain. I will not put you in harm's way until the time that it is necessary to do so. Save yourself a headache and stop asking, my answer will always be the same. I quit asking, when my father gets that way he is like a snapping turtle and will not open his mouth. Going to O'Sangha and not seeing my father every day is going to be quite an adjustment. I will miss him terribly; he has promised me that I will have his undivided attention when I am able to come home for visits. I am not sure who is going to miss whom more.

As the Queen of Zanzi, I need to be able to step in and rule if I am called upon to do so. I must be the best queen I can be for the people. I need to know what that role is and master it. A good king and queen must complement each other. If the king is the warrior then the queen must be the nurse, if the king is the hunter then the queen must be the cook. Running a kingdom is about balance. That is one thing my father lacks as a ruler. There is no one to balance him. Doctor Tenjin and I try but my father knows that he does not have to answer to either one of us. Sometimes he listens and sometimes he does not. If he had remarried then he would have had someone who was not afraid to keep him in check. When he is angry, watch out if you have to step before him. If he is in a jovial mood then he tends to let certain transgressions slide. It is always either one extreme or the next. Overall, he is a fair and just ruler but there are the rare occasions that he just enjoys the suffering he has the power to inflict.

    The party was grand; everyone was there except my Kimo. I asked my father where he was. I was given some lame excuse about some errand he had been sent on. I acted cool like it did not matter. Deep down inside though my heart was breaking, I knew this was the last time I would be able to spend time with him. It hurt that he was not there. I knew that the next time I saw him I would be preparing to wed and would have to treat him as a stranger. Maybe it was for the best that he was not there. Anymore, seeing him was just as hard as not seeing him. I have grown up with him. He was my best friend. Slowly our feelings evolved into something more. Our parents thought it was cute so we allowed our feeling to grow for each other. We made promises to each other of a lifetime together. When I wanted to help Mr. Sula and his family escape, Kimo helped to me help them. He is the one who secretly took the canoe to the other side of the island for me. I would have never been able to do all of that myself. I have loved him in different ways for as long as I can remember. After that, we would sneak away whenever we could. When I found out about my father's past and what he did to my mother, Kimo consoled me. I wanted to hate my father, the things that he did, I was in shock and did not know what to do. Kimo made me realize that I did not know that man from the journal. He reminded me of all the good my dad had done for me and for the people of Zanzi. That was not the awful murderer written about in those pages. I felt anger towards the woman that wrote those things about him. This caused a lot of guilt and confusion for me. Kimo reminded me of the love he has for me. After that, I knew that no matter what I could never hate my dad. I felt guilty though because I could never love my mom nor could I be angry with her. What she wrote was true, that is who my father was but is not any longer. I had never met my mom. How can you love words in a book? I am sure had I grown up with her it would have been a different story, that was not so, therefore the feelings did not exist. Kimo made me realize that I did not have to feel guilt for not loving her yet loving the man that brutally took her life. I love my servant boy with all of my heart.

After Kali's torture and helping her family flee into the dark night, I sought out Kimo for comfort. Normally, we were very careful about being seen together. We were still allowed to hang out but we did not want to push the envelope. I was so upset though that Kimo left his palace chores undone and we stole away to our secluded spot. We talked all afternoon, Kimo held me as I cried. We lost track of time and when we returned, my father caught us. He sent Kimo home, "Your parents will deal with you, they are waiting for you Kimo, go home." I had steeled myself and was preparing for a stern lecture; I would have preferred a stern lecture to what my father was going to tell me. He sat me on my bed and took my hand (here it comes I thought.) "Yana," he began, "You are fourteen now, it is time you started acting like the princess you are. Yana, you know when you get too big to play with certain toys so we put them up or give them away? You are too big now to play with Kimo. He is a young man and a servant; you are a young woman and a princess. You are like oil and water, you do not mix. People are starting to talk, we cannot have anyone ever doubt or question your virtue. Like it or not Yana, you are a role model for all the young maidens. We cannot have you acting inappropriately." I tried to interject, "But father, Kimo is." He stopped me, in a slightly raised voice he said, "Kimo is a servant Yana, lest you forget that, he will never be more than that. You are a princess who will someday be the queen of Zanzi. Tomorrow you will tell Kimo that he needs to forget you and that you two are not allowed to hang out together." Big teardrops threatened to cascade down my face and I looked up at my father pleading with my eyes that this was not so. He looked at me, "Yana, it is time to grow up. You have responsibilities to your kingdom. Fun, games, and childhood promises are over. Kimo is a servant and when you see him you, look at me Yana (I raised my eyes to meet his) you will treat him as such. If you disobey me, I will have no choice but to punish him and send his entire family away. There will be no impropriety under my roof and definitely not from my daughter. Tomorrow you will tell him or I will. Somehow I think coming from you will be nicer than if I tell him." My father got up from my bed and dropped my hand a he started to leave my room; he turned and looked at me, "Tomorrow Yana, you tell him tomorrow." He turned, left, and shut the door behind him. I crumpled into my bed and sobbed all night long. I thought to myself, how am I going to tell my heart to stop beating? How do I tell my one true love that we are over even before we began? I will never love the prince I am to wed. For how can you love someone when your heart belongs to another? I felt hopeless, devastated, and just wanted to die. I mocked my father, "Tomorrow Yana, you will tell him tomorrow." I fell back into my bed and cried myself to sleep.

Tomorrow came too soon, with swollen eyes I went to the Great Hall in search of Kimo. When he saw me coming, he broke out in a big smile. Then he noticed the state I was in and his smile faded and a look of concern crossed his face. His parents had lectured him all night about impropriety. Kimo stubbornly stated that he and Yana loved each other and that would never change. Now looking at her, he was not so sure. Did she stand up to her father? Did she confess her undying love for Him to the king? He did not want to find out but was afraid he was about to. Yana walked right over to Kimo and she did not care who saw her. She stopped a few feet from him and turned to all of the kitchen workers, "I hope you go run and tell the king. We were not doing anything inappropriate; he was the only good thing in my life, you, all of you (she pointed around the room.) You all have destroyed our happiness, so go run to the king, I do not care. While you are at it, tell him this." She crossed the few feet that separated them, stood on her tippy toes, and kissed Kimo full on the mouth. Totally shocked Kimo pulled away at first, and then he bent down and picked me up, put his arms around me and kissed me back. This was the first and the last kiss we would share for a long time. We could hear all the shocked gasps behind us and all around us but for that brief moment in time, no one mattered but the two of us. Hand in hand, we walked out of the kitchen.

I knew I had given Kimo the wrong impression. I knew it was wrong what I did in the kitchen and it was going to make what I had to tell my Kimo all that much harder. I just wanted to give the kitchen gossipers something to gossip about. I wanted it to get back to my father; I just never meant to hurt Kimo in the process. I was selfish and had used Kimo to get back at dear old dad. Kimo was talking so much that he did not realize how quiet I was. We went to our secluded spot and that is when Kimo finally noticed the tears in my eyes. He looked concerned, "What is wrong my sweet Ku'u ipo?" That, was his pet name for me, it meant my sweetheart. I just sat on our boulder that jutted out across the bay. Subconsciously tracing our names, we had carved into it as children. Finally, I looked up into his eye, the eyes of the man I loved with all my heart, "My Love, I don't know how to say this, I don't know how I am going to survive this (I started to cry again.)" Kimo took me in his arms, "Ku'u ipo, what is it? You can tell me anything." I pulled myself out of his arms, wiped the tears away, "Kimo, I love you, but my father has forbid us from seeing each other anymore." He sat straight up, "What? He cannot do," I stopped him, "Yes he can stop us, my love lest you forget, he is the king. If we do not stop, if we, we do not end our love, he has threatened to punish you and send your entire family away. (I hung my head) I cannot allow that, will not allow that to happen. This is the last time we will sit here together. When next we see each other we must act as strangers, you must treat me according to my station. You must not look into my eyes; you mustn't smile familiarly to me. Even if it is not true, you must treat me as if I mean nothing to your heart. It has to be this way; I am a princess who will one day rule Zanzi next to another." I grabbed his chin in my hands and made him look into my tear-filled eyes, (he was crying too.) "Kimo, my love," I began, "I love you and will never love another. I will marry for the sake of the kingdom, as I must. He will never possess my heart, which has always belonged to you. I gave it freely and it is yours. I will watch you fall in love with another, I will wish you well. Today my love, my heart is shattering in a thousand pieces, today I hate my father for what I must do. You will haunt my days but at night when I lay my head on my pillow to wait for sleep, I will smile because you will be there. In my dreams is where I will find you. In my dreams, you will be Kimo and I will be Yana. There will be no servant and there will be no princess. No one will tell us we cannot love in my dreams. That is the one place they cannot take you from me." Kimo hung his head, tears slid down his face; he had never felt like a servant around Yana until now. Sadly, he realized that he was not good enough for her. He would always be just a servant, Yana she was to be a queen. He looked into her eyes, slowly stood up, turned, and walked away. Yana turned and watched him walk away; she started to call to him but stopped. It was over; this day she had lost her best friend, her love and her happiness. When she could see him no more she stood up and left their spot. She would not return there for many months.

Kimo avoided her whenever he could. Whenever there were chores away from the palace, he volunteered to go. He hoped that by not seeing her the pain would lessen but it never did. She was never far from his heart. He tried to forget her in the arms of other maidens but that just made him more miserable. She was his first thought in the morning, he breathed her in throughout the day and at night she was his last thought as he closed his eyes. His dreams were always filled with her smile and laughter. Days grew into months and soon a year had passed. They busied themselves with other things but if they happened to see each other in passing all those feelings came rushing back. Each wondering if these feelings would ever go away or forever torture them.

Yana's sixteenth birthday was a few months away; the king had summoned him to the throne room. "What was this all about?" Kimo wondered as he made his way there. As Kimo entered the throne room and bowed in a show of respect for the king, he noticed that there were no guards, no Doctor Tenjin either, it was just the king. When Bart saw Kimo, he motioned him to come in. After Kimo recovered from his bow, he made his way to the throne and stood before the king with his eyes cast down to the ground. Bart said, "Kimo, come closer to me, sit here," he pointed to a stool that had been set next to the throne. Confused, Kimo sat and looked at King Amir, "Why have I been summoned here Your Highness? What is it you ask of me?" Bart looked at the boy, he noticed the sadness in his eyes, and it was the same when he looked at Yana. He knew now that he was making the right choice. He sighed deeply and began his story, "Kimo, things are changing drastically, I can sense it, there is something I need you to do for me, for Yana. Kimo sat straight up and looked at Bart, "Is the princess alright? Is she in danger?" Bart put his head down, "Kimo, I have done things in my past that I fear are coming to exact their revenge. I am not proud of the man I was before I came to Zanzi; you have to believe me when I say that man does not exist any longer and has not for a very long time. I knew this day would come and it is almost upon us. Yana will not suffer for the sins of her father, not now and not ever. I am not going to order you to do this I am asking you to do this, if not for me then for sweet Yana." Kimo looked very confused, "Your Highness, I ask once again, what is you will have me do?" Bart began again, "I am going to ask you to travel a far distance and locate a place that is suitable for Yana to live out her days. It must be private and money is of no consequence. You must purchase it and furnish it. You must assume an alias and make your present known. You must learn all you can and become someone that people see on a regular basis, you must make friends but keep them at arm's length. You must make it known that you await your wife's return." Kimo quickly looked up at Bart, "My wife? Your Highness you well know that I have no wife." Bart smiled at him, "Kimo, you are going to be a very rich man, you must treat my daughter like the queen she is. I already have a passport and ID card for you with your new identity. You must never mention Zanzi, when you leave here with Yana. Do you understand son? You must never return here. If you do, Yana will suffer for the sins of her father and be put to death." He paused and looked at Kimo, "I have no right to ask this of you, I ask because I have watched both you and Yana, your love is true and I know once I am no more you will make her very happy. Will you do this for me? Will you give up your family and your life here for Yana?" Kimo thought for a moment, "I will protect her with my life and love her unconditionally. Your Highness, why can you not accompany us? Why must you die?" Bart looked down, "I am going to distract them while you get my daughter to safety. They will scour the island for her when I am dethroned and no longer the king. Custom dictates that if a king disgraces the crown the bloodline is to be eradicated. They will hunt Yana as long as she remains here. I am depending on you to save her. There is something else, Yana must not know of this until the time comes. This must stay between us until I have to involve the others. If it gets out, both Yana and I will pay the price." Kimo looked at the king, "I swear on my death this will not pass my lips. When is this supposed to happen Your Highness? When do I leave?" "Kimo," Bart began, "You are to steal away on the night when the moon is full, make haste to O'Sangha and gain passage on the Supply ship headed to the Mainland. You will have four months in which to accomplish all the tasks that have been set before you. You must be back here no later than the fourth turning of the moon. If you are late, Yana will die. I have a calendar for you so that you can mark the moons." (Bart handed the calendar to Kimo.) Kimo had never seen one of these. It was strange looking, there were many boxes with the days of the week and numbers. He asked the king, "What does all of this mean?" Bart explained the calendar to the young man; gratefully he caught onto it very quickly. "Kimo, you must hide this, no one must see it." "Your Highness you said I am to have a new identity, who am I to be?" Bart laughed, "Your new name is to be Matteo Rossi and you are from Italy." Kimo thought for a moment and smiled, "I like the name Matteo. When I get to the Mainland, I will by a book on Italy. Do you know where in Italy I am to be from?" Bart said, "Your family owns a wine vineyard in the hills of Milan. Bart looked at the time, and realized that he needed to cut this short lest someone see him talking to Kimo. Ok Kimo, I think you have a lot to think and plan. Start taking your things to the cave on the other side of the island a little at a time. In two weeks' time you will make your trek to O'Sangha." Kimo nodded, and before the king could say anything, "I'll make sure no one sees me leave you Your Highness." Bart smiled with relief...He had chosen well, gods permitting Yana would be safe. Two weeks later a lone figure in a canoe slipped into the sea and with the moonlight as a guide disappeared into the night.

My father had pulled out all the stops for this party. He had my favorite meal prepared in too many ways to mention. My father made a special trip to Manu Island for my party. He brought back the biggest crabs I had ever seen, the shrimp were the size of my hand and the mussel were so fat they almost did not fit in their shells. We had octopus that could probably swallow a baby and the fish, oh my god; they were big and so colorful. Doc's wife made strawberry pie; strawberry cake, strawberry pudding and something we rarely ever have here were ice cubes. Hers were special, they were strawberry. Honi made me a backpack to keep all my things in while I was in O'Sangha and Kimo's mom knows that I love chocolate and made all kinds of different candies for me that just melted in your mouth. I nonchalantly asked her where Kimo was, she was about to answer when my father (who had overheard us) came rushing over to us rudely interrupting me and said, "Yana, the cook needs you in the kitchen, you better hurry because he seemed desperate." I left and went to the kitchen to see what all the uproar was about. My father stayed back to speak with Kimo's mother, when I glanced back they had moved off to the side, Kimo's mother was waving her hands in the air and getting very animated. My father was just shaking his head. I knew something was up and reminded myself to ask my father later. I had overheard some of the servants saying something about Kimo earlier; as soon as they saw me, they quit talking. I am guessing I am no longer their favorite person. Where was Kimo I wondered? I at least saw him in passing at least once per day. Come to think about it, I had not seen him in a few weeks. That was not like him at all. I did not realize I had entered the kitchen and had just been standing there this whole time. Embarrassed, I looked up and everyone had stopped what they were doing and just stared at me. The cook stood there with his hands on his hips impatiently tapping his foot and said "Well?" I looked at him and realized that I had not heard a word he had been saying. I quickly composed myself, put on the biggest smile I could muster, "Cook, you will create magic, of this I am sure." I turned and ran out of the room. I was not paying attention during my hasty retreat and ran smack dab into my father. He grabbed my hand, there were presents to open. He pulled me away from the kitchen and took me to the table in the Great Hall. I had never seen so many gifts, and they were all for me.

My father came up to me and asked me to take a quick walk with him. I looked at him, "I thought it was time to open the gifts? Is that not why we came in here?" He smiled and said, "Yana, just humor me and take a walk with your old man (he gave me his sad puppy dog eyes,) I rolled my eyes at him and took his out stretched hand. "Where are we going?" I asked dear old dad. He just smiled and urged me on. I stopped and put my hands on my hips, "You have been acting weird all day. I know that I am leaving after the party but I do not think that is it. Dad, please stop." Bart stopped and looked at her, "Yana, I was wrong, I was so wrong. Love must come before all else. Without love, none of it (he pointed north, then east, then west and south,) none of this means anything. Life is too short and I want you to be happy above all else. Whether it is with a prince, or a mere servant, if it is love then it is destiny. I just brought you out here to give you my birthday present." I was too stunned to speak so I just looked at him. "Yana, my sweet, sweet, Yana, I thought long and hard about what to give you on this special day. I was at a loss, and then it hit me like a ton of bricks. I am the king, which means I can change the laws and the rules whenever I want. I did something that has never been done. I opened up the challenges here on Zanzi to every man that wants to compete. Regardless if he is a prince, a commoner or a beggar on the street." My mouth dropped, I did not know what to say. Bart continued, "I thought about it long and hard, I came to this decision for a few reasons, the first being that whenever I need someone to stand and fight for my honor (he looked at me,) it is not princes that volunteer, it is the common folk that fight and sometimes die for me. If they can fight for the king's honor then why can they not fight for the right to be the king? Bart was thinking of himself now, he was not royal blood yet he had been the king now for sixteen years. He had made many positive changes, the palace as well as the island was thriving. He figured if he could do it then he was sure that any of his fellow man royal or not could do it as well. He continued, "Yana, I have found that when someone works for something they appreciate it and strive to be the best at it. They know what it took to get there. Royalty on the other hand almost as if they are entitled to it. They take it for granted and do a half ass job." I agreed with him, "Is that my birthday present then father? I think it is grand and extremely thoughtful. It makes me proud to know that you care about the commoners that way. Is this not something that would have been better told where all could hear?"

Bart looked at his daughter, "I remember when you were a babe, I was so afraid I would crush or break you if I touched you. We learned together, you and I what it meant to be a family. You have saved me child, I wanted you to know that. You have enriched my life in ways I cannot even explain. You have given me a reason to live, a reason to want to be better tomorrow then I was today. Because of you, when I look in the mirror I respect and like the person that is looking back at me. Away from you, I am flawed but with you, I am whole. You have given my life meaning and you have taught me throughout the years how to be vulnerable and trust and most importantly how to love not only you but also my fellow man. You have brought me so much happiness. If I died tomorrow, Yana, as long as I knew you were safe I would have no regrets. I started living the day you reached your little hand out of your crib in the infirmary and grabbed my finger. When you looked at me, I was done. I love you sweetheart, no matter what you hear, please know that I love you. You turned a bad man good." Tears were falling down my face, I climbed in his lap and snuggled my head against his chest, looked up at him, "I love you daddy; I am who I am because of your love for me. I remember everything you have ever taught me. I am proud to be your daughter.

This is the best birthday present ever." Bart laughed, "Oh baby girl, that was not your birthday present," he fished around in his pocket and brought out a wrinkled piece of paper. He held it out for me, "I give you my blessing." I took the paper from him and looked at him very confused. "Do not be out here too long; there are still presents and a mountain of food to eat. Somehow though, I don't think the rest of the gifts will shine as bright as that wrinkled piece of paper you are holding in your hand." He smiled, blew me a kiss and left.

My hands trembled as I carefully opened up the wrinkled piece of paper. My breath caught in my throat when I read the first line.

Tears slid down my face when I realized that this was from my sweet Kimo. It read....

> My dearest Ku'u ipo,
> I am sorry I am not there to celebrate your special day with you. I am away doing something very important. I will be back soon though and we can be together like
> We belong. I tried really hard to get over you but I never could. I know you feel the same. Your dad and I had a long talk and we came to an agreement. I am going to enter the challenges for the right to rule Zanzi. I am going to win and make you my bride. Your father has given me his blessing. Well my love have a beautiful day and I will see you on your first break from O'Sangha.
> Always & Forever,
> Kimo

I read Kimo's latter a few more times and carefully put it in my pocket. My father had been right; nothing anyone could give me could compare to the selfless gift my father had given me today... His blessings. He gave me back my heart; he gave me back my Kimo. For the rest of the day I was on cloud nine, the presents were sweet, and thoughtful, the food was amazing. Before I knew it, the time had arrived to give kisses and hugs and say bittersweet heartfelt goodbyes. I made my way up to my room to make sure I had everything I would need. As I was about to turn off my light and head to the dock, I turned and sat on my bed not really thinking about anything. That is where my father found me. "Come on Yana, the canoe is waiting for you." I got up, shut off the light and closed the door. This was goodbye to my childish ways and hello to the future Queen of Zanzi. Head held high, I walked down the worn path to the beach on my father's arm. Life as I knew it was about to change. As I got in the canoe I glanced over at my father, I briefly caught a sadness in his eyes. When he realized I was looking at him he quickly placed a fake smile on his face. He wanted Yana's memories of him to be happy. When he could see her canoe no more Bart returned to the palace, locked himself in his room to come up with a plan.

CHAPTER SEVENTEEN

THE GIG IS UP

Yana has been on O'Sangha for a few weeks now and is fitting in quite well. She has made a few friends and enjoys her classes immensely. She and her friends have found that they love to visit the market place on lunch and breaks. Being from Zanzi there was so much that Yana had never experienced. She found that one of her favorite things to drink was Star Bucks it was her favorite place. Finally, Friday came, the weather was bad and seas were choppy so Yana had to stay put this weekend. She and her friends were goofing around when one of them stepped on her foot. "Ouch, that hurt! Be more careful next time." She said playfully. Someone had overheard one of her friends call out Yana's name and give her shoulder a push.

Soon the girls walked off to go investigate another storefront display window. The stranger name was Mina.

Mina is Kali's younger sister, after they got safely to the Mainland she had vowed to avenge her sister's death. She was going to make King Rayno pay dearly for what he had done. Mina's life on the Mainland was very different from her life growing up on Zanzi. She was given the opportunity to go to college. Towards the end of her first year, she had to do a Thesis. For her Thesis, she chose was on Island Monarchy. She decided to concentrate her topic on Zanzi. Having grown up there, she knew a bit about how their monarchy ruled. While researching she came across some things that did not add up. While there were no recent pictures of Zanzi, she had come across some from when the ships were still allowed to dock there. The people of Zanzi were pretty short in stature except King Rayno. She thought that odd, they were never allowed to wed outside of their bloodline so how it is that almost everyone on the island was between 4'3" to 5'3" and then you have Amir Rayno who is all of 6'5"? The monarchy are light tan in skin tone and yet King Rayno has an olive complexion like that of an Italian or someone from that part of the world. The facial features did not add up either. King Rayno had a very pronounced chin and dark blue eyes while the islanders had pointy noses and hardly any chin at all. The more she dug, the more curious she became. She decided to see what she could dig up on Amir Rayno. The more Mina researched the more things did not add up. She finds the newspaper clipping in regards to the sinking cruise ship. She tries to find out information on Amir Rayno…she comes across a photo of the real prince and it is not the Amir Rayno that is ruling Zanzi. In addition, there is no record of prince Rayno ever being married. No mention of an infant daughter. She finds a picture of the supposed prince Amir from when the cruise ship sank. Using the facial recognition software from the forensic lab at the college, she is shocked when it pings the name Bart Randolph.

Mina calls Cato (her father) and tells him everything she has found out and asks about someone by the name of Bart Randolph. Cato has no knowledge of anyone named Bart Randolph and begs her to leave this alone. Mina disregards his request and petitions the

Island of Zanzi for entrance – she says she is an exchange student and is doing research. Rayno as usual denies admittance. Not one to give up Mina decides to travel to O'Sangha and plead her case to the monarchy there. She arrives on O'Sangha and checks into the hotel. She submits everything she has dug up n King Amir Rayno and requests an audience with the king. No one would tell her how long she would have to wait for a response but she knew she was not leaving until she had her "day in court." Mina is a very impatient girl so she decides to take a walk along the small boardwalk to check out the shops etc. She spies a group of young royals (probably in between classes hunting lunch) about to give a no never mind attitude she hears one say Yana and affectionately and playful push a young girl's shoulder.

All day Mina wonders to herself why the name Yana sounds so familiar to her. She calls Cato- after the initial shock of learning where Mina is she asks him if the name Yana means anything to him…he is very quiet then tells Mina that she is the reason they are alive. She planned and executed their escape. He once more begs his daughter to leave it alone Kali is in hallowed ground. If they find out who Mina really is and Rayno does some digging he will find out that his very own daughter not only let them escape she planned and carried it out all the while she was only fourteen years old. Mina assures him no one will know, at least until it is too late. She is going to go after king Rayno aka. Bart Randolph. Cato's begging and pleading falls on deaf ears. Mina is still trying to reason with her father, she is greeted by dead air, Cato has ended the call. Mina thinks to herself, "He will be proud of me for doing what he is too much of a coward to do himself." She was convinced of this.

Later she makes her way down to the café where she saw Yana earlier and strikes up a conversation with a much younger boy who thinks he has a chance with her. Mina toys with him and nonchalantly ask a few questions about princess Yana. She finds out that the princess is here apprenticing with the queen, as she has no mother or queen to teach her. A little more flirting and a few more questions later she finds out the story about the cruise ship yada yada yada. She shuts the kid down, breaks his heart and heads to her room.

Mina decides the best way to learn about King Rayno is to become friends with unsuspecting Yana Slowly she starts conversations with Yana until pretty soon they become fast friends. Mina tell Yana all about the USA and Yana in turn answers her questions about Zanzi. About 2 months into the friendship (still no answer about a meeting with the monarchy) they are such good friends that Yana stays overnight with her friend sometimes. On one of those occasions, she introduced Yana to the television. Yana was memorized by it and vowed to own one of her own. Yana gets bored and starts thumbing.

Through Mina's photo album and comes across Cato's picture. She knows him, but from where…she asks, Mina who this person is…Not thinking about the impact this was going to have she said, "That is my father Cato." Yana looks up at her friend in shock, "You, you are Mina Sula? Why are you here in O'Sangha? Did your father not warn you? Do you have any idea what my father will do if he realizes you are here….Do you have any idea what he will do to you? I still have nightmares about your sister and I did not know her. You are my friend. At least I….Are you my friend? Mina, please tell me what you are doing here." Mina sat down next to Yana and told her the entire story. When she is done, she adds one more thing, "I never intended to become friends with you but I am our friend now. Yana, you have to believe me." Yana looks at her, "I believe you but I need to go, I have a lot of things I need to think about. I have some decisions to make. We will talk more tomorrow." Yana squeezes Mina's hand, gets up and leaves her room. Yana walks to the dorm she is staying in; she has a lot to think about. She had a feeling that things were not as they seemed and life was about to change. Was dad's past catching up with him? She felt as if they were living on borrowed time. She wondered what would be discovered and who the other players in this game were going to be. Yana was trying to concentrate but found she could not focus and was getting sleepier by the moment. She could not fight it and pretty soon she drifted off into a fitful sleep…Voices, she heard voices.

On Zanzi, on a secluded street there was a faint of a drumbeat and soft chanting. Mama Samedi was in a trance-like state, "Oh sweet young Yana, you are correct when you say change is coming.

Oh child, you have no idea. You talk about a game, you are correct. Your grandmother began this game long ago when your daddy was just a young boy. Sleep child and glimpse your father's past life…. You will glimpse where the sweet changed to the hard. You will see innocence be replaced with desperation born from fear. Sleep sweet girl. As Yana slept Mama Samedi took control …."hmmm, hmmm, hmmm." Yana repeated in her sleep, "Mama has control, mama has…." She was now in a deep sleep. Mama smiled, "You, my sweet child are going to see the where your father's destiny changed, this was the start on the long road to Zanzi. You are going to see your daddy become whom he fears the most. It starts with a choice. He chooses bad. His choices haunt him now. You are going to see, sleep child, Mama Samedi is going to take care of everything, just sleep."

In a dream-like state Yana follows Mama's voice….Alice (*that is your grandmother child*) moved away after Bart was sent to the Boys Home (not because she wanted to lose contact with Bart.) The "nice" officer did some research on her and saw that her bank account goes from thousands to almost nothing on a constant basis. He did some more research and conducted discreet interviews (her father's neighbors, the schools etc.) What he finds troubles him tremendously. He goes to the Boys Home and talks to Bart. Bart does not give away much but towards the end of his conversation with the officer he does let something slip that rather confirms what the officer was fishing for. He off the cuff says "Ah hell, she is a baby-making machine and she has probably already replaced me by now. That's what she does when you're of no use to her anymore" (he is hurt and jealous that Alice has never come to see him.) That is what Officer Cain was afraid of. He digs up reports from the Welfare office.

Apparently, every time Alice is pregnant she gets additional money from the state to help with the pregnancy etc. Officer Cain uncovers fifteen cases that were reported….who knows how many were not. He also discovers a pattern, Alice moves maybe every two years. Through census and tax records, he tracks down at least five of the places she lived in the last ten years.

(***This is a smart one Mama Whispers to Yana's subconscious***) He interviews all the neighbors. Because of the areas she tends to live in there are very few of the same neighbors still living there - he finds a few. Some fondly remember Bart's grandfather (**Yes Child had that man lived, but he did not, Mama Comments**). All of them confirm that every time they saw her she was pregnant but strangely come to think about it they never saw any babies. They remember many different cars coming and going. Some were extremely expensive at that. Armed with everything he found out Officer Cain decides to make a surprise home visit.

He knocks on Alice's door a young girl; (maybe fourteen) answers the door. She is shocked and scared when she sees a police uniform. "Please don't tell her I let you in…please? Big blue eyes beg of him. Officer Cain then hears, "Can't you do anything right? Are they here? Well, bring them back here and show them the baby! Oh my god girl…Do I have to do every damn thing around here? What is wrong with you?" Alice is still yelling when she walks into the living room…she stops dead in her tracks when she sees Officer Cain and her cigarette falls out of her mouth onto the floor. Quickly she dons a huge smile, ***(This one spews only lies, this one is the reason….more soft chanting)*** "Why Officer Cain, what in the world are you doing here today? I was just getting ready to drop her off at school…seems she has missed the bus yet again. Children, I swear, if it is not one thing it is another." Sweetly she looked at the girl, "Honey mommy cannot take you to school looking like that, please go get dressed." A baby cries in the background. Cain eyes her suspiciously, "Alice, whose baby is that?" Alice, not missing a beat, "That is my neighbors little one. Poor thing got called into go to work and her regular babysitter is sick…I told you once that I love children so how could I say no?" Cain continued to play the game; he had no warrant so he was trying to waste time for what he thought was a possible illegal adoption getting ready to take place. Alice was no dummy; she had been around the block a few times. She smiled sweetly at him and said, "Oh my, where are my manners, please sit down Officer Cain and I'll make some coffee and we'll catch up a bit. Unless of course you have to rush off?" Cain was a bit confused but played along, "No

Alice, my shift is actually over (I worked the night-shift last night) I just wanted to come by and see how you are. I could sure use a cup of coffee if you have any though?" Alice thought quickly and said, "I keep it in my bedroom, lord knows these brats…I mean kids have enough energy, can you imagine them on coffee? She nervously giggled…"I'll be right back; I'll just go fetch it."

She went back to the bedroom, glancing back to make sure Cain stayed in the living room. She grabbed the girl that was huddled in the corner of her bedroom, "You…oh I'll deal with you later for letting him in. Right now I need you to go out the window (do not get caught!) and tell the people that are coming for it (she points at the baby in the crib) that I had to go to town…formula or some other excuse. Tell them I will call them and we will schedule the pickup. NOW GO!" The young girl scrambled out the window.

Alice returned to the living room with a bag of coffee and a big smile, "I'll go make a pot of Joe now…so, Officer Cain how have you been?" Alice keep herself busy making the coffee. After they talk awhile (both of them knowing why he is there but playing along as if it is just a visit between old friends), the front door to the rundown trailer opens and the little girl from earlier comes in. She looks at Alice and nods and gives Officer Cain a very nervous look. She goes straight to Alice's bedroom and shuts the door. Cain senses that somehow, Alice has distracted him and the illegal adoption has been postponed. He needs to get back to the office, get a search warrant, and come back. He gets up says his good byes (feigning that he is tired) and leaves. He wonders to himself, "How in the hell did she pull it off? I was with her the whole time…her phone never even rang?" He drove off to get the warrant.

Alice knowing exactly what he was doing went into action. This was not the first time she was in this situation. She started barking out orders, "pack everything NOW! Anything that has my name on it goes in this bag NOW! We do not have much time. We are out of here in less than an hour." The boy and three girls scrambled to get it done. No one wanted to deal with her wrath. They have been through this before, quite a lot actually. Cain returns in an hour and half with a search warrant and finds the trailer empty. Damn he says,

"She is smart, but I'll catch her sooner or later. I still have her favorite boy in the Boys Home." (**Your grandma was a sly one Yana that is where your daddy got that from**).

Alice is headed out of town; Denver is getting a little too small for her liking. She is on Cain's radar and needs to disappear (that is something she is good at.) She stops to make a phone call, when she gets back in the car she looks at the boy and three girls (she never considers them her actual children, they are just a means to an end.) She points to the boy, "We are stopping at McDonalds, keep the car running and park around back. Then she eyed all of them…No one, I mean no one comes in. If you have to use the bathroom then pee on yourself. If I see any one of you trust me there will be hell to pay. I will be in and out, I am going to be paid for this brat and then we are out of this one-horse town! On to bigger and better scams!" The children nodded, no one said a word, like mindless robots they would obey. Alice met with the prospective parents, took their money, handed them the baby and she was gone.

Two years later, she anonymously calls the Boys Home and finds out that Bart had been released the week before. She knew right where he was going but she also knew that he would be watched. She had people that she could have watch him without being seen and that is what she did. She watched and waited. Off and on, she checked up on him. She just needed to know where he was in case she needed him…Another means to an end and of no consequence other than for her gain. She finds out that he married a rich girl with a trust fund – (she adds that to her notes.)

(**Now you are going to learn about your Uncle Ian Mama whispers to Yana**) Meanwhile the other boy (Bart's younger brother) is turning out to be quite useful. He is not big like Bart but he is smart. She has sent him a time or two to Denver and he has actually met Bart (although to Bart he was a nerd out-of-state bookie) that handles some large betting deals for him. Alice had to call him something so she named him Ian Bilke. Ian was getting ready to go see Bart to place another bet for him once again. This maybe happened every couple of months. Alice tells him to try to get in a conversation with him this time and bring up the trust fund, "Talk about investing it etc." She laughed and said, "Momma needs a piece of Bart's pie." Ian nods as he packs for his trip. (***Mama Samedi whispers, this one is the master of the game. She has made all the rules and changes them when it suits her needs.***)

(*"Now they are going to talk about your mama child."… Yana stirs uncomfortably, "Sleep little one, Mama Samedi's got you."*)

Ian meets Bart at the usual bar. Bart who is usually in a foul mood is actually laughing and buying drinks when he gets there. He see Ian, walks over, and slams his hand hard on his back, "Welcome my friend! What are you having tonight? Drinks are on me." Ian responds, I'm guessing marriage suits you?" Bart laughs and almost spits beer everywhere, "I don't care about…What's Her Name, but I can tell you that her money suits me fine!" Dumb Bitch has finally agreed to sign her trust fund over to me. Ian, in four months I am going to be a very rich man!" Women are only good for three things, cooking, satisfying a need and this one happens to be loaded." Ian quickly sent Alice a text message with his newfound information.

Later that night, after everyone left, and it was just Bart and Ian left, Ian decided to talk to him about the investing scheme Alice had cooked up. "So Bart, what are you going to do with all of your wife's money?" Bart eyed him suspiciously, "Why are you asking Ian?" Ian uncomfortably cleared his throat and fidgeted with the button on the pocket of his coat. "No, no reason" Bart cut him off laughing, "Ha ha, I got you man, damn you are squirmy. I have not thought that far ahead, first I need to see exactly how much I am getting and then I'll get a hold of you and we'll talk turkey. I like you (even though you are a nerd,) besides if you scam or cheat me I will just kill you and everyone you care about." He stood up and went to get another drink. Ian, who did not realize he had been holding his breath through the entire exchange, let a sigh of relief. Once again, he sent out a text to Alice.

(***Mama's voice drifts into Yana's head, your daddy's momma finds what she can use to make them do her bidding, revenge will be sweet when sighs are turned on her…Watch Yana, your story with your grandma is yet unwritten….***)

Ian's trip to see his big brother was a success. Alice was pleased with him. When he got home, she had a special surprise for him waiting for them in their basement. She thought to herself, "I am so glad I screwed the contractor. Extra favors got her everything she ever needed. Ian had a fetish, when he obeyed her and did things the right way (Alice's way) he was always very happy with the reward. Alice told him over the phone that he had a special reward waiting for him. Before Ian, left Bart told him to contact him in 4-5 months and they would see how Ian could make both of them very rich. Ian shook his hand and thought to himself, "Poor sucker, don't fight her, she gets everything she wants and it is always easier to go along with her." He hailed a taxi and was on his way to the airport and then home. He could not wait to get home.

When Ian walked in the door 12 hours later, Alice smiled and pointed towards the basement, "Have fun honey....you definitely deserve this one." Ian walked over to the door that led to the basement, took a deep breath, turned on the light and said, "Ah honey, you don't have anything to fear....Daddy's home." Alice heard the basement door click and lock, before the door shut all the way though she heard, "Don't cry little one, I hate it when you cry...then a sound slap that met skin." She sighed and said to herself, "Poor depraved sick bastard, good thing I never adopted that one out. He's very easy to handle and very easy to please." Ian was down in the basement for three days. He only came up to eat and shower.

Five months later, Bart called Ian. A meeting was scheduled. He was in a foul mood, why Ian wondered. He just had his wife's trust fund of over a million dollars. Oh well he would find out in a week. Right on time the brothers met in the bar and Bart was still in a foul mood. "Dumb Bitch went and got herself knocked up. Can you imagine me with a screaming brat? I will drown the damn thing. Ian smiled to himself and thought, "I never imagined having one that young. Maybe when it is born I can talk him into giving it or selling it to me?" Ian could not contain himself at the thought of that. Bart noticed how excited Ian was getting, "What is your problem man? Got ants in your pants? I know you are squirmy but damn man sit still." Ian quickly composed himself, "Sorry man, I just won big on a bet I placed." This visit with his big brother was also very lucrative. He was set to swindle Bart out of all his newly acquired trust fund money and he had brought up the baby. Bart was going to wait until she had the brat and then give it to Ian to sell for him on the black market. In the end, everyone was going to be happy, well accept Bart. However, as Alice said, he was a means to an end and of no consequence.

(*Mama chanted to Yana…this is not the fate the god's chose for you, this was not to be your fate my child.*)

In the beginning of April, Alice got a phone call in the middle of the night from one of her "friends" in Denver. All her screaming woke Ian up from a very good dream. He through on his shorts and ran down the stairs to the living room. When he got there, Alice was pacing and saying into the phone, "No, no no, he did what? Everything was all set for next week. Ian was going to, uh huh, I know, but he…Oh my god what an idiot. Where is he now? What do you mean you do not know? I pay you to know. Well find him!" She slammed the phone down so hard she almost broke the receiver. She looked at Ian, "Call your brother, find out where he is, do it NOW!" He grabbed his phone and dialed Bart's number, it rang repeatedly and Bart never picked it up, ever. They tried to track him and had all but given up hope until Ian happened to be watching the news, "Hey Alice, there is another Cruise ship down in the Pacific. What, wait a minute, I know that mug. Hey Alice, you might want to see this." Alice begrudgingly came into the living room, "What is so friggin important, she looked at the TV and there was Bart. He was impersonating a prince and holding a baby?" Her head was spinning now, "I got to sit down." She sat and listened to the reporter intently. When the broadcast was over, she looked at Ian. He was already packing. Ian missed him by a day and it would be 10 years before he had another chance. (***Decisions were made long ago sweet child that bring us now to present time. In your troubled dreams you will visit these glimpses….Just know, things are not always, as they seem.***) With that, all was quiet on Zanzi. The strange humming and beating of the drum had ceased. On O'Sangha, sweet Yana tossed and turned in very troubled sleep.

Yana kept Mina at arm's length. She had wanted so badly to confide her strange dreams to her friend. She just was not sure she trusted her. After all, she had found out that their friendship (which was true) had begun as a lie. Mina's intentions were true; Yana's experience has been that a lie based off the truth is still a lie. For every action there is a consequence, was the price this time to be their friendship? Yana was not yet sure, time would tell. She threw herself into her studies and thinking of her sweet Kimo.

Back on Zanzi, Bart was having a hard time settling down. He could feel that things were getting ready to change. He was uneasy. A few weeks back he had been walking with his court advisor (Doc Tenjin.) Doc was babbling about something and Bart was only half listening to him, his mind was blank. All of a sudden, out of the blue he blurted out the name "Ian!" Shocked at his own outburst he looked at Dr. Tenjin and laughed, "Sorry Doc, I have been troubled these past weeks and I think my subconscious just answered my question for me." Tenjin gave him a very puzzled look. Bart quickly said, "I'll explain later, do you know if the courier to collect supplies from O'Sangha has left yet?" Doc replied, "He was making his way to the beach as I came to find you…Why?" Bart took off running towards the beach; he turned his head and almost ran into someone, "I am sorry, excuse me." He then stopped and trotted backwards (never stopping), "Doc, no time to explain…later!" With that, the king was gone. He had to catch that courier before he left…this could not wait a minute longer.

Three months later, a response to Bart's letter came. Not quite in the way, he expected it to. Dr. Tenjin had him summoned to the throne room. When Bart arrived, he looked at the doc a bit perturbed. "Really Doc, you are summoning me? I am the king and, I am supposed to do the summoning, not the other way around. This had better be good….Well Doc?" He crossed his arms and again said, "Well? What is it?" Tenjin was quite excited, "Your Highness, there is a person on O'Sangha that says you summoned him and he wants to deliver your response in person?" Bart was flabbergasted and stumbled a bit over his words, "Tenjin, listen closely, you go fetch him. He talks to no one but you or me. Take him to your home and make sure no one sees him. Send me a courier when you are securely in your home with him. I will come to you. He then grabbed Tenjin by the shoulders and looked him square in the eyes, Doc; I cannot stress how important this is. It is a matter of life or death. No one and I mean no one is to know he is here." Doc looked a Bart, "You can count on me. No one will know he is here." Tenjin looked up at the sky, "Do you want me to go now? You do realize it is dark out?" Bart stopped and thought for a moment and turned to Tenjin, "Now Doc, not a moment to lose."

The courier came and the king left silently in the night. He rapped on Tenjin's door and entered the room. He looked at Tenjin, "Doc, this is private." Tenjin took his cue, grabbed his wife's hand, "It is a nice night for a stroll along the shore." Once they left, Bart turned towards Ian, "A simple return note would have worked fine." He laughed and took Ian's out stretched hand. After the hellos were out of the way, Ian looked him over and said, "Son, you have a lot of explaining to do. And I have all the time in the world, so start talking." He sat down and waited. Bart took a deep breath and told Ian the entire story. He even told Ian about his childhood and Alice." Ian, of course was a little taken aback when Bart mentioned Alice. He never let on; he needed to process everything Bart had just told him. He decided he would save that conversation for another time. Ian leaned in and said, "So, why me and why now?"

That is when Bart told him about Yana. Ian smiled, "Ahhh, the baby I never sold for you." Bart was ashamed of himself and hated himself at that moment. He thought to himself, "What would have happened to her if I had done that, what if things had worked out differently and I would have destroyed the one person that turned my life around, the one person that saved me? It was hard to believe that he did everything he had just told Ian he did. He looked at Ian and said, "Man that little girl saved my life. I am not that person anymore. However, I have a bad feeling that something is going to happen and she is going to be in grave danger.

I have signed the trust fund over to her (she does not know anything about it or my past.) Or (he paused) her mother." All Ian could think to say was, "Ok, Bart, semantics aside, where do

I possibly fit in? You live on a private island that no one can access without your permission. You had me snuck over here in the middle of the night, which I do not recommend taking a five hour canoe ride with a man that not only talks to himself, he actually answers himself too. Besides all that, Bart, my friend, how can I possibly help you?" Bart looked at him for a minute and then replied, "Ian, if the worse happens and somehow I am found out. I am going to set it up so that you get $3000,000.00 for getting Yana and Kimo to safety. You receive the money once Yana herself goes to the bank and withdraws it. Ian looked at him questioningly, "You don't trust me my friend? You call and I drop everything and travel half way around the world? Does that not prove to you that I am your friend?" Bart stopped and looked him square in the eyes, "Ian my friend, and I do mean friend, you and I are cut from the same cloth. I may not be that man anymore but I think you still are. I am not judging you by any means, you know the living in glass houses thing. Anyways, you do whatever with whoever you want, young or old; it makes no difference to me. You ae the only one who will answer for your sins, no one else. When it comes to my daughter, sadly my friend I do not trust anyone. She is the only good thing I have ever had in my life besides my Grand Dad. I do not think I would have trusted him with her either. I would and have killed to keep her safe. So, please do not take this personally. ." Bart paused and then continued, "The trust fund money will only be released to Yana. Another fail safe is that it will not be released all at one time. She will personally have to go to the bank and request it each time she wants or needs it. A house, college or whatever it is she needs. I have people in place to watch over her. I know how people like you and me think, pretty girl, probably an easy mark. At this point in her life, she could run rings around you here on the island. The big bad world though, that is another story. Kimo has been abroad. He is familiar with the Western Culture."

Ian respected Bart for doing everything in his power to protect his daughter. He too had finally found the love that made him whole and healed him. She found him and now they have a son Todd. He too would kill for his son. He too had been a victim of Alice. He once again looked at his big brother, "Got it loud and clear. Back to my question friend, what is my role in this?" Bart smiled, he knew that Ian would understand, "Ok, when the shit hits the fan (my gut is never wrong) I need you to get Yana and Kimo off the island and away to safety. I will enlist Dr. Tenjin to help you." Ian responded, "That is all fine and good, but am I to stay hidden in the good doctor's house and wait?" Bart laughed, "Oh god no, his wife would kill you! The west half of Zanzi is uninhabited. It actually has a nice clearing with a cabin and running water etc. I always had a backup plan if I needed to escape. When Yana became my number one priority, everything changed. You even have a phone there and plumbing!" With that they both laughed.

Bart realized how late it was and remembered that he was still in the doc's house. "We better get you to the palace; everyone should be asleep by now. Put this cloak over your head, to hide your face, do not speak to anyone." Bart opened the door and let the doctor and his wife in. "I'm sorry we took so long old man, come find me tomorrow we have a lot to discuss. Bart looked at Mrs. Tenjin, "I'm sorry we kept you up so late. Tomorrow the wash can wait; Kings Orders are for you to rest and tend your garden. Yana will be coming home for a visit this weekend and we all know how much she loves your strawberries." With that, he smiled and bowed to her. Mrs. Tenjin smiled and hurriedly left the room to get ready for bed. Bart looked over at Tenjin, "tomorrow then my friend." He and Ian said their goodbyes to the doc and left into the black night from whence they came.

Ian had a lot to think about. He and Alice had a falling out about six years ago so she is not even a consideration anymore. He no longer acts on his fetish. He is actually normal He understood where Bart was coming from. Nevertheless, damn he thought, the money would be nice. Bart did set it up so that he will be handsomely compensated, and this was his niece. He knew the answer; he was going to come clean with Bart. "Let the cards fall where they may."

Right around lunchtime, Bart shows up in the three rooms that he had sequestered for Ian. Even if the servants were to question his actions, he is the king so they will never ask or try to find what he had in there. His word is law and everyone knows what happens when King Rayno's laws are broken.

"Kali" Bart thought back to that horrible day. He sees things in a different light now because of the situation he finds himself in. His past sins are about to catch up with him, not only he will pay the price though. Innocent, pure beautiful Yana will be made to suffer as well. He now regrets what happened to Kali's family. He was correct in the torturing and killing of the girl. He was very wrong in holding her family accountable for her actions. He was wrong and had they not committed suicide and walked out into the surf he vowed he would have made amends to them.

He felt no shame for torturing and killing their daughter, she deserved what she got. He felt shame for persecuting the family. He made a mental note that if he still had time enough he was going to right many wrongs. He brushed these thoughts from his mind and swung open the door to the main living quarter.

"Ian....Where are you man?" Ian entered from one of the other adjoining rooms. "What's up my friend? I thought you forgot about me?" Bart looked at him and laughed, "Not on your life." Ian looked at him seriously now, "Bart you came clean and told me everything last night, I kept quiet (you know our type,) I am now ready to tell you all about Ian Bilke, if you are ready to hear the story?" Bart sat down and motioned for Ian to sit as well, "Tell me all about Ian Bilke....please." Ian nervously sat, "First of all, you know Ian Bilke as Errand Boy." Ian quickly looked up at Bart to see his reaction. Bart sat straight up, "You, you are Errand, you are my brother?" Ian hung his head, "Alice is very controlling and all I wanted to do was please her. Then I got to know you and....Do you want to hear the rest?" Bart looked at him, another victim of Alice's, "Please little brother, please continue."

Back on O'Sangha.... Mina feels bad for lying to Yana. She calls Cato to talk to him. He tells her something very alarming, "By turning in the king, you have now put Yana's life in danger. If the king is dethroned for any reason then (just like your sister Kali) Yana must also pay the ultimate price. She as well as her father will be put to death. The custom dictates that the bloodline must be severed.

""Oh Papa, what have I done." She frantically asks Cato, "What can be done to stop this?" Cato sadly replies to his daughter, "I asked you to leave it alone, I begged you to stop before it was too late. Now sadly nothing can be done. It is up to the gods now." The phone line goes dead. Mina drops the receiver and slides down the wall to the floor sobbing.

Yana had forgiven her friend, they had made a coffee date, she is concerned her friend is always very punctual and she was now 30 minutes late. Yana pays for her coffee and makes her way up to Mina's room. She finds Mina crying on the floor, "What is the matter Mina? Why all the tears? Is everyone at home alright?" Mina looks up at her friend, "I'm so sorry Yana, and I didn't know, I should have listened to my father but all I saw was my opportunity to avenge my sister." Yana is completely puzzled now, "Honey slow down, you are going to have to start from the beginning, and you are not making any sense." Mina tried to control her breathing, Yana waited patiently continuously stroking her hair and telling her it was going to be alright (whatever "it" was.) When Mina was composed enough she relayed everything that Cato had told her. When she was done, she looked at Yana, "Do you hate me? I never meant, I mean not you of all people." Yana looked at her and quietly said, "Oh Mina, none of this is your fault. Do not blame yourself one minute longer. This weekend on my visit home, I am going to confront my father. I held something back from you too. I also have my own proof about my father. After your sister's, well after that I found my mother's journal." Mina looked at her, "Your dead mother?" Yana responded, "My only mother and yes she is dead. My father killed her." Mina was shocked but started to cry again, "And now my sweet friend I have killed you." Yana just hugged her, telling her it would be all right. In her own thoughts, though she wondered if the sins of the father were her now her own to bear. After Yana was sure her friend was ok, she left to make the trip back to Zanzi for the weekend.

Bart met Yana on the beach when she arrived home. He hugged her and told her that he had some important things to discuss with her. He said they were taking a small trip this weekend. She was alarmed because her father never left the comforts and safety of the palace grounds (at least not that she was aware of.) He told her to unpack quickly and come to his quarters. They were leaving from there before sunset.

Before she goes to Bart's rooms, she uncovers her mother's journal from its hiding place and securely tucks it inside her shirt. She is about to knock when he opens the door and pulls her in, "Did anyone see you? You did not tell anyone we are leaving did you?" Yana assures him that no one saw her and she spoke with no one. "Why all the cloak and dagger stuff dad? What's going on?"

He looked at his daughter, "No time to explain, here put these clothes on and don this cloak over your head and shoulders, I'm going to do the same When they each emerged, it was

astonishing, she was no longer staring at King Rayno, this man looked like a commoner (just a bit taller.) When Bart looked at his daughter, he marveled at the fact that no matter what you put her in she is still stunning and carries herself elegantly as only the royals do. He worried if someone looked at her too closely they would recognize her immediately. At that moment, the doctor appeared from the other room, "Are we already to go? Your Highness, my god you are even stunning as a commoner." Yana curtsied and blushed, "Thank you Doctor Tenjin, will someone please tell me what is going on?" She looked from one to the other and no one said a word. (A knock on the door) "Doc go see who it is," Bart said. He looked at Yana, motioned her to go in the next room, once again, she obeyed. She quickly went to his bedroom and did as she was told.

Kimo entered and Doc locked the door behind him. Doc asked Kimo the same questions, "Did anyone see or question you Kimo? You spoke to no one right?" Kimo too assured the doc and the king that he spoke and saw no one. Bart asked him, "Kimo you know why you are here right? All the trips to the Western world make sense to you now right? I am trust you with something more precious to me than any gem and she is worth more than all the money in the entire world to me. Please Kimo; take care of her as if your life depended on it." Kimo assured the king that he would watch over her all the days of his life, "I promise you, as long as there is breath in my body, no one will ever harm her. I promise that if there is only one piece of bread left, it will always go to her. I will put her before my life now and always." Bart seemed satisfied, "We have wasted too much time it is too dangerous for Yana here now. Doc is everything set. Are we ready to go? Doc (who had been looking out the window) said, "Just a little while longer, I want to make sure that there is no moon out tonight. I do not want to take any chances of us getting caught."

Bart paced back and forth, a movement caught his eye and he stopped. Yana was peaking her head out of Bart's bedroom door, "Is it safe for me to come out now Papa?" She had not yet seen Kimo. However, he saw her and she was even more beautiful then he remembered. There was no way to disguise her not even in paupers clothing. Bart motioned for Yana to exit her hiding place. When Yana entered and peered around the room she saw him and he still took her breath away, "What is Kimo doing here? Papa, what is going on?" Bart stopped pacing and looked at the doc ignoring his daughter's question, "Now doc? Is it time to go now?" Tenjin (lost in his own thoughts) looked out the window and sighed, "Yes Your Highness, now we can go." Bart then addressed the entire room, "We are going down to the beach, and no one is to say a word. We are going to stagger the procession and go one or two at a time. Once there the doc will take over."

Bart turned and hugged his daughter so tight she thought he might break her in two. He cupped her chin in his hands and looked into her eyes, when he spoke his voice was filled with emotion, "My sweet daughter, I want you to know that no matter what you hear about me, I want you to know that you, Yana, my sweet Yana, you saved me. I have done some terrible and horrific things in life. I am willing to take my punishment. As a matter of a fact, I deserve my punishment. However, you my child deserve none of it. I will not let you suffer for what I have done under my own free will. I will not make any excuses for the things that I did and when you hear them, you may just hate me. I deserve that and more my sweet girl. Just know that you turned my life around and I love you and will protect you until my dying breath." Yana wiped a single tear from her father's face and whispered to him, "Papa, I know and I don't hate you. I did not know the man in mama's journal. I cannot hate what I do not know. You have loved me and comforted me all the days of my life. Papa, I am proud to be your daughter. People that matter will not slander you and people that do not matter are of no consequence. Papa, I know and I love you more right now for speaking the truth." Bart put his head down, and Yana snuggled up against his chest (as she used to so many years ago.) He brought both of her hands to his lips and kissed the top of her fingers, "Yana, it is an honor to be your father but it has been a privilege to be your friend."

He got up off the bed, "Time to go, they are getting near." No one but Bart had been paying attention to the faint sound of steady drumbeat for the past hour. It was the sound the royal guardsmen from the neighboring islands used to keep their rowing synchronized. He knew what it meant and he knew why they were coming to Zanzi. The end was near; Bart knew the game was up. It was time to get Yana to safety. One sometimes two at a time made their way down to the beach in the cover of night. Bart had made his peace. It was time to say goodbye to his daughter. Everyone was in the canoe accept Bart, that is when it struck Yana, "No Papa, no, you have to come. I cannot live without you Papa." She tried to climb out of the canoe but Kimo held her securely, "Yana, it has to be this way. He loves you." Bart shoved the tip of the canoe until it was free from the shore. He looked at his daughter who was still struggling against Kimo with tears streaming down her face, "I love you Yana, never forget that I love you." Bart stood on the beach and watched until he could no longer make out the shape of the canoe. He turned and slowly walked back up the path to the palace. He thought to himself, "It is time for him to pay for his sins." Then he smiled a little, Yana, his beautiful little girl was safe.

EPILOGUE

As he left the beach and walked up the path to his palace, Bart could feel that the end was near. He had time to reflect on his life. Overall, it had been a great life. Through hook or crook, he experienced things most people only dreamt about doing. He did some terrible things in his past and deserved his sentence. Yana was going to be safe and live a healthy and happy life, Bart felt at peace as he rounded the corner and saw the entourage that awaited him.

At the palace gates stood King Branoi and King Tula. Bart knew why they were here and it was not for a social visit. At least he would not die among strangers. As he got nearer to them, the look on their faces told him that this was the last thing either of them wanted to do. Bart smiled and said, "Tula, Branoi, my brothers, please do not look so sad. I am glad it is you that will deal the mortal blow. If I must forfeit my life, at least it will be in the arms of my brothers. Please do what you must." Branoi signaled the head of his royal guard to place the shackles on the king. Bart held his arms out in front of him with no resistance. Once shackled the king was led away to a cell in the dungeon to await his death.

There was a manhunt for Princess Yana, she must be held accountable and the bloodline is to be wiped out.

Custom dictated that two kings and one member of each royal house must attend to witness the execution.

Bart was led out and as he gazed around the market place, where the execution was to be performed. He spied a young girl that was around Yana's age (Mina he guessed.) Moments before he was to die the elders asked him if there was anything he wanted to say. Bart stood and looked at Mina, "Mina how is it that you are here today?" Mina stood, smiled, and told the tale of a brave young princess that risked her life and the wrath of her father to help her and her family escape. Bart smiled with tears running down his face, "Mina, I was wrong in prosecuting your family. I know that now, let the sins of the father die with the father and not fall to the daughter." He then looked at the monarchy and the elders and said, "Yana is safe, she will live a healthy and happy life. You will never find her and she will never look back." The elders had wanted to make Bart watch his daughter take her last breath before they killed him. They were sure she would be found by the morrow so Bart's execution was stayed until sunrise. Later that night in the prison, Bart had three visitors.

At sunrise, Bart was once again led out of the dungeon; his head was encased in a black cloth sack that matched the black robe that he donned. His arms and legs were shackled behind him so he had to be led everywhere. He was pushed down into a kneeling position. The last blessing was bestowed on him by Somas. When the blessing was concluded, Somas took his foot and pushed Bart into the Pit. The occupants of the pit for this execution were, Vipers, Black Mambas and a special visitor. They had captured a saltwater croc just for Bart. As not to hear the screaming, the heavy stone cover was slid into place. "Somas smiled a little and said," The deed is done, the king is dead. Where is the princess, she is next, find her. No one sleeps until she is here at my feet begging for her miserable life. Now GO!"

Because there was no family to claim, his remains Dr. Tenjin stepped up and assumed that responsibility. Traditional island custom afforded the family members of the deceased permission to take the body to their home to prepare them for burial. Quite a few islanders later Bart (Still clothed in black with his face hidden) was laid across the dining room table in Tenjin's home. When he was sure everyone had left, he pulled out a small satellite phone that Ian had slipped him during Yana's escape and made a quick call. As Ian hung up he whispered, "God Speed Big Brother, God Speed."

Ian found Yana and Kimo sitting on the reef, he cleared his throat as he approached, and they stopped talking. The news he had for her was just going to deepen the sadness he saw as he looked into her eyes. "Yana," he said in a very comforting voice, he is gone honey. I am so sorry." Yana felt as if someone had hit her hard in the chest, she could not breathe and everything was spinning. She had held out hope that her dad would have found a way to beat this as he always did. She wiped the hot tears that were streaming down her face and took a deep breath, "Where, where is he Uncle Ian? I am his only family; there was no one to claim his body?" Ian put his hand on her shoulder, "Dr. Tenjin claimed him, and he is being washed and wrapped and prepared for burial. He is in loving arms." Yana jumped up, "I have to see him, Uncle Ian? Kimo? Somebody please….I have to tell him that I love him." Both of the men shook their heads and told her that was not possible. She looked at them and said, "Someday, I will come back to Zanzi and they will rue the day that I return."

A few months later, on the deserted Isle of Manu, a lone figure tends a small fire as he gazes over the sea with a faraway look in his eyes. A slight limp as he gathers more wood for his fire….

ABOUT THE AUTHOR

This is always the hardest part for me. What can I tell you about me? I can tell you that against all the odds I am still here. I am the mother of four beautiful girls. I have been blessed with a beautiful granddaughter. I am with my soulmate and in the loving bosom of his family, especially his daughter and two sons. All I can say is never be afraid to follow your heart. Always look forward, give your imagination wings and follow your dreams. You only live once, make it best it can possibly be.

www.ingramcontent.com/pod-product-compliance
Ingram Content Group UK Ltd.
Pitfield, Milton Keynes, MK11 3LW, UK
UKHW022227230426
12048UKWH00016BA/1112